The Lost Witch

ALSO BY PAIGE CRUTCHER

The Orphan Witch

The Lost Witch

Witch

Paige Crutcher

ST. MARTIN'S GRIFFIN
NEW YORK

First published in the United States by St. Martin's Griffin, an imprint of St. Martin's Publishing Group

THE LOST WITCH. Copyright © 2022 by Paige Crutcher. All rights reserved. Printed in the United States of America. For information, address St. Martin's Publishing Group, 120 Broadway, New York, NY 10271.

www.stmartins.com

Designed by Gabriel Guma

Library of Congress Cataloging-in-Publication Data

Names: Crutcher, Paige, author.
Title: The lost witch / Paige Crutcher.
Description: First edition. | New York : St. Martin's Griffin, 2022.
Identifiers: LCCN 2022034624 | ISBN 9781250797391
  (trade paperback) | ISBN 9781250797407 (ebook)
Subjects: LCGFT: Fantasy fiction. | Romance fiction. | Novels.
Classification: LCC PS3603.R876 L67 2022 | DDC 813/.6—
  dc23/eng/20220721
LC record available at https://lccn.loc.gov/2022034624

Our books may be purchased in bulk for promotional, educational, or business use. Please contact your local bookseller or the Macmillan Corporate and Premium Sales Department at 1-800-221-7945, extension 5442, or by email at MacmillanSpecialMarkets@macmillan.com.

First Edition: 2022

10 9 8 7 6 5 4 3 2 1

For my mother, Marilyn Jo Weaver, and in memory of my grandmother, Frances Mack Weaver. Two queens and goddesses who taught me love is eternal.

When I sound the fairy call,
Gather here in silent meeting,
Chin to knee on the orchard wall,
Cooled with dew and cherries eating.
Merry, merry,
Take a cherry;
Mine are sounder,
Mine are rounder,
Mine are sweeter.
For the eater
When the dews fall.
And you'll be fairies all.

—Robert Graves

ONE

1922—Before

Brigid Heron was a mother and a witch, and she refused to give up being either. There was nothing a mother wouldn't do—and no power a witch wouldn't master—to save her child. Fortunately for Brigid, the power she needed was right beyond her doorstep.

The town of Evermore floated outside the ring of Kerry, off the coast of Ireland. It might have appeared sleepy if anyone could see it. Mists circled the island most of the year, and when they didn't, there was a wildness to the land. A once celebrated abbey crumbled along the lone mountainside and multiple croppings of ash and hawthorn trees made the land there near impassable. A coven of unruly witches, seeking an ancient and unattainable power, was rumored to reside on that side of the town. To the other side, though, were stretches of beaches and a dock, and inset from the dock a once thriving and inviting town. Almost five miles outside of the center of town, and there wasn't a lot of town to begin with, was a slumbering lough. A lake rumored to contain power to heal any ailment, to best any enemy, to transform the world . . . if only a witch could tap into the rebellious magic swirling beneath its surface.

Just over the hill and down the lane from the lough of Bri-
onglóid, the lake of dreams, sat Brigid's house. A white stone
house with a slate roof and a bright blue door, the house (like
Brigid) bucked tradition. She planted a sprig of a hawthorn
tree in her front yard in honor of her mother. She grew lavender and roses and hydrangeas out of season, vibrant pinks
and purples and blues that seemed to grow even more alive in
the rain and the frost. Her yard was always a brilliant green.
Irish green, she called it. It was the perfect garden for walking
barefoot across, letting your feet sink into earth softer than
the best rug money could buy.

"It's blessed by the fairies," Molly O'Brian, Brigid's closest
neighbor who lived three kilometers away, liked to tell anyone
who would listen. She would stand in front of her iron gate and
push away the curls perpetually falling in her eyes, glaring in the
direction of the lake. "That lough is, and I wouldn't be going
into it after the sun sets. There's an angry howling that comes
from it, like something awful is trapped beneath the surface
waiting to get out."

"It's not just anything trapped under the surface, but the
heart of magic. That lough is sought after by dark witches,"
Peter McGee, with a shock of white hair and who was never
without a pick of some kind between his teeth, often said from
his teetering perch on his pub stool. "It's that damn beating
heart, has been calling to them centuries it has."

"Not just *any* witches," Sera McCarthy told friends over tea
when they'd stop in to see her at the Bake House. "The Knight
witches are the ones who want that lough. The four of them live
on the other side of Evermore and only come out on the eve of
a full moon. Beware the dark-eyed one with pale hair, she's the
worst of the lot and uses that godforsaken lough for all manner
of ill repute."

Brigid, with her copper hair, freckles, and skirts that were far shorter than was considered societally polite, knew herself a thing or two about ill repute.

"That Biddy Heron is a witch. No doubt about it, and the child's most likely a changeling. It's the only answer for how she came to have a babe with no husband and no known suitors about either," Molly O'Brian was fond of saying to whoever would pass by while she was tending her own garden.

"There's something strange about a redhead who talks to herself," Peter McGee liked to declare of Brigid. "She's got a calmness as eerie as the still waters of the lake, and that girl of hers is too smart for a lass. She does the numbers in her head, doesn't need a paper to add 'em up, and if you ask her, she can't even tell you how she got them."

Sera McCarthy tended to disagree. "Brigid's odd to be sure, but she's one fine healer. Fixed up my Johnny and Violet when they had the flu, and I wouldn't wish on anyone what her child's going through."

The child, Dove Heron, *was* exceptional at math. And climbing trees, reading, telling tall tales, and most especially drawing. She was Brigid's greatest wish come true, her deepest dream realized.

Dove was a special bit of magic, born from a deal Brigid made. A deal not struck with her Goddess, whom Brigid trained under, but with an outside power. The only deal she'd ever made to go against her Goddess, and the deal had proven to be worth its cost . . . even when things grew complicated.

Brigid came into the world knowing exactly what she was missing. Love. She sought it all her childhood and into adulthood, and yet it remained elusive. She didn't fit in with other children. She had a funny habit of singing to herself and preferred staring at the stars and reading to gossiping. Her mother grew sick when Brigid was still a teenager and didn't have the capacity to do more than suffer in pain, and Brigid, for all her skills as a healer, failed to save her mother. Her lone friend, her sister Agnes, was much older than Brigid and had left when Brigid's father attempted to raise his hand to her one night after failing to keep yet another position of work in the village. Her father officially abandoned them not long after that, and the townspeople wondered if the Herons were all just a bit cursed when it came to normal things like love. The longing in Brigid grew as her work as a healer in town spread, and she witnessed the true love of a mother and child. Brigid knew, into the very marrow of her bones, she was born to be a mother.

On the eve of St. Brighid's Day, she slipped out into the forest that rested between the lough and her home, laid a basket of freshly baked bread (thanks, Sera), a full pint of beer (stolen from Peter), and a newly cooled pie (courtesy of Molly's windowsill) at the base of a tree adorned with ribbons and a small spring that ran beneath it. The clootie well of Sainted Brighid, the best and most beloved goddess of them all, and Brigid Heron's mentor.

"Goddess Brighid, hear my plea, for life and strife and all I believe. I ask of you to gift to me a child of my own, a light in my life, a beautiful soul to love and nourish in the ways I dream."

Brigid lowered a cup into the well, with her desires cast into it as her spell.

The Goddess, who was never silent, did not reply. Brigid went home and, in the morning, found the Goddess waiting for her in the pasture beyond her home. A beautiful spot that boasted hazelnut and sloe trees with nuts that Brigid could never crack. It was the Goddess's favorite spot in all of Ireland, a hill that featured a fairy ring, one the Goddess never entered but loved to sit beside and lay back in the grass, studying the passing clouds. She wrapped her cloak the color of night around her, her ivory skin and gentle green eyes shaded, her fiery red hair and crown made of flowering flames covered by her hood.

"I cannot give you what you seek," the Goddess said, her eyes on the heavens.

"You've taught me to harness the wind and tame the tides, but you cannot teach me how to gain what I truly seek?" Brigid said, laying a fresh basket of fruit at the Goddess's feet.

"Child, I would give you all of the universe if it would make you happy, but it would not. What you ask would never work. You cannot serve the nineteen with a child."

"Of course I can."

"You can't complete your mission to become one of the nineteen and tend the eternal flame when you're caring for a babe."

"You don't need me right now," Brigid said. "I could wait and instead of taking my place in a few years, I will serve you later."

The Goddess sighed. "It would go wrong, child. I cannot give you what you seek." Instead the Goddess gifted Brigid a book, a history of magic and a grimoire of spells in one.

Brigid took the book back to her home and read it forward and backward. For one year she studied the spells inside and perfected them. Then one day, as she was walking up the road, she came across a power unlike any other. It tasted of smoke and cherries, and she had to push against the urge to turn and walk the other way.

A man too handsome to be real stood leaning into the stone wall that separated one side of the lane from the other. He slouched against the stone, his gray pants, and black boots too crisp and clean for the countryside, his white buttoned-down shirt with the sleeves rolled up revealed defined forearms and hands that looked like they belonged to an artist, not a farmer. Long and lean fingers that matched his tall, angular body. His eyes were dark, and glinted as they gazed at her, unrelenting in his study of her from head to toe. He had an aristocrat's straight nose, sharply chiseled jaw, and delectably full lower lip. Brigid wondered at first if he were a mirage, if she had somehow dreamed him out of thin air. Then he dipped his chin, and her heart skipped a nervous beat. Dark unruly hair came down to his chin, the wind tousling it back, and she thought he wasn't so much angelic in his beauty as a fallen devil in her way.

She swallowed, considering turning back, and then he smiled and her stomach flipped at the dimple pressed into his cheek.

"You don't tend the lough," the man said, his voice wafting out and around her like a dense fog.

She blinked and he was right in front of her. For a moment, Brigid forgot how to breathe.

Brigid Heron did not believe in love. It was why she had asked the Goddess for a child and not a man or a woman to lay with. She had seen what marriage did to her parents, what it did to those in the village, and she did not have time to fight unnecessary battles of heartache and self-preservation. She knew enough of lust to fill her needs when she traveled off island, but as she inhaled the musk and mint of the ridiculously tall and brooding man standing before her, she realized she did not understand desire.

It punched at her core. The man's smile shifted into something so delicious, Brigid bit back a whimper.

"Will you not speak to me?"

"What?" she managed, after untangling her tongue.

"Your lough. You do not tend it."

Brigid gave her head a shake. "It is unwell. No one tends the lough."

He lifted his brows.

Brigid cleared her throat. "Or no one should tend it."

"So, it's true. You avoid the lough *and* your fellow witches. I thought the story must be wrong, written in the wrong ink, on the wrong page, in the wrong chapter even." He leaned down just enough to bring them level eye to eye. "Why do you hide from who you are? A witch needs her coven."

"I hide from no one, and I am not alone," Brigid said, setting her shoulders back. "The lough is not well, and my Goddess does not reside there."

He inclined away from her, and Brigid shifted her arms one across the other at the loss of his presence. It was foolish to feel such a way, and she would search the book of the Goddess later for a spell to address whatever malady she was clearly suffering from.

"What is it you want and why are you here?"

"Can't a body take a walk and find a witch he wishes to speak with?"

"There are other witches you could speak with. I am not a member of the witches of Knight. I work with my Goddess."

"Your goddess, the Goddess Brighid, you mean? Tender of the eternal flame, *the exalted one*, who enjoys healing those who harm themselves, stealing milk from cows, and has poor taste in poetry?"

Brigid's eyes narrowed and she took a step back. Who was this stranger to be so bold? "You dare to tarnish the name of my Goddess?"

"I dare a great many things, but I cannot tarnish that which is rust. I can only hope to help it shine." He took a step forward. "You shine already. I could see your glimmer from the skies . . . and feel your sorrow through the earth. Why are you so sad? What has your Goddess done?" Whatever he saw in Brigid's face had him tilting his chin. "Or not done, rather?"

Brigid swallowed, her hand unconsciously going to her stomach. "Who are you?"

His gaze followed her hand and when he lifted his eyes to hers, she had to press her heels in the road to steady herself at the compassion she saw there. "You may call me Luc."

Brigid knew enough of men to know when one wasn't saying something. "What do others call you?"

The corner of his mouth gave a single twitch, as though it were fighting a smile, and the dimple flashed. Brigid decided, watching it, dimples should always win. "Most around here call me Knightly."

The breath whooshed into her lungs at the name. The master of Knight, the being the coven of witches known as the witches of Knight served. She had heard of his cruel beauty, but she had never crossed paths with him before.

"I need to go," Brigid said, lifting her chin higher, refusing the nerves that flooded in at the recognition of his name.

"What do you know of my lough?"

"I know it is not yours."

"The lough was made by Manannán, god of the sea, and my foster father. As such, kingship over the lough and this land rightfully should pass to me."

"And yet it remains shut."

"Because your Goddess doesn't like to share."

"Or because she is wise and wants to protect the people of Evermore."

"She took what was mine, and I want it back."

Brigid leveled him a look. "Good luck with that."

"You need me," he said. "And I need you, so why don't we help each other?"

Because Luc Knightly never helped anyone but himself.

"There is but one other deity in the realm that dares to enter Evermore," the Goddess had written in the book she gave to Brigid. "The man whose essence is as dark as the night himself, who seeks to pervert magic for his own gain and to rule all of your kind. You cannot control the fates and they bend for no man. That lough he seeks to harness is incapable of being healed because it was made to lead to chaos. It must stay shut, or the world as you know it will be in grave danger of destruction. Remember, he is not to be trusted, for he will bewitch any mortal's eyes or ears with his lies and false promises."

Like the lough, the Goddess did not trust Luc Knightly or

the magic in him. Which meant Brigid should not trust him either.

And yet.

Brigid's hand was still cradling her stomach, and the emptiness there. Her days had been full, yes, of spell work with the Goddess, healing in the village, and tending her small garden. People opened their doors to her, but rarely to allow her inside, for a healer was an asset in the small town of Evermore, but her unusual talents and penchant for seeing people too clearly were off-putting. Brigid's attempts at making friends were always vaguely successful, villagers were happy to have her services but wary of claiming her companionship. She lived, but she longed. Her nights, well, they were the toughest of all. Consisting of solitary meals by a fire, silence in a room meant to hold laughter, with only the sound of a heart breaking slowly, over and over, one day at a time.

"How can we help each other?" she asked, knowing she should run home, put as much space between herself and the man who made her palms itch, and yet she did not wish to move an inch. Not if there was a chance he might have the power to give her a family.

His eyes stayed on her stomach for another beat, before meeting her eyes. "You desire a child. I can give you one."

The craving for him, the one that had wound itself around her foot as soon as he stood before her, slithered up her leg and climbed onto her thigh.

"I don't think so," she said, her breath hitching.

"We can make a deal," he said. "I give you what you most desire, and you help me."

"How can I help you?"

"With . . . a little information."

"Information?" Brigid did not think he was planning to ask for directions to the nearest pub in town, and she shuddered at what he might want.

"I need a peek inside your mind," he said, his voice soft as though that might lessen the horrifying truth behind the words.

"No."

"Please."

She shook her head. "I am not letting another witch inside my mind. I've read the *Book of the Goddess*, I'm not a fool."

A glimmer of heat flashed in his dark eyes. "And I'm not a witch."

"I said I'm not interested." But she couldn't keep her other hand from coming up to cover the first as the idea rooted in her mind.

"I only need a quick stroll," he said. "Your thoughts for your future." Knightly pulled a small circular looking glass from his pocket and it shifted into the form of a coin, before he flipped it into the air. When he caught it, he held it palm out to Brigid, who looked down into it before she could stop herself.

Mirror magic was unruly magic, so of course Knightly courted it. As soon as Brigid stared at the coin, it shifted once more into the looking glass, and she was transported into the vision inside. To a grassy stretch of land, the pasture beside the fairy ring, where she sat with a baby in her arms, beneath a sun-kissed sky. Her eyes were bleary from lack of sleep, her hair a muss, but her smile was as wide as the cosmos. The baby cooed in her arms, and Brigid dipped her chin. She hummed softly, and the wee babe shifted into the sweet slumber of one who is loved and is safe. Brigid felt the weight of the child, smelled its powder-fresh skin, her heartbeat contented as a peace she had never known sank into her veins.

Then Knightly was calling her name and she was blinking up at him, a grief as fast as the rushing tide pressing against her.

Her hand flew to her mouth to hold back the sob building at the loss, and he pocketed the coin. Something like regret flashed in his eyes, there and gone in a blink, and he held out a hand. "One minute in your mind, Brigid Heron, and I will make the vision you saw real."

This time Brigid did not hesitate. She slipped her palm into his, and shook.

Knightly kept his promise. One year later, Brigid had her child, a girl. With her cooing voice and the peace she brought to Brigid, Brigid named her Dove.

The Goddess did not ask Brigid about the child, but she came to her less and less after Dove's arrival.

"You have chosen a different path as a mother," she said, "and while I wish you well on it, you cannot follow the one you have agreed to for me, until the child leaves home."

Brigid's magic did not wane. She grew in power, teaching Dove the spells she most loved, and guiding her hand in healing and caring for those in the village. One year turned into another and the next, as time has a funny way of doing. Brigid thought of Knightly often, of the time he spent with his hands pressed to her cheeks, cradling her face. She wondered what he needed from her mind, and if he had gotten what he sought.

She did not hear from him again, until the year Dove turned twelve, and the wasting sickness struck. Dove grew gaunt and tired in the span of a month. Food lost flavor, energy refused to stay in her skin, and the sparkle that always flared in her eyes dimmed.

One night just as the evening star was lit fully in the sky, Brigid heard a noise on the front stoop. She went outside to check and saw a small circular object on her porch. She bent down to better see it, and realized it was a mirror in the shape of a coin. Knightly's looking glass.

She picked it up and turned it over and saw reflected in it a body of water. The lough.

The lough of dreams, reputed to heal any ailment, hid untapped and unruly magic. It was foretold in the *Book of the Goddess* to have the power to unmake the world . . . if only one could figure out how to access it. That was why the witches of Knight wanted it, why the Goddess refused to go near it or let her healers use its water.

Was Knightly telling her to use it? She turned the mirror again and saw herself standing next to Dove, her blond hair no longer stringy and matted to her face, her sunken cheeks full, her lips pink and parted in laughter, her bright hazel eyes shining. Brigid nearly dropped the coin. She ran into the house and gently woke her daughter, bundling her up in a quilt and grabbing her bag of oils and crystals and salts, and guiding her daughter to the shore of the lough.

"Mama," Dove said, her voice barely a whisper. "You said the lough was dangerous and we had to avoid it."

"Sometimes you need a bit of danger to break the rules and change the course of things," Brigid said, her arm tightening around Dove as the child stumbled.

When they reached the entrance to the lough, Brigid paused. The grass beneath her feet was a thriving green leading to a dusty shoreline of sand and rock. Large stones the size of serving dishes clung to the far side of the lough. To the right was a curving of trees and shrubs, and to the left the water met the shoreline before the earth rose into a hill and the land leveled off. The water of the lough was a near perfect mirror for the sky, reflecting cumulus clouds and blue-gray skies. She searched the banks, until her eyes caught on a small, gold cauldron sitting partially submerged up the bank.

She helped Dove sit along the shoreline and hurried to it. Her hand hovered over it when she heard a splash and looked up.

Ten feet away, a woman rose from the water, her eyes a frosty green, her dripping wet hair as pale as the moon.

"That does not belong to you," the woman said, swimming

for the shore. Her voice echoed out into the lough, layers of tone and cadence woven into it like there were multiple people speaking instead of one.

She walked onto the bank of the lough, her movements slow and methodical, her pale hair clinging to her back, her dark dress dripping wet, power rolling off her. The water rippled out, waves following her as she drew closer. East Knight, the leader of the coven of witches that haunted the lough, was as formidable up close as she was from afar. Brigid had seen her before, but they had stayed out of each other's way, their paths crossing only from a distance. Brigid did not frequent the lough or tangle with the witches of Knight, and so they pretended Brigid—like the rest of the town—didn't exist. Nothing existed for these witches except tending the lough.

Even when the lough did not respond to their efforts.

It was no secret the lough was sealed shut, at least not to Brigid. The Goddess had told her such a power should not exist when there were those who would wield it for harm. The Goddess herself had closed it, and her will would not bend to opening it. It was also no secret the coven wanted its power, but they and their leader could not force the Goddess's hand. There were two powers who ruled on Evermore, but Knightly was no match for the Goddess.

Most of the locals enjoyed the story, a few bought into it as truth, and yet no one worried overmuch, because to them the lake was as silent as a cemetery.

Brigid's fingertips tingled from the power calling from the water. Her toes itched to turn and run for the center. The power under the surface was as deep and dark as the water, and it called to her.

She had a momentary flash of Knightly's eyes and turned to look behind her for the man. The air was empty, and she cast her gaze down to Dove, who sat with her toes dipped into the lake, watching her mom speak to the drenched stranger.

"I didn't know the cauldron was yours," Brigid said, the lie rising up in a flash. "I brought herbs to soak in the water and forgot my own mortar and pestle."

East stared at her, her eyes narrowing. Brigid did not lie for sport, and what she said wasn't entirely false, but a warning flared in her as soon as she'd seen the other woman. Along with an urgent insistence. She needed the tiny cauldron, and she needed it for Dove.

"It isn't mine," East said, crossing her arms over her chest. "It belongs to the lough."

"I don't understand."

"No one has ever taken the cauldron up. I guard it, along with my sisters. We are waiting for the day when it opens and we along with the master of Knight claim its power as our own."

"Oh well," Brigid said, "then don't worry about me. I've my own goddess and don't see any need to interfere with yours. Or their immovable objects."

"Are you mocking me?"

"I'm trying to understand you."

"Are you threatening me?"

"I'm simply speaking to you."

"Then why are your hands glowing?"

Brigid looked down. Her hands *were* glowing. She lifted them up and stared. "I have no idea."

East gave her head a shake. "You can't have it."

Brigid started to ask her what she was referring to, but she was already moving away from the witch. Her feet knew better than her mind, and she was running for the small, gold cauldron. She reached out and plucked it up, off the shore.

A roar erupted from behind her, and Brigid did not pause to look back. She hurried to where Dove sat on the shore.

"Drink," she told her. "From this."

Dove's hands were shaking when Brigid tried to transfer

the cauldron to her. Dove knocked the water out, unable to hold it steady.

"Mom?" Dove said, her eyes focused behind Brigid, her voice full of terror.

A sense of purpose shifted in Brigid, protective and unbreakable. She turned and, as East charged forward, lifted her hand not holding the cauldron. East rose into the air, power spilling from her in the form of rain that burned as it fell. It spilled out onto Dove, and the girl let loose a cry that knocked the breath from Brigid's chest. Brigid's hand closed into a fist, and East screamed. Her bones cracked as Brigid squeezed her fist and crushed East's legs. Then Brigid's hand opened, and East dropped with a thud into the water.

Dove let out a moan and Brigid scooped up water into the cauldron and pressed it to her lips.

"Drink."

Dove opened her mouth, her face contorting into an argument, and Brigid tipped the water in. She waited until her daughter swallowed and held her breath.

Color seeped back into Dove's cheeks, a sparkle twinkled awake in her eyes, her cheeks filled out, her posture straightened, and even her hair regained its shine.

Dove threw her head back in a laugh—

And a tentacle of water slipped out of the lough and wrapped itself around Dove's leg. It yanked her up in the air. Brigid screamed and reached for her daughter . . . and Dove disappeared into the lough.

Three nights later the moon hovered, reflected on the surface of the silvery water. Brigid ran a finger through the lough, watching the ripples fan out. She thought the stillness of water was one of nature's most proficient lies. It was like a murderer wearing a smile. Beneath the deep water's still surface anything could be concealed. Plants born to poison; sea life designed to maim.

Brigid did not care. She had only one purpose now, and she could not fail.

After Dove disappeared, Brigid dove into the lough. She had swum as far across it and as deep as she could go, looking for her child. The lake was endless. Deeper than anything she'd ever dreamed. Colder, crueler.

She'd called for Knightly that night, to no avail. Had seen the markings where his witch, East, had pulled herself out of the water and somehow managed to leave. She had a fairly good idea who had helped East and had not helped her. Brigid had heeded his assistance with the mirror, and in the process broken one of his witches.

She only had one choice left.

"Why are you here, daughter of mine?"

Brigid turned to see the woman, who was not only a woman, in a cloak the color of midnight standing at the edge of the cropping of trees that circled the far side of the lough. The Goddess had not aged but grown more beautiful in the passing of time.

"I must save my daughter." Brigid dropped to her knees before the Goddess. "I will set things right, but I need your help. Please."

Lightning struck at the edge of her property, a bolt of bright white that sparked as it hit the trees.

"Witches' fire," the Goddess said, looking from it to Brigid. "The witches of Knight know you are here. They are hunting you, child."

"The Knightly coven is always hunting," Brigid said, undeterred.

"You broke the seal," the Goddess said, her eyes shifting to study the water before her. "If you leave the lough untended now, they will take it."

"I don't care about them; I care about Dove."

There was steel in the Goddess's voice when she spoke. "You mortals do not ever seem to understand the power you're playing with. If those witches harness this lough, it will damn the town and those in it." She lifted a single brow. "They will damn *your* line as well as those who have been here for a millennium, and all that can come after."

A low thrum beat beneath Brigid's feet, a calling of power, seeking.

"They will be here soon," the Goddess said, her eyes seeing beyond the forest.

Brigid rolled her shoulders back. "My line is no longer here. I am already damned."

The Goddess made a sound a lesser human would call a sigh. "Your vision is too narrow. There are always other ways around a problem."

Brigid shifted her weight, turned to look at the woman whose power was infinite, whose name was revered. "I've lost the most precious child in the world. Only I can fix this. What other way would you have me walk?"

"She drank from the lough. She made her choice."

"She is my *child*, and it was my choice for her to do so."

"And you are mine, yet you are a fool." The Goddess did not alter her tone or raise her voice. She stared at Brigid, seeing into her, beyond her. The night breeze stirred between them. "To go where you seek, you are bargaining. Your destiny for her. Taking your place in front of the eternal flame cannot come to pass if you do this." She stared straight into Brigid's eyes. "This is a mission of failure."

Brigid swallowed, a barely perceptible movement. She had not wanted to give up her place as one of the nineteen who served the Goddess Brighid. Yet there was no other way. "There are some things more important than destiny."

The Goddess shifted her cape, seeming to pull the night in closer to her. "What you're doing is not an act of love. This is not selflessness. This is the opposite of it."

Thunder rumbled across the sky, the power of the Knightly witches announcing them as they grew nearer.

Brigid looked at the lough, how it expanded as far as the eye could see. A sprinkling of bluebells grew along the edges; a pretty promise of spring and a lie because Brigid would stay immune to the poetry of every season if she had to spend them alone.

"I *must* find her," Brigid said and looked over to her once mentor and friend.

"There will be no coming back from this."

Brigid did not hesitate. She nodded once, her mouth firm. Brigid pulled the small coin-shaped mirror from her pocket she had gotten from Knightly, a bit of his unruly magic, and broke it on the rock beside her. She took a fragment and dipped it into her palm. Blood pooled in it.

The Goddess inclined her head, and for a moment Brigid was certain she caught glimpse of a single tear pearling down her cheek. But that was impossible. Deities did not cry.

"Be well, my Brigid," the Goddess said, and Brigid sagged in relief. Her plea for help would be granted.

The Goddess began to chant and smoke rose from the water. Mists of white and gray.

Beneficial and baneful magics, split and splintered as two were pulled from one. The consequences of such a magic were unknown even to Brigid; she could find only one mention of them in the *Book of the Goddess*. *To pull the light from the dark is to splinter the very vibration of magic and all it affects.*

But when you have only one choice, there is only one choice to make.

Laughter, too high and forced, broke through the trees. A group of four women charging forward toward the lough, their arms outstretched, their faces rapt in rage. East was fully healed and leading the coven of Knight.

Brigid reached for her Goddess, whose lips curved in a smile so sad a crack splintered in Brigid's heart.

"As I will," she said, pressing her palm to Brigid's bleeding one.

"So mote it be," Brigid finished, squeezing the Goddess's hand once.

The air rippled and Brigid looked up to see the stars swimming overhead. Her gaze tracked the brightest star in the sky. The evening star. The witches closed in, and Brigid Heron closed her eyes and thought impossibly of Knightly's dimple, and then of Dove's beautiful hazel eyes.

She made what some might call a prayer, and others a wish . . . and then Brigid Heron disappeared.

TWO

2022—Now

BOOK OF THE GODDESS (P. 10):

How to Call the Goddess

The Goddess waits, she watches, and she is open to hearing your call. To bring her to you, simply recite your desire and set out an offering pure of soul and intention. Be mindful of the call, for if your intention is not pure, the Goddess's wrath is swift: If you call me, I will hear you.

If you need me, I shall free you.

If you harm me, I will end you.

If emotions wore clothes, Brigid Heron's feelings would be wearing a tattered burlap bag stuffed with the shards of cutlery, or so it felt to her as she sat on the floor of her cellar. Pearls of perspiration beaded her brow and upper lip and dripped down her spine. She tried to swallow and managed only a smacking of dry lips.

Brigid knew she was in her cellar because, when she had

awoken five minutes earlier the first thing she saw was the rickety dining chair she had carted down from the kitchen to fix after its leg broke. The light from the small window over her shoulder fanned in shadows across her legs. The air smelled stale and old, like a forgotten book had been opened and the dust of its pages freed into the room, and the sound of her breath was too loud, whooshing against her ears. Brigid coughed to clear the fear pressing against her throat.

She was in her home, in her cellar, lying on the floor with her wits scattered about her. She closed her eyes and tried to remember *why* she was on the floor, with her tongue tasting of overripe cherries as it clung to the dry Sahara of her mouth. There was a blank space in her mind, and that blank space filled her with dread. She *never* ventured down here, to the place where unwanted memories were tossed and forgotten.

She opened her mouth to remind herself she wasn't imprisoned anywhere, to breathe, but what came out was a harsh command. "Don't forget."

Forget *what*? Brigid took a painfully deep breath. She couldn't remember a thing.

She blew out and in and repeated the process three more times. When she found she could swallow, she did so gratefully, before rolling her head from side to side, scooting all the way into a seated position, then slowly standing.

The light in the cellar was dim. It was daybreak, early, and she stretched, poking at the blank spaces in her mind and finding they shoved back.

Brigid Heron was a witch. She reminded herself of this as she conducted a quick mental rundown. She was thirty-three years old, unwed, and she loved long walks—preferably while reading a book—and hated small talk, which was unavoidable considering her position as healer. She lived in the town of Evermore, a small island off the coast of Ireland. She did not travel off it much anymore, except when in need of satiating her sexual cravings for a quick mind with an interesting face and capable hands. There was a reason she didn't travel often . . . but she could not recall why.

While not precisely a recluse, she was private. She had to be. Witches, a hag as she'd heard herself once called, were little understood. She trained under the Goddess, had grown strong in her craft and mission.

She rubbed her bare arms and whispered all of this to herself as she sought to free the panic slinking along her skin. She took a tentative step, found the room did not spin, and took another. With every step forward, Brigid found the world righted. By the time she reached the top of the stairs, she was feeling more like herself and gave a little laugh at being so scared in the first place. Of course, there was a simple explanation. She'd remember what had transpired as the day wore on.

While she wasn't precisely sure what day it was, every week the mayor stopped by for a basket of protection and a tonic for patience. She also had a small roster of women in the village who came for their herb sachets to keep their monthlies regular and a few who came for sachets to keep their men away from their beds. Not all married for love in the village, which was another reason Brigid considered love a fool's errand. She opened the door, thinking on whether, regardless of the day, she should prepare rose water for Mayor O'Malley to help his wife with her digestive issues of late. She walked into the living room and stopped.

Brigid's heart climbed back into her throat. Her eyes and her mind went to battle over the former trying to convey what they saw and the latter working to understand what that meant.

Brigid's very tidy living area was not empty, as it should be. In fact, had she not come from the cellar, she would have thought she was in another house entirely. Instead of her threadbare rug and wooden chairs, there was a cream-colored sofa shaped like the letter L offset by two strange square tables. Lamps with bases the color of the sea after a storm sat inside a curio cabinet, and pale green glass jars filled with wax adorned nearly every surface in the living room.

Her heart beat a rapid staccato, and she had to put a hand to her stomach to center herself and prevent the swoon that rose up. She forced herself to take measure of what she was seeing. Her house filled with new and strange belongings.

"*What* is this?" she asked, and spun in a circle, her mind racing.

Brigid turned back to where she had come, to the cellar. She never went into that dark and dingy storage room. So why *had* she been down there?

Brigid gave herself a shake and did what she always did when faced with fear. She lifted her chin and faced it. She hurried through the rest of the house. The other rooms featured new furniture and hardware, bits and bobs that didn't belong and yet here they were. Hanging lights with pale blue shades, chairs the color of avocados, rugs that had intricate prints across them, see-through side tables, and paintings of the ocean that looked like you could step inside them hung on the walls. The most shocking items were the framed photographs of two young women she had never seen in her life. It was like being in her home, but not. By the time she'd done the full tour, her shirt was soaked with sweat and her legs trembled so strongly, she could practically hear the bones knocking together. Brigid needed air, and she needed it *now*.

With her heart pounding painfully in her chest, she opened the front door and stepped outside. Her eyes drifted to the shrubbery along her house. Shrubs she had *not* planted. It was bad fortune to bar the way to the door, and these bushes could not have grown overnight any more than the fairies could have come through and replaced all her furnishings.

What in the name of the Goddess is going on? Brigid took five deep breaths, reminding herself she was Brigid Heron. She did not cower. She lifted her hands to her heart to call the Goddess, and a wave of power shimmied down her arms. She looked at her hands, checking for sparks. She sent the wave of power out into the ether, calling the Goddess. Summoning her friend.

I have need of you.

The Goddess did not respond.

Brigid looked up at the blue of the sky, the same as it ever was, and shuddered. Something was very, *very* wrong. She looked across the yard, and her heart plummeted at the sight of a lone hawthorn tree. It was a tree she planted in honor of her mother. One her tears had poured life into. It had sprung into a sapling when last she saw it. The tree should not stand tall and proud, wearing age like a general brandished his metals. Its chest round and puffed forward, its arms thick and wide. Her hand flew to her mouth. She fell back into the side of the house, out of sight, her breath coming too fast.

A metal beast pulled up the drive. A box on wheels with doors. Brigid stumbled behind the shrubs as a voluptuous female with large eyes and a smile as bright as a ray of sunlight exited the beast and hurried to the front door of Brigid's house. The woman entered the home with ease, and another wave of shock ripped through Brigid as the power of the woman reached her, a current of electricity threading up her legs. She smelled lavender and hibiscus, and tasted a sweetness in the air.

A witch was in her home.

Brigid started to go in after her but hesitated. She needed more information before she challenged an unknown witch, particularly when everything seemed to be completely upside down. She turned to look through the window but could not see inside. She looked up and down the exterior of the house and realized all the windows were warped. The glass pebbled as though from age.

All materials in life were of the earth, to some degree, including Brigid, including the very pieces of the home. That was the secret to great spell work. The world was made up of energy. Elements. One need only to understand how to move energy to use them. Brigid had long ago learned how to work with, and manipulate as needed, the matter around her. Her knowledge came from the *Book of the Goddess*, written by the Goddess herself. There was always a bit of a cost, but she was happy to pay it.

Standing beneath the squat window, she glared into the house and forced herself to think of sand, of soda. Of the bits of earth that went into a recipe for creating glass. The tingle started in the tips of her toes. It shot up through her feet, crested over her legs and on to her belly. It raced along her spine, traveling to her lips. Magic. Power so pure it let out a pulse. She grimaced at the pinch of pain between her thumb and her forefinger, drew the power in and sent it back out. It flowed around her, down into the earth, rushing back up again. She smiled and pressed her hands into the brick wall of the home, and the brick began to melt beneath her fingertips.

Brigid leapt back, aghast. Magic *always* worked *with* Brigid as an extension of herself. Yet the brick before her *bubbled*. She looked back to the window, took a slow, measured inhale.

Her magic might be acting out, but that did not change what she needed to do. She only had to focus, lighten her touch. Brigid rose onto her tiptoes. As she blew out a breath, the window rippled where air met glass. It melted and remolded before her eyes, taking with it dust and age and grime. She could feel the power pooling. She released it with every exhalation of her breath until the age in the window was gone and she could see in to where the small, curvy woman stood.

Brigid called the power up a second time, ready to send it forward and into the witch. A sneak attack. The stranger held a rectangular object to the side of her cheek. She was . . . talking to herself. Brigid's eyes widened with the way the woman threw back her head and laughed at no one.

Empathy pushed in against her rage, diluting the latter. Brigid wondered if the woman was a bit mad, if maybe she had broken into the house and somehow shut Brigid in the cellar because she needed her help. The urge to aid tugged at her like a child yanking on her mother's skirt.

The woman read something from a book open on the side table, and one of Brigid's treasured jam jars filled with yellow daisies from her meadow floated into the air. Then the side table levitated as well. The stranger screamed so loud it shook Brigid's bones and ricocheted into her teeth. The jar dropped, shattering into a hundred pieces.

The strange woman bungled a simple spell and broke the glass and . . . was she *laughing*? In that instant Brigid tasted lemon so sweet it should have been a mango. She heard a low laugh, thought she heard a baby cry, and the fear she had been fighting crackled along her spine at the holes she was missing in her mind.

What was going on?

She turned and the shadows at the edge of the path leading into the forest deepened. Eyes in the woods watching her. Someone was there, out of sight, cloaked in magic. Waiting.

Hyperventilation pressed against her throat, choking her. It was too much. Brigid, who had never run from a fight in her life, ran for safety. She sprinted down the lane and over the hill just beyond her home.

Her mind flew through possibilities as she moved. The most

obvious answer was that none of what she was experiencing was real. She was dreaming. It certainly wouldn't be the first time she'd suffered the nocturnal state, lost between real and unreal.

Her feet tripped over each other, and she stumbled forward, her hands reaching out to catch herself. Yes. She was most likely asleep in her bed, suffering this horrid delusion from oversampling her latest batch of anti-laudanum. She was drugged and confused and hallucinating, again due to the new batch of anti-laudanum. That could absolutely be it.

She pushed on past the grouping of trees and around the bend. She hadn't thought of where to go, but her feet led her to a source of magic. Not the well of the Goddess, but a different spot. One she avoided at all costs but felt compelled to seek now.

A lough, at the edge of the small wood, that before had seemed as large as a small ocean, its magic as old as time and as off-limits as the secrets of the gods themselves.

Brigid blinked as she stared down into the water, the truth of things setting into her skin like a fever. The lough had trickled into a small pond. The house she had run from was not hers. The Goddess had not heeded her call, so perhaps the old gods were gone.

Brigid was a lost witch, one with no memory of where she'd been or how she could get back home. She couldn't help but wonder how things could get any worse.

Ophelia Gallagher believed a great laugh and a long sleep could cure anything. She told herself this as she dusted salt from her pants and tightened her grip on the steering wheel. Her bright pink glitter nail polish glimmered back at her; the thumbnails chipped yet again after having to rush through the salting of the perimeter at the edge of the village.

She met her honey-brown eyes in the mirror and growled at the salt dusting the tip of her brown nose, coating her sharp cheekbones and the top of her full upper lip. The truth was she was surviving on far too few hours of sleep and couldn't remember the last time she'd had a proper laugh. Life in Evermore, where for the past one hundred years the villagers had remained stuck and unable to leave while mythical monsters roamed free, didn't inspire a ton of joie de vivre.

She slowed down as she took a curve to let the grouping of sheep Farmer Joanie clearly needed to wrangle, pass through and huffed out a breath. At least nothing had eaten them this season. Yet.

To top everything off, she was running late to meet her roommate and best friend. Finola McEntire, who refused to keep time because she thought it was an out-of-date construct likely thought up by a mediocre white man, was usually the one who was late, but today Ophelia couldn't help it.

She was late because of said monsters (and a few too many power-hungry witches) trying to cross into the center of the village yet again. So she'd spent one more morning trying to protect the villagers who didn't have magic and were defenseless to creatures that should only exist inside the pages of a children's fairy-tale book.

The salting had proved fruitful, thankfully. The mist that had been pressing in was receding, and that was a relief. The mist always came before a creature, but the salt wouldn't hold forever. Soon one would break through. Too many had broken through of late. What Ophelia needed was to go over the family letters the house had coughed up last night, the ones telling her change was coming.

Thirteen years earlier Ophelia and Finola had moved into the abandoned home of Brigid Heron. A home forgotten by the town, and as hidden as any stretch of stray sod. Ophelia had a dream where the house, a forgotten house that no one had set foot in for almost one hundred years, revealed itself to her and invited her in. It was such a convincing dream that Ophelia dragged her best friend to the front door, and found it swung open as soon as her fingers brushed it. Inside they discovered an oven full of letters, and a tale of a powerful witch who was the key to sealing up the cursed lough and saving them all. For years Evermore had been overrun with monsters, with Ophelia and Finola the only two witches in town willing to fight to save it. The townspeople had tried to force back the monsters when the curse first came to pass, but repeated failure over the decades led to their eventual acclimation of life as it had become and strategic avoidance.

Ophelia and Finola felt it was up to the two of them to break the curse, particularly as they knew there was but six months until the lough would completely unseal and all that was contained would be released. Not that anyone listened to them about it or knew for sure what was on the other side of the lough. But the nightmares they'd encountered so far left them terrified at the thought for what remained.

Ophelia pulled over at a roundabout, removed her wide-brim fedora, and tried phoning Finola again. Earlier, Finola had screamed in decibels that should have cracked the glass of the cell phone, then hung up on Ophelia. Ophelia had been trying to reach her ever since. She wasn't overly worried. Finola was prone to antics and had once told Ophelia, "All the world's my stage and the people members who haven't yet awoken to the fact that they are my audience." Fin loved drama, lived for it. Drama and magic, and Ophelia. And, from time to time, girls with a gap between their two front teeth and shiny hair.

"Argh," Fin finally answered, sounding like a pirate.

"Fin?"

There was a cough, the sound of clattering, and then a long exhale. "Sorry, was chewing on the middle of my pencil, trying to convince it to levitate."

"How'd that go?"

"Can you get lead poisoning from a number two?"

"So you're not on the floor bleeding out, then?"

"What? Oh. Shite, no, sorry. Didn't you get my texts? Don't they read themselves to you in that fancy car of yours?"

"I turned it off after you sent me ten eggplant emojis in a row."

"Well, bully for you," Finola said, and took a deep breath. "I read out a spell from the *Book of the Goddess* and it worked."

Ophelia blinked. "What?"

"I found a spell on levitating objects and thought, 'What the goddess, it's Beltane, why not give it a try?' It would be brilliant if we could set up a floating safe space for the villagers to escape from whatever comes out of the lough next, wouldn't it? So I gave it a whirl, a jar of flowers floated. Into the air. Then the table *levitated*."

"Have you been drinking?"

"No, it's only seven o'clock in the morning. And I don't think there's enough Guinness in all of Ireland to make things float. I need you to try it."

"Copious amounts of Guinness?"

"No. A spell. *From the book.*"

"Now?"

"Yes, but if you can't handle a purple penis metaphor while driving, then perhaps doing this sort of magic while motoring will send you over Lugh's cliffs."

"I pulled over." Ophelia blew out a breath. "Which spell?"

"Any of them? You've got so many memorized by now, don't think it matters which so long as they don't involve anything you wouldn't want Father O'Malley to see should he drive by in his ancient lorry on his way to diddle Farmer Joanie."

"They're just friends," Ophelia murmured, for the tenth time that year, and she thought of one of her favorite spells.

Finola's and Ophelia's magic were quiet powers. They could work charms and protection, but they had never been able to master the spells of Ophelia's ancestor Brigid Heron. There was a simple spell she had tried a number of times over the last decade, one that always stuck with her. How to send a thought to another. Her stomach gave a happy flip at the idea it would finally work. She closed her eyes, saw the words in her mind, and whispered.

From me to you, a bit of truth.

She whimpered as a pinch tugged at the back of her scalp and Finola gave a gasp.

"I knew you still weren't over Thorpe."

"Oh gods," Ophelia said, the truth of it bringing a bronzed glow to her cheeks.

"Yes! Okay, I'm going to try to Judy Blume one of these. A little 'I must, I must increase my bust' and see what I can do. Hurry home, Phee." She shrieked in a decidedly Finola way and hung up on Ophelia, again.

Ophelia heaved out a breath around a laugh and rubbed the back of her neck. Her spell had worked. Finola had heard her. The thought, that she wondered if Thorpe ever woke up reaching for her, had rumbled from her mind to Finola's before Ophelia could replace it with a less painful one.

She turned back onto the road, the scent of freshly mowed grass drifting through the window.

There was only one reason the book of spells would work. Its owner was back and the magic within it returned. The house had been telling her it would happen, sending her messages in the form of a story for months, but Ophelia had been reluctant to believe.

Ophelia's gaze shifted across the horizon as though she might find Brigid Heron waiting in the field, but only the sheep waited, grazing and dozing. Ophelia let out a soft laugh, that hiccupped into an excited call of hope. Ophelia was ready to believe.

If Brigid Heron was back, she could seal the lough and stop the monsters.

If Brigid Heron was back, they were saved.

"This is a sign," Ophelia whispered to herself. "A damn good one."

She told herself to ignore the kernel of worry as it unfurled in her belly, and her phone pinged three times in a row with a series of indecent produce emojis.

—0

The sound of wind rustling across bright green blades of grass, then brushing through the leaves, had always been a comfort to Brigid. But as she stood looking over the lough, she found relief an impossibility, high out of reach.

The surface of the lough was a deep blue. The sun should have glinted off its surface, but the lough ate the light. Brigid's nose tickled, as the faint smell of sulfur drifted in the air. Bubbles floated up in the center of the water, a sharp gurgling escaping with them. A cold chill worked its way down her arms and Brigid took a step back.

The ground beneath her feet was dry and cracked. Brigid knew this earth, understood how it would feel between her fingertips before she touched it.

But she did not know this lough. What could have happened, to diminish it so? Standing at its shrunken edge filled her with a dread so deep she had to clamp her teeth against it. She took a deep breath and shook off the fear trying to scurry up her spine.

She stepped to the water's edge. Dipped her toes into the lough her Goddess had refused.

A roar came into her head, the blood in her body rushing upward to meet it, her mind eerily quiet as the power of the lough swelled over her in a vision of moments. Brigid tried to catch the pieces it showed her, hold its memories from the past. She saw a circle of women, taking their place at each of the four corners around the lough and calling to the power beneath it. The water gurgled, and a creature made of shadows crawled from the water's surface, dragging itself to the woman on the farthest end, the witch's face hidden by shadow.

The sun shifted into the moon and day and night sped up. The moments tripped one after the other. Brigid watched a creature fighting to be freed of the lough, then another, then five more. Her breath froze in her lungs, and she pressed a hand to her lips as she bore witness to a slew of monsters not of this world pouring from the water's surface.

Finally, the vision slowed on a flash of two faces, the woman from inside with messy curls and killer curves and the other woman from the photograph with sleek black hair wearing a white dress that popped against her brown skin, circling the perimeter in salt.

Then Brigid was stumbling back, away from the lough. She blinked and the Goddess stood before her. Her cloak shielded her almost entirely from view. Brigid reached for her, and the sky spun. Brigid was no longer by the lough, but at the clootie well, listening to the Goddess.

"We do not tend to the lough of dreams," the Goddess said. "It carries ancient magic, unruly and unwell."

"Can't we heal it?"

"You are no god, Brigid Heron." The Goddess shifted back, something a lot like sadness flashing across her delicate features. "Lugh is a god of mischief and knight of sovereignty. I tried once to compromise with him, and he nearly undid your world. He can't help but deal in chaos and it can't help but follow him."

The world tilted and spun, and Brigid was back by the lough. The fragments of memory mingling with the vision of the water. She swallowed terror, as she tried to make sense of what was happening.

The only thing she was certain of was that she needed her Goddess and she needed her now.

She held her palms skyward. "I call thee, Goddess Brighid of the eternal flame. I need thee. I seek thee, Goddess Brighid, hear my plea."

For a minute, two, twenty, Brigid waited, her palms open, her will true. The lough sat still before her, bubbling ominously, a sharp contrast to the breeze stirring the grass beneath her.

The Goddess did not come.

Brigid dropped her arms and tried to swallow past the emotion building in the back of her throat. Her Goddess would not ignore her twice. Had her Goddess abandoned her?

She gave a soggy laugh, and the lough bubbled back. The sky above her shifted from a soft blue to a gunmetal gray. The wind began to whistle through the leaves. The bubbling expanded out, toward where Brigid stood.

Brigid's gaze tracked to the center of the lough. The bubbling stopped. The lake went as quiet as a sleeping mouse, and the hair on the back of Brigid's neck rose as a chorus of voices speaking as one reached her.

"Why are you here?"

Brigid turned. Standing behind her, dressed in cloaks of gray that matched the sky, stood four women. Power rolled from them, smelling of ashes and burnt cinnamon. Brigid squinted as the woman in the center stepped forward. Her features were obscured, the light refusing to rest on her face as though it were made of shifting shadows.

"What is wrong with the lough?" Brigid asked, darting her gaze to the woman to the right, with dark hair and amber eyes.

"We are the keepers of the lough," they said, speaking again in unison. "You are trespassing."

"Trespassing?"

"The lough is under the dominion of our god; no others may pass without his permission."

"Which god?"

"We belong to the darkness, we welcome the magic of the ancients gifted to Lugh."

Brigid's eyes widened. "Do you only speak at the same time?"

"We speak for the power of the lough. For the ancients who came before us. We are the witches of Knight, protectors of chaos."

Brigid's breath caught. She knew of the witches of Knight. The Goddess warned they were trying to take the power of the lough, to draw its power into themselves.

She flicked a gaze to the lough and back to the women and schooled her features. "Not much of a lough anymore, whoever's it is."

"The lough is endless. You do not belong here."

"I can't say I disagree," Brigid said, biting back her irritation. "But—"

"You *do not* belong here," the one with the distorted face said, and for a moment, Brigid could almost see her. A flash of pale hair set against green eyes, a scowl marring her shadowed face.

Then the four witches began to chant and the lough responded.

The water rose fast and high and Brigid spun on her heel to fight it down, but the witches were quicker than she, and the wave slapped down against her.

Brigid didn't have time to utter a single curse before she was sucked into the lough.

• ⊶0

Brigid kicked against the water that held her beneath the surface of the lough. She fought, pulling and pushing against the
invisible current, and when it tried to suck her deeper, she gave
in to her primal urge and let out a scream.

The vibration of sound whooshed through the lough, the
water stilled, and released her. Brigid clawed her way up and
out, onto the banks of the lake. Her breath hitched in her chest
as she looked for the four witches.

They were gone. Brigid coughed, gave a shriek of frustration, and burst into tears. The lough was clearly, somehow, unsealed. She was broken and alone and had nearly been drowned
by a parroting coven of witches. There was so much wrong with
this world. Where Brigid's memories were, why the Goddess
did not answer, what had happened to the lough and Brigid—
all knowledge was just beyond her grasp.

Brigid slowly made her way back to the house that was not
her home. She pulled the sunshine to her, drying her clothing,
and wove a concealment spell around herself. She did not trust
this world and was wary at the notion of running into the angry
coven again when she was so unprepared.

Clear blue skies framed the tall, sturdy white stone house
like a crown sitting on top of the head of a forgotten queen.
Bright green ivy ran along the foundation, creeping until it
wound into a series of looping circles up a lone trellis interwo-
ven with pale pink roses. The roses were the only adornments
the house bore. The aging cobblestone walk leading up to the
house featured the solitary flowering hawthorn fairy tree.

The thick base of the tree, curved trunk, and overreaching
limbs shot out in one direction and gave the remarkable appearance of a woman standing in a windstorm, her back arched and

her long hair blown back from her face, streaming behind her. Brigid's gaze drifted to the shadows beneath it. She cocked her head, watching the undulation of light shifting into dark and spreading across the earth.

The shadows along the ground were large, larger than the sun demanded them to be. She squinted, and one shadow shifted away from the tree's growing and expanding until it met the form it belonged to.

A man who looked like he'd fought his soul and lost stood not ten feet from Brigid. He was beautiful, with a mouth she could only describe as clever, though she did not know why. His eyes were dark, and she found herself wanting to see herself reflected in them.

She moved closer, thankful she had woven herself invisible . . . until his gaze dragged from the tops of her feet to the crown of her head. The corner of his mouth twitched, a hint of dimple flashing above a scar that cut through the edge of his top lip, and Brigid's mouth ran dry.

He couldn't see her and yet . . . her fingers twitched as he took a step closer to where she stood. He sighed, and the sound swam around her, mournful notes that tried to seep under her skin.

It sounded like relief.

Then he looked from her as though she weren't there. She paused to see what he might do, but he went back to studying the house. In return, she studied the dark slashes of eyebrows, high cheekbones, and those deep-set eyes. They were heavily lidded, and she wondered how they'd light up when excited, or aroused. His black hair brushed the top of his collar, too long and yet somehow just right. He reached up and rubbed the back of his neck and his scent, cedar and mint, swarmed around her. Her mouth went dry, and her head swam. Yearning crested through her, and she shook it off as she noticed how his shadow stretched out from him.

A strange clawing sensation worked its way up her feet, climbing onto her legs, and shimmying up her thighs to clamber onto her back and scurry up her spine. Brigid was hit with a wave of need so strong it nearly knocked her over.

She was an empathetic witch; it was part of what made her such a strong healer—being able to sense what another might need even when they hadn't yet worked out that need themselves. This was altogether different.

Brigid blew out a slow breath and *pushed* with her mind.

The man stumbled backward a step, nearly losing his footing. Surprise danced across the sharp angles of his gorgeous face.

"Is that you, Ophelia?" a woman from inside the house called, walking out the screened side door, peering into the yard. There was a glow to the woman's eyes, a lightness to her step. She reminded Brigid of a balloon in the hand of a child, bobbing along, only slightly anchored.

She saw the man, fisted her hands on her hips, and frowned. "Oh, it's *you*."

"Still trying to save the world, Finola?" he said, his voice low with amusement and something darker.

"I think you're a bloody turnip and should go fester somewhere else, you demon of a god."

"What the devil does that mean?"

"It means, Luc Knightly, the winds are changing," Finola said, biting off the last word with relish. "Evermore is ours."

The man, Knightly, only grinned. It was the sort of smile that made a flower wilt and Brigid rubbed her arms at the chill in it.

He looked over his shoulder in the direction of Brigid and dropped the newspaper he carried. Once he was far enough away, and the woman had returned inside, she hurried over, bent down, snatched it, and slipped behind the tree.

She opened it and stared at the date: May 1, 2022.

Her heart skipped a beat, then another, before it slammed back into motion, speeding up. Brigid's eyes scanned over the article circled, seeing but not reading. She forced her mind to slow enough to help her unjumble the words on the page.

EVER MORE NEWS

May 1, 2022

Two monsters captured last Friday on J. McCarthy's property, three km outside of village center. Both reported to be banshees, though the witness couldn't be certain because he went blind and deaf for "a good four hours" after they tore through.

Rollins McGee, the main witness, also stated, "I had been drinking a bit, ye kin, but I knew there was something wrong with their faces. No lass likes to wear that much black gunk around their eyes, even if goths are making a resurgence in Evermore thanks to those bloody witches."

The lough of annoyance, also known as the lake of dreams, continues to spit out creatures every full moon, and occasionally every new moon, and some nights when the moon just appears to have a bad attitude. Our resident monster buster, Ophelia Gallagher, has kept the perimeter salted, and outside of McGee's strange attempt to bed a monster, it's been an okay month.

McGee's misadventure may serve as a timely reminder that we at *Ever More News* urge you to use the protection charms we deliver each month on your front porch in case the perimeter fails. Nobody wants a repeat of what happened when that Pooka got out and attacked the Devon twins. We have a low enough crop supply this spring as it is.

For all inquiries and tips or sightings, please contact Finola McEntire, editor at large, or Ophelia Gallagher, reluctant field reporter.

Fmcentire@evermorenews.com

Ogallagher@evermorenews.com

THREE

BOOK OF THE GODDESS (P. 22):

How to Sew Together a Lost Memory

    Magic is energy, tapped into and manipulated. Memories are moments, made up of time and promise. Beware trying to keep them all—they grow heavy and burdensome, as some things are better let go. If you must recall or retain that which hopes to be lost, then you must barter. A moment of pain for pleasure, the loss of another memory, or any second of joy will do.

Brigid stood beneath the tree, gripping the paper until she no longer felt it in her hands. It was impossible, unfathomable.

May Day, in the year of *2022*.

Monsters in Evermore.

She swayed where she stood and tried to recall her most recent memory. The day before or before that. Something trivial but familiar, the feel of dried rosemary between her fingers before she dropped it into the mixing bowl to grind into powder, the way the floorboards in her hallway creaked when she hurried down them.

Anything.

Her mind was a perfect blank, and she swallowed panic like she used to gulp swigs of wine after having to procure a tincture for Baird Overman. There was a pinch against her rib and then . . . Baird. She remembered him. An obnoxious villager who never failed to smell of dung and ale, he was her worst and best client, paying anything she asked and staring at her backside the whole time he doled out coin. She considered poisoning the man more times than she could count but could never quite convince her hand to pour the distilled cherry laurel into his flask. Brigid didn't usually prescribe baneful magic. Baird might have been a brute, but, unlike some of the other small minds in the village, he didn't wish to judge her over her apothecary remedies or explain how a female's work was in the bedroom—he was simply an entitled ass.

Brigid let loose a hysterical laugh at the memory. That was real.

Why could she remember Baird, while so many other memories were scattered free? She looked down at the paper in her hands. Banshees in Evermore. Women fighting the monsters with salt, which could only mean they were witches trying to protect the town. Brigid thought of how the coven of Knight ambushed her at the lough, how they existed, what, a hundred years in the future?

The paper shook in her hands, and she forced herself to breathe.

The lough was shorter in length, the forest had grown in closer on one side and the rocks that stepped out into it were now pressed to its side, and yet it was deeper than she'd thought a body of water could be. So it was diminished in length, but not power. The witches of Knight had tapped into it, clearly, pulling monsters and mayhem from it, feeding on it.

They had said they were witches of chaos. They appeared to thrive on creating it. Why?

A memory itched at the back of her mind. The water, the Goddess, and dark eyes staring deep into hers. When she tried to draw this memory to her, it faded to nothing.

The sound of a loud clang had her straightening where she stood. A statuesque Black woman with impeccable brows and lively eyes came around the side of the house. She wore a bright green dress and carried a wide-brimmed fedora. She looked like she'd stepped from the pages of a well-glossed advertisement . . . except for her boots. Work boots. Covered in salt.

Brigid stood up straighter. She'd seen her face in the photos in her home and in the lough and knew another witch when she felt one. Much like the other from inside her home, this witch's power was an electrical current shifting and swirling from her out into the world around her. Brigid tasted ambrosia and had the strongest urge to move toward the witch. The taste was one she associated with only one person, her sister Agnes. Whom she had not seen in a very, very long time. This new witch did not feel like the witches at the lough; this witch, like the other from earlier, left Brigid with curiosity and something close to longing—not fear. The woman stomped her boots at the mat in front of Brigid's door and slipped inside the house through the door off the kitchen.

Brigid sighed, because this day was nothing but trouble, and followed the woman up the walk to the door. She reached for the handle, and it flew open. Brigid came face-to-face with two witches.

"Sweet Charlie Berkins," the shorter one said, her eyes going so wide she looked like a child's depiction of a ghost.

The other woman said nothing, her lips moving but no sound coming from them.

Brigid looked beyond them, to her counters where once

upon a time she had rolled out dough for biscuits to try and tempt her mother, to the window where she had gazed into the gardens beyond, dreaming of a better life before the Goddess found her. Her gaze flicked back to the interlopers. "*What* have you done with my home and where is my Goddess?"

The two women gaped at her, before the taller one stepped forward.

"I'm Ophelia Gallagher," she said, her tone crisp, the cadence faint. "There is so much to say." She swallowed, her hands moving forward and then back to dust at salt on her skirt.

"You're Brigid Heron, aren't you?" Finola asked, taking in Brigid's tattered inside-out dress. "I'm Finola McEntire."

Brigid's only response was to raise a single brow.

Ophelia cleared her throat. Twice. "We have been keeping your home for you, and—"

Suddenly there was a swarming of sound, like a cacophony of buzzing bees and honking geese. Finola and Ophelia peered around the side of the house.

"Shite, one's breached the perimeter," Finola said, her wide eyes on the lawn. "Phee . . ."

"I know," Ophelia said, wiping her brow. "Woman your stations. We can explain everything," she told Brigid. "But first we need your help."

"*Help?*" Brigid asked, the noise—rising voices, clopping steps—sending her shoulders inching up toward her ears. She took an instinctive step back and tapped her left shoulder. *Cloaked from sight, I hide what doesn't belong.*

Ophelia let out a little gasp as Brigid's cloaking spell hid her from view, then reached out and grabbed Brigid's arm.

The spell dropped away.

Brigid squeaked out in shocked protest. "How did you—?"

Ophelia pointed to herself. Tall, Black, beautiful, and imposing. "Blood of your blood, Brigid Heron. You cannot hide from me."

Then Ophelia was dropping her arm to take up her hand and she and Finola were pulling her from the room.

They darted out the side of the house, into the lawn, and Brigid skidded to a halt.

A creature, if you could call it that, was slinking up her yard. It wore a suit, or something that perhaps had once been a suit, and carried a long stick. It dragged its back leg, and yet with each step it sounded as though a hundred people were marching. Noise followed it, expanded out from it, and Brigid sucked in a breath at the sharp cry of pain barely audible beneath the noise.

"It is hurting," she whispered.

"It is one of the Damned," Ophelia said, her words weighted in what Brigid recognized as grief. "The lough of dreams is overrun with unruly magic. The ancient monsters, beasties much of the world considers myths, keep coming from it. They are called forth by the witches of Knight, and bring chaos magic. They infect anyone they touch. Damning them. Damning the townspeople who do not listen and wander too far out of bounds."

"We are cursed," Finola said, her eyes on the creature, speaking to Brigid. "No one has left Evermore for one hundred years, since the day you disappeared, and the lough awoke. The witches of *fright* grow more powerful, and we try to keep the monsters out. Sometimes we grow so weary we give up. That monster is Brian McKinney, when *he* grew desperate and tried to leave, one of the monsters met him at the harbor. This was his fate."

"It is not a fate to become that," Brigid said, her hand shifting up to her throat.

"It has been ours," Ophelia said. "Since the seal was opened."

The creature was only twenty feet away now, and it growled,

a low and mournful call. The earth beneath them trembled and Brigid braced her feet.

"I don't remember," Brigid said, shaking her head.

Ophelia looked to her. "What don't you remember?"

"Anything. I can't tell you why the lough is open, if that is what you expect. I don't know how to close it. I don't know where I've been or why I'm here. Or why there are *monsters* on Evermore. But I know how to fight, and I know how to heal."

Brigid lifted her arms as Ophelia cried out in warning. "Wait—"

The wind parted through the trees and dove at the creature that was once Brian McKinney. It caught and pinned him to the spot. Brigid lifted her other hand, and lightning struck down.

"I didn't mean to do that," she said, dropping her hand, and wincing—as the lightning continued to strike.

Once, twice, three times, in a rapid fire, it danced around the Damned and spurred him on. A heavy mist moved in, sweeping across the field. Ophelia and Finola joined Brigid, trying to draw the wind from Brian and send it toward the mist, but the elements refused to cooperate.

Energy sparked in the air, flickering bits of golden light. The wind grew fierce and wild, and rain slashed down from the skies.

"We have to stop the mist," Finola cried.

Brigid lifted her hands again, trying to draw a shield of protection, but the magic refused to yield.

The energy built and built. Brigid looked to the creature and thought she saw the mask of magic fall from his face.

"Now!" Finola shouted as the Damned was caught in an upswell of wind.

The creature's eyes met Brigid's and he opened his mouth, trying to call out. Brigid drew her hands together, trying to bring the spell down, and instead drove all of the elements straight toward the man caught in the cyclone of air.

Her own magic would not obey. The creature shrieked before he was thrown from the property, the wind and rain and energy following him down the road, as far as the eye could see.

Silence fell across the women, the world eerily quiet. A roll of horror turned her stomach over at the look on the man's face, the Damned, before he was cast out. Like he was trying to call for help.

Brigid heaved out a ragged breath and looked over to the other women. They were *smiling*. Then laughing. Then shouting in joy.

Finola threw her arms around Brigid, and Ophelia threw hers around Finola. "Holy shit, that was epic! You flung him into the next pasture."

It did not feel epic. To Brigid, it felt like the start of a disaster.

When they finally let her go, Ophelia pulled a pouch from her pocket. "We have to check the perimeter fast before he slinks back this way. I'll take the northside if you'll take the southside, Fin. Brigid, stay here and blast him with whatever that was if he comes back."

She walked backward away from Brigid, who was still shaking from the rush of the fight and the realization that Evermore was truly cursed.

"We won't be more than a few minutes, and when we get back, we have so much to tell you," Ophelia shouted, flashing a grin.

Finola let out a whoop. "Yeah, we do. Welcome home, Brigid!"

Then they were off and running, and Brigid's breath was whooshing back into her body as she tried not to hyperventilate.

—0

Brigid had almost killed a man possessed with unruly magic and Ophelia and Finola hadn't noticed. Brigid's magic was misfiring.

She was a hundred years in the future, and the monsters invading Evermore coincided with her disappearance. There was something she needed to remember, nudging the back of her head, crying to get out.

"Oh gods," she said, bending over at the waist and trying to catch her breath.

As Brigid straightened, a shadow slipped out of the shade of a cluster of hawthorn trees budding with red berries at the end of the yard. The man with mesmerizing eyes and hair the color of a raven's feather crossed to where Brigid stood. Luc Knightly, Finola had called him. As his gaze fell on her, a burn traveled up the length of her arm. Magic. Brigid took one step in his direction, and a vibration ran up her feet all the way to her head. He gritted his teeth and huffed out a grunt.

He wore all black, and it seemed like he'd wrapped himself in the dark. His eyes glinted, and as he reached her, they settled on hers. Deep brown and adorned with impossibly long lashes. For a moment, as she stared into them, Brigid was certain the light around them drew inward and he pulled the night from the sky. She looked up and saw the stars glistening in the deep purple horizon. She felt her name spoken by his low, velvety voice. Air brushed across her collarbone like fingers trailing along her skin. Thunder clapped. Light flashed across the atmosphere.

She gasped, and when she looked back at Knightly, the morning sun glowed bright against his dark hair. Not a single star shone overhead. He gave his head a shake, his brows drawing together as his lips curved up. Brigid forced a slow inhalation, wrapping her arms around herself.

She looked down and found his shadow looking up at her; it lifted a hand and waved. She stilled, awareness flooding in. His was an ancient magic, magic beyond this world. A magic of the gods.

She swallowed hard.

He took a step back, turned from her, then swiveled around again. He was surprisingly graceful, considering his height. She felt an insane urge to offer her hand and invite him to dance. There was still dew on the morning grass, here beneath the shade of the tree. She'd like to spin under it until the twirl made her dizzy. She blew out a breath, sending the auburn locks that had fallen across her face up and away. She didn't know *why* she was here in the wrong bloody century, with pieces of herself missing. Her feet were tired, her head ached behind her eyes, and this person with unruly magic stood before her.

Was *he* another monster?

"You don't scare me." She lifted her chin. "What is it you want?"

He studied her face. Whatever he saw had him taking a step closer. "I . . ." He narrowed his eyes. "Can't find the words."

Brigid forced herself to look away from his mouth. His mind was whirring so loudly she could practically hear the gears.

"Are you Damned?"

"Am I what? Oh. No." He licked his lips. "Well, maybe a little, but not in the way you're asking."

She took a step away, crossed her arms over her chest. She didn't like how he was looking at her, like he saw into her, when she couldn't even get her fingertips around the blank spaces in her mind. She didn't like how she wanted to stare right back at him.

"What about you? Are *you* Damned?"

When she only blinked in response, he leaned closer. His breath smelled of peppermint, and up close she saw his eyes were a deep cinnamon and held flecks of gold. The long lashes fluttered and cast shadows across his sharp cheekbones. Her gaze drifted over to the stubble coating his finely chiseled jaw, and she bit her lip. Brigid refused to let herself get distracted by him. He was so . . . tempting.

She dropped her hands, tilted her chin up.

He looked deep into her eyes, and she swayed at the intensity there. "You've been gone a century."

Her stomach somersaulted twice. One hundred years. What an unfathomable truth. It meant Brigid had lost her life, and the people in it. Her past was six feet under, and she had no idea how to get back home. She swallowed and forced her mind to clear. Fear the size of Grendel didn't change the fates. There would be a way to fix this. There *had* to be.

The air stirred around them, brushed against the branches of the hawthorn trees, the newly flowered leaves dipping to tickle the tip of Brigid's nose. The wind brought the smell of an oncoming rain, crisp and clean . . . and the scent of him. Woodsy and fresh like a spring. Brigid breathed it all in.

"You know me?" she asked him.

"You"—his voice deepened on an unidentifiable emotion— "came back."

Brigid blinked as the memory of his voice wrapped around her. She knew it. Was it also a trick of the imagination, her mind trying to give her something to distract it, to hold on to so she didn't lose it completely?

He ran a hand over his face, a strange expression flitting behind his eyes as the hand beside him uncurled from where it was fisted and the fingers stretched long before curling back in again.

Once again, she had the strange urge to reach for him.

"You didn't answer my question," she said, refusing to be waylaid by the myriad of distractions pressing in on her. "Do you know me?"

He rubbed the stubble on his chin and Brigid wondered if it was soft as a feather or sharp as a pinecone. Then cursed herself for wanting to find out. He was bewitching, but she was no novice wise woman. She was of the Goddess, she could resist temptation.

"Yes," he said, showing a flash of straight white teeth. "I know you."

A fluff of dandelion floated in the air, hovering as it dropped between them. She reached for it just as he did; and as soon as the tips of their fingers touched, a sharp crack rang out. Brigid was underwater, struggling to catch her breath, then she was in the air, trying to remember how to fly, then she was back on the ground, staring into the eyes of a man who didn't know the night sky was crashing down over his head.

He pulled magic into his hands like a cloud calling for rain. His lips moved too fast, but she understood the words well enough.

Welcome home, Brigid.

Then a whisper of a girl's voice saying, "Do not trust the gods. They are as fickle as they are powerful, and whatever you do, *do not* fall in love—"

His hand reached for her, his fingers curled into Brigid's, and the light in him spilled over, burning her skin. It spread across her arms, up her chest, down her legs, across her face. It filled her up to the brim.

Brigid's eyes rolled back in her head, and everything went dark.

FOUR

When Brigid shook off the dregs of a deep slumber, she discovered she had fallen asleep on her own settee in her home. She blew out a breath in relief, having awoken from the most perplexing dream, and shifted to sit up. Her back ached, her lips tingled, and there was an ache just behind her shoulder blade, like an insistent reminder had curled against her in the night. She lay still, assessing her body, wondering what it was she could have forgotten. The soft voice of a woman reached her, its tone deepening as its whisper sharpened.

"Well, for fuck's sake, is she under a sleeping spell? What do we do? Get out the sage, build a shrine from amethysts, check to make sure her ears aren't haunted? Huh. Do you know, up close like this she actually looks younger than you, Ophelia?"

"I'm thirty, not thirteen, and you're just jealous because you've always looked at least five years older than me even though we're the same age."

"I used to love looking older," Finola mused. "When did that change?"

"Everything changes," Ophelia said. "Except this bloody town."

"Until now," Finola said.

"Until now," Ophelia agreed.

Brigid jolted upright, knocking the unfamiliar blanket off her legs. She looked over her shoulder to where Ophelia and Finola stood staring at each other with wide eyes and perplexed brows.

"Oops," Finola said to Brigid before looking back at Ophelia. "I think I woke her."

Brigid's head spun as everything came rushing back to her. She was a century in the future, in her home, with two witches who were staring at her like she was their salvation. The events of the morning crashed down on her like a beam falling on her head. Waking in the cellar, her home being taken over by two strange but kindly witches, facing a coven of angry witches, the creature in the yard they called Damned, and the man who had pulled at Brigid like the moon calls to the ocean's tides. She stood, the room swam, and she reached for the side table. She gripped it gratefully.

"Water?" Brigid said, her voice hoarse.

"Of course," Ophelia answered, giving a curt nod. "Fin, be a dear, get the kettle steeping and a glass of water for Brigid?" When Finola looked about to argue, Ophelia offered the arch of a single imposing eyebrow, and the shorter woman gave a huff but walked from the room.

Brigid looked around. Her house had always been a carefully curated collection of the things she cherished. She had devotedly arranged tables and books, vases and pens and writing paper in her living room. But her belongings were gone, and in their place were fragments of someone else's life. Fat candles and picture frames, soft rugs and flowers plucked from the garden on almost every table. Looking at these adornments was like trying to put the wrong pieces of one puzzle into the frame of another.

The memories of her things—echoes of where they should be—swirled around her, her nervous energy mingling with grief and confusion, making her jumpy.

Don't forget.

The reminder was awake, settling under her skin. The words she'd given herself when she first awoke in the cellar. Brigid tried to pull up the memories at the edge of her mind and peek under them. While she might be able to recall the day she'd collected the wishing stones sitting in this very room, trying to remember where she'd been and how she came to be here was *impossible.* Her mind was splintered into fragments of thought, and she did not know how to stitch them together.

Brigid wanted to stamp her feet like a child. Instead, she patted the pockets in her dress, a dress that was both inside out and looked nothing like the clothes the other people in her home wore. She slipped her hand into the wrong-sided pocket and tried to weave the shards of memory into something familiar. It was a child's magic, sewing together basic thought. The spell from the *Book of the Goddess* was one she'd used after blacking out during a particularly horrid fight with her father after he'd spent two months away and returned to scream at her mother. After the spell, she recalled the potion she'd slipped in his pocket and the effect it had in sending him away. For good.

Brigid's hand moved as she tugged at a slippery bit of the past; a shiver of pain worked its way up her calf, and she leaned into it. She wove the words of the spell through her mind as the magic of her fingers sought to find a hint of what was lost.

Reknit, resew, return
the words I wish to relearn.

She glanced to the edge of the room. A slip of memory, a bit of truth—there. Just out of reach. Brigid stretched her mind and grabbed it, bound it to her. Brigid's stomach rolled over as the essence of the memory, but not the memory itself, settled and she felt a hint of what she was missing.

She *had* been somewhere far away, and she had been there for a very long time. She tasted cherries on her tongue as she tried to unspool the memory. Her heart gave a terrible thump as if in warning. There had been a field, flowers that grew as tall as her waist, and . . .

The sound of the girl's voice again. "You can do this, *don't forget*—"

Do what? Forget what? The harder she tried to unravel the twisted memory, the more beads of sweat broke out along her hairline and brow. Ophelia's fingertips brushed against her arm, and the memory whispered into next to nothing.

"Brigid," she said, "you are safe here."

Brigid wiped her palms along the inside of her pockets. She had dug her nails so deep into her palms she'd drawn blood. She swallowed and remembered Knightly, how when he'd looked into her eyes, she'd nearly been tempted to offer him anything if he'd only keep seeing her. How strange and wonderful it was to be seen after years of feeling etched into the background of her life except when she was with the Goddess.

Unruly magic, ancient powers, and chaos were everywhere, and they were terrifically seductive.

"None of us are safe here," she said.

"Let me rephrase, you are safe with us," Ophelia said. She offered a wisp of a smile. "You were asleep under the tree when we returned. I imagine the shock of your journey, whatever it has been, overcame you."

Finola, emitting the kind of energy that should create sparks, returned to the room and handed Brigid a glass of water.

"There was a man waiting in the shadows," Brigid said. She pressed a hand to her chest, as the urge to close her eyes to the world, as strong as the urge to burst into tears at waking up here, again settled over her.

"A man?" Finola said, handing her the bottle. "You mean the Damned you vanquished out of our property; he came back?"

"No. Knightly." The name tickled under the edge of her nose. "The witches of Knight. He is theirs. The god of mischief."

"What?" Ophelia asked, exchanging a look with Finola.

"He's a right pain in all our asses," Finola said. "But a god?"

"Yes." She could feel his power, the ancient truth of what he was as though it were stuck in her palm like a splinter, itching for her to draw it out. "He crawled out of the shadows of the hawthorn tree."

Ophelia's eyes roamed over Brigid. "Did he hurt you?"

Brigid drank deeply, grateful for how the cold water eased the dryness in her throat. She couldn't get her bearings, didn't know if she might ever again.

"He didn't hurt me," she said, once she had swallowed half the contents of the glass. "He knew me and I believe he came to challenge me. To test my power."

"Brigid," Ophelia said. "He's the mayor of Evermore. Supposedly his family line has always been here."

Finola nodded, scratched her temple. "He doesn't age, though."

Brigid sat the water on the table. "At all?"

"Not really," Ophelia said. "No one in the town notices but us, but we just assumed it was a glamour and he was a witch like the others."

Brigid rubbed at her eyebrow. "He is a god, and he has been at war with my Goddess for eons." She thought again of the way each time he saw her, he looked relieved, grateful even. "It is interesting. He doesn't look as wicked as his witches."

"It's his pretty face," Finola said. "Looks can be deceiving."

"Yes." Brigid nodded. This she knew to be true. She looked across the living room to the hall that led to the front door.

"What do you mean, your goddess?" Ophelia asked.

Brigid turned toward her. "I mean Brighid the exalted, the Goddess of the well who watches over Evermore."

"There is no goddess watching over Evermore," Finola said with a snort. "Unless you count us, and well, people really should."

"No Goddess," Brigid murmured, her failure to call her shifting from an annoyance into a sense of foreboding. "How long have you been here?" She asked Ophelia. "You said you're my blood, so the house must have let you in because of it."

"We are the daughters of Adel, who was born to Agnes, who—"

"Who is my sister," Brigid said, wrapping her arms around her waist. "Was. She lived off island, my mother sent her away when . . ."

"When your father tried to hurt her."

Brigid nodded. There was a hole in her heart in the shape of Agnes's face. Heart-shaped with a pointed chin, wide almond-shaped eyes, and a pert nose that she'd said was good for sniffing out trouble. Dark curly hair and a mouth that was always smiling, unless their father was around. The sister she had loved so very much, who at least had escaped the curse of being a daughter of Miles Heron.

Or so she'd thought.

"I have her journals," Ophelia said. "She came back when news of your disappearance reached her. You were gone, but she stayed in the village to protect the people there. When she eventually tried to leave, she found—like all those here—she could not."

"Your house was locked away and cloaked in magic until we found it," Finola said. "Ophelia had a dream about it. Told us where to come."

"I think the house knew you would return and need us," Ophelia said.

Brigid thought of Agnes, back on an Evermore without the Goddess to guide and protect it and her. The sacrifices she must have made, how alone she must have felt. Brigid blinked back the sting of tears and cleared them from her throat. There would be time, later, for her sorrow. "You're my nieces? The both of you?"

They nodded, and Brigid looked from one to the other. Ophelia with her Black skin and striking beauty, Finola with her pale skin and gorgeous curves. "You're sisters?"

"What, we don't look like twins?" Finola asked.

Ophelia snorted. "Fin's adopted."

"Ah."

Brigid took another breath, letting the information settle and root. "How many years ago did the house invite you in?"

Ophelia hesitated. "Thirteen."

"Of course. The alpha and the omega." She thought back to the newspaper Knightly had dropped for her.

The year. 2022. The god had dropped the paper for her, he had been testing her, or playing a game.

Gods loved their games.

"You didn't know Knightly is a god, the lough is open, and the Goddess gone," Brigid said. "They are all connected. They have to be."

"Who was your goddess and what could she have to do with Knightly?"

Brigid settled back on the couch. "That's a bit of a tale, you see."

BRIGHID V. LUGH
(AS TOLD TO BRIGID BY THE GODDESS)

Once upon a time, there were many gods and goddesses who ruled over the magical island called Ireland. Evermore, tucked away off the coast of the ring of Kerry, was no exception. In fact, it proved exceptional.

The Goddess Brighid fell in love with the island, and the people of it. How the soil in the island needed little nudging to grow and harvest the ripest of fruits and vegetables. How the people were gentle and kind, with a love of singing and dancing and for one another. A half god, Lugh, with a penchant for mischief and a need for power, also grew besotted with Evermore. He too was mesmerized by the way the people of the island needed nothing more than what they had, and how they knew so little of mischief or tomfoolery. What a wonderful place it seemed and in need of him as much as he needed a home.

Lugh's foster father had blessed the small island with a lough of infinite magic, in honor of Brighid because he, like so many gods, was a bit in love with the fiery champion.

Lugh wanted the island and the sacred water on it. He was a proud demigod and believed the magic of the lough should be his as it was his right by sovereign laws, being the next in line for it as it was his foster father who had blessed it. Determined to claim in, he grew restless and bored, as many a demigod will do, and spent his days infiltrating the peace Brighid was cultivating on Evermore.

She created weaving, and he invented chess to drive the mortals half mad. She brought horses into the realm, and he introduced horse racing and betting. For each good turn Brighid provided, Lugh had a twist on how to make it better.

Brighid did not need the magic of the lough, but she wanted to tend the people of Evermore, and she wanted them free of Lugh's interference.

She agreed to give him his sovereignty over the lough if he would give her peace.

But Lugh was a god of mischief, and so he drew into

himself the power of the lough and used it to create another world. A pass-through world on the other side of Evermore. One where magic grew and twisted, reshaped, and evolved as the demigod who watched over it advanced. He tempted mortals to his side, stealing from Brighid without a second thought of consequence, playing his games his way.

He forgot who ruled Evermore, and therefore, who wrote the rules of the land. Brighid punished him for breaking their agreement, and she sealed the lough and Lugh out of it and cast him from her sight.

But Lugh would not be outdone, and he made his own deal with the witches of Knight to amplify his power and began to work toward undoing all Brighid had done, and getting his lough and power back once and for all.

"Wow, your goddess was a badass," Finola said. "Too bad she peaced out on us."

"Fin," Ophelia said, nudging her. "I'm sure there's a very good reason why she's no longer here."

"I can't imagine what would drive her from this land," Brigid said, taking a deep breath and drawing in the strong scent of their magic, the sweetness of it as they relaxed into listening to her story. Orange and strawberry.

"I can smell your magic. It's in the air," Brigid said, blowing the breath back out. "You were amplified by me when we faced the Damned. It happens when witches join together, or so I've read. I've never had a coven before. What sort of witches are you?"

"We are made of hope," Ophelia said, with a quiet smile.

"I did not realize *that* was a power."

"We've learned it's a superpower."

"We're not as strong as you," Finola said. "Or the coven of

assholes who guard the lough. But we're capable. We've kept the town safe."

"Who showed you how?" Brigid asked. "Your mother? Father?"

"Our mother died when we were fifteen," Ophelia said, her expression shifting. "We never knew our father."

"I'm sorry."

"So are we," Finola said.

Brigid wanted to ask what happened, but the angry pinch of Ophelia's mouth told her it was not the time to poke at this wound.

Brigid turned and looked out the window. For a moment, she thought she saw a flash of teeth beneath the fairy tree.

Knightly. She dug her heels into the rug, his magic calling to her like a butterfly is called to a wicked flame. His dark hair blew back from his face, and he stared at her through the window. His eyes drifting over her, drinking her in. She watched desire replace his intense focus, his eyes widening, the dimple on the side of his cheek flashing. She could practically taste him, cherries and honey wine.

"Brigid?"

She looked over at Finola and Ophelia and then back to the window. He was gone.

She sat down. "What does Knightly want?" She spoke the question out loud, though she had been asking herself, trying to see what she could not name but could feel. The truth was trying to settle, but couldn't find a way in.

"The coven wants to take over Evermore," Ophelia said, her voice weary. "To reclaim the island as theirs."

"Then the mission of the coven of Knight has not changed in a century," Brigid said.

"The lough was a slow trickle of monsters and mayhem for years, but it's been increasing," Ophelia said.

"We've kept numbers," Finola added. "Our family has for the past century. We've scried, cast runes, and all portents point to Samhain. If we don't find a way to stop Knightly and his coven by then, Evermore and every single one of us trapped on it, which now includes you, will be lost forever."

—0

Brigid sat on the floor of the house that was not quite her house, with journals and ledgers scattered around her. She had spent hours reading. She'd drank vanilla and star anise tea the two witches, daughters of her sister's daughter, had brought her. Made to help bring on any psychic visions of the past and restore tranquility. Eaten ravenously the cheddar and chive scones they'd laid out with homemade butter and honey when the clock struck midnight, and then fallen asleep at the hearth in front of the crackling fire on the soft, plush rug. She awoke to the sound of a log snapping, the sizzle of the fire, and the scent of hickory on the hearth.

Her limbs ached, her mouth was parched, and there were still holes in her memory, but she knew where she was . . . even though she didn't know where she'd been.

Brigid picked up the journal at her feet and sighed at the words there. Agnes's writing was slanted and spotty. The last of her entries, it told Brigid what she had begun to fear when Ophelia and Finola told her the lough opened the day Brigid disappeared.

I do not know what happened to Brigid. I fear the worst, that she is dead and gone. I've tried to pretend otherwise these last thirty years, but I grow weaker by the day and can no longer deny it. Whatever happened the last day Brigid was in Evermore did something to the lough, and something to Brigid. There is no other reason for it to have unsealed.

I will join her soon, and then, at least, I will have answers.

Brigid stood and crossed through the parlor. She opened the cupboard with the hidden compartment beside her writing desk. She needed her supplies and she needed them now. As her thoughts shifted from the women to Knightly and the coven, she flexed her fingers. There was a spell that might be able to give her answers to the past. It was a spell she'd never used, one the *Book of the Goddess* cautioned against. Certain spells required sacrifices, and Brigid had never before been willing to employ the baneful side of things.

That was before she was the cause for them.

Because Brigid had analyzed it from every angle while reading the journals before she'd fallen asleep, and after reading Agnes's last entry, she was certain. Whatever had happened the day she disappeared one hundred years ago is why the monsters were set free.

If she could access her memory to that day, Brigid could fix this. She had to believe that. She simply needed something powerful to sacrifice. She thought of Knightly and his coven, and the monsters in the lough.

Yes, any one of them would do.

(CLIPPING PASTED INTO AGNES HERON'S JOURNAL)

EVER MORE NEWS

Sean McDougal lost himself on Ash Road for the better part of two days last week, according to our town historian Gilda Keough.

"I found him crouched down, covering his head, and staring up at the old abbey like he'd never seen it before," Keough told me. "When I gave him a shake, he looked at me like I wasn't there at first, and then he blinked and shook his head, before he took to screaming like the soles of his boots had caught fire. Says he in a voice I'd never heard, 'The lough is waking. *Monsters.* Monsters are coming for us all!'"

McDougal's not the first Evermorian to overindulge at his local pub, but he swears he'd not had a drop of ale that night. McDougal has been refusing to walk on Ash, taking the longer and more arduous route of Acorn, when he leaves the shops of Evermore. Keough, on the other hand, has taken to standing beneath the old abbey when the moon is high. "Stray sod isn't a trap. It's a warning and, perhaps, a curse. It could be a harbinger of things to come or could simply be the start of a new tale," she tells me.

Either way, after the last eight villagers tried to leave and were struck by lightning, the full moon refusing to wane, and the latest slew of sheep missing, I'd say it's important we stay together when leaving a pub—no matter the number of ales we've had.

This is Agnes Heron reporting ever more news in our Evermore. Stay safe, friends.

FIVE

*T*here were many stories the Goddess had told Brigid during her training . . . if only she could remember them all. There was a blank space in her mind, not only from where she'd been but stemming from a specific conversation with the Goddess. She'd asked her for something, and been told no. Was that why the Goddess was gone? Had Brigid offended her or, worse, betrayed her?

Brigid gave her head a shake. She'd never betray her Goddess. But the gaps, they were alarming for so many reasons. There was something crucial she had forgotten, something she needed to do. And it had to do with the lough. Each time she thought of it, she couldn't help but think of the god claiming its water, and his devastating smile.

Brigid tried to convince herself the thought of him was only haunting her because she was currently on her way to the lough. She carried with her a journal, a copy of *Ever More News*, a bottle of anise, and an old needle carved from bone.

She suffered a twinge of guilt at leaving Finola and Ophelia behind, but she did not want to drag them into the darker side of magic, and she planned to go as dark as necessary to find out what had happened to the lough and to her on the night she disappeared. It was risky, returning to the waters that were guarded by the coven of Knight. But Brigid was a hundred years out of time without her memories. Risks were all she had.

The air was warm, and the wind whistled as it blew through the trees, carrying the mild, sweet scent of the hazelnuts and sloes. The grass swished and whooshed beneath her feet, the damp earth making the ground pliable. Brigid's heart beat a steady thump in her chest, her eyes focused ahead on the path and the water that waited. The grass beneath her feet was well tended and emerald green. Large boulders dotted the path and she climbed atop each one, giving into the need to feel the hard gray rock beneath her. Grounding her further into the land. There was a stone wall and wooden gate and it gave with ease. She pushed through and walked on to where the rocks diminished, and the land led to the lough. The landscape changing from inviting to warning.

When she reached the small shore of the lough, she paused, and stepped out of her shoes. Rooting herself deeper into the land. She refused to let the cruel shudder trying to press between her shoulder blades erupt. The once mirrored lough had lost its luster and grown opaque and ominous.

The water was dark and deep, and wrong, but then, Brigid felt wrong too.

She gathered the fallen sloes that fell from the trees bordering the left side of the lough bed to cast her circle, using the fruit of the land to make her protective barrier.

"There are times one must look back in order to go forward," she said to herself, as she set the perimeter of her circle, letting her fingers drag against the coarseness of the sand and the softness of the grass.

She was so focused on what she was doing, she lost track of

time, and that was her first mistake. When she finally looked up from her circle, she was surrounded by a thick mist the color of *Verbena bonariensis*. One of her favorite flowers, with their pretty lavender petals and ability to offer protection and work as a love talisman. She lifted a hand to push the mist away, and then she heard the chanting.

> *"Little orphan Brigid has come to our lough to play*
> *to try and stop our god*
> *and she's getting in our way.*
> *We call to these waters*
> *that bring chaos to our shore*
> *to drown dear Brigid*
> *so she won't bother us anymore."*

There was a break in the mist and Brigid saw through to the four women, who had taken the four corners of the lough. They shifted in the wind like smoke, their capes the color of the lake's dark water. Shadows obscured their faces, and their voices came out as one, echoes on echoes drawing the hair up on Brigid's arms.

Then, the shadow that wore the face of the woman nearest to her parted, and Brigid saw straight into the eyes of East Knight. She let out a surprised puff of breath and stood on unsteady legs, staring at a woman as out of her proper timeline as Brigid was out of her own.

East Knight looked the same age as Brigid, her pale blond hair longer than before, her eyes a deeper, more violent green, so bright they practically glowed. She was beautiful in a cruel and ethereal way. Brigid had never seen her this close, having tried to give the witches space as they served two very different gods. Yet, here East stood with the determined set of her glossy lips, staring at Brigid as though she wanted to peel her skin from her bones and fry it up for the monsters of the lough. There was such hate rippling across the planes of her face, and for what? Because Brigid was in their way by casting her circle at the edge of the water?

The mist pressed against Brigid's circle, but it could not pass the boundary she set. Brigid looked to the water of the lough. They were here for it. To pull from it. To draw out another of the Damned.

She tapped her third eye three times, and then her lips twice.

"I see the future and speak to the present.
What was once open will now be hidden."

She meant for the water to shift behind a veil, to move forward in time—at least in appearance—to appear empty, desolate, so they would think there was nothing to draw or pull. In hopes they would go.

Instead Brigid blew out a breath, and the air tinged in gold. Her exhale fled from her and dropped into the water. A ripple spread across the surface as the lough froze.

A *tap tap tap* resounded in the air, and Brigid blinked to see the floating face of a person knocking from beneath the water.

Her magic had misfired yet again.

"You should *not* have done that," the witches said as one.

"You should not push me," Brigid said, her gaze shifting from the face of the Damned to the leader of the coven of Knight. "Whatever your god has promised you, it isn't worth what you're doing to these poor creatures and the people of Evermore."

The four women let out a low laugh, the rise and fall of their giggle following one after the other like children singing rounds of "Too-Ra-Loo-Ra-Loo-Rai." Brigid swallowed and looked back to the feature of the woman trapped beneath the water. She had hair the color of the sun, her skin a glowing amber. Her mouth was pinched and her eyes, oversized and lidless, flitted left to right in terror.

"You're hurting her," Brigid said.

"No," they said together, their hands coming out to their sides and up to their chests as they cupped their palms together. "We are freeing her. We are freeing them all. We have claimed Evermore and the people here. We are making this land into something new, better."

"This is *not* better," Brigid said, as the woman trapped beneath the lough screamed against the ice, her body bucking, her hands slapping at the frozen surface as her dress tangled around her legs.

"But it is. Evermore is what it could be, what it was meant to be before your Goddess interfered. We couldn't have done it, if not for you."

Brigid's gaze snapped back to East. "What did you say?"

"The lough," East said, her voice rising a decibel higher than the others. Brigid focused on the rasp of the sound. It was like the hissing of a snake trailing along the ground, and she fought her instinct to take a step backward and out of the circle to get away from it. "We spent long years attempting to break the seal of the lake of dreams. We came close, but we could not decipher how the Goddess was protecting it. What magics she used was a mystery to our Knight, eluding him. Until you. You gave him the key."

"I would never—"

"Go against your Goddess? Make a deal with a god that is more devil than angel? More deity than mortal?" The coven laughed and the sound rose and fled like ravens taking flight. "You may not remember but we do. You, Brigid Heron, are the reason the Damned are set free. The reason our power grows."

"Is that so?" She fought the panic that sped along her arms and drew her fear into her palms. "Then how come you keep trying to kill me?"

"You are in our way, interfering with our mission to free the Damned, so we will send you where you belong," they said.

Brigid looked from one shadowy face to the other of the four witches, their bodies somewhere between smoke and corporeal. Each staring at her with the same mutinous expression. She might not have come here with the express purpose of a fight with the witches of Knight, but she wasn't about to back down from one.

Brigid lifted her hands and pushed, the wind rising to meet her and blowing the witches back from their posts. The anger in East's gaze was so visceral, Brigid could nearly smell it.

The water of the lough splintered. The ice thawing.

And the creature breaking free.

Ophelia walked out of her cozy bedroom with its oversized pink shag rug, Himalayan lights, upcycled side tables, and hung moon charts and calendars, and looked into the living room where she had left a sleeping Brigid the night before. The thick Sherpa blanket and plush pillows she had set out remained undisturbed, so either Brigid was exceedingly tidy, or she hadn't bothered to use them. She walked into the kitchen and turned the kettle on, and her eyes drifted to the floorboards by the side door. Underneath them was the box where Ophelia kept some of her most precious of treasures: a folded stack of pages the house had gifted to her and Finola.

They were peculiar pages, with whole sections blacked out, so only a few words remained uncovered. Spelling out sentences that could have been poetic but proved prophetic instead.

It was easy to remember when they found the first page, on the night she and Finola moved into Heron House thirteen years earlier. The house had been a whisper of a mystery for as long as she could remember. The white stone cottage that varied in size depending on who was describing it washed away or sunk into the land after Brigid disappeared as payment to the fairies. It had existed, that much she knew, but beyond that it was all lore. When they walked up the macadam country road, with the stone wall running along each side of it and the errant sheep eyeing them lazily, they'd suspected to find the land of Brigid Heron as empty and bereft as it had always been.

Instead, they found a home with white stone and a blue front door that looked as inviting as a plate of freshly baked biscuits. It had flowers traipsing up and down the sides, blooming with all manner of things that should not grow out of season, or even out of region. Ophelia swore she saw a bush that grew raindrops that first night, but when they went out in the morning it was simply a sprig of tiny roses trailing up a vine.

They took their time walking up the little stoop and studying the blue door. When Ophelia reached for it, her fingers brushing the handle, the front door sprang open.

Ophelia and Finola had entered the house, carrying bags and lanterns, flashlights, and a bottle of Jameson they nicked from O'Maggie's, their favorite local pub that had the best fish and chips. Back in those days shipments still came with a little more regularity from mainland.

"Why does it smell like the inside of a lint trap in a dryer?" Finola asked, as she unceremoniously dropped her bags on the floor, sending up a cloud of dust.

"Because it desperately needs clearing out," Ophelia said, waving the dust away with one hand and covering her nose and mouth with the other. She hurried over to the front door and threw it back open, then worked to raise the windows. Finola went on to open all the kitchen doors in the process, including the cabinets and oven because, as she said, "You never know when you'll bust a borrower in action." Instead, they discovered a single sheet of paper resting in the oven like a pie baking.

Ophelia and Finola took the paper out the kitchen side door and sat on the stoop outside, gulping in the clean night air and scrutinizing the page with a flashlight as grasshoppers serenaded them and a long-eared owl gave a low, breathy hoot from somewhere off in the distance.

"'Welcome, witches,'" Finola said, holding the flashlight high above the page before turning it over and looking for more. "Is it a joke, do you think?"

Ophelia held out a hand and Finola passed it over. The paper tingled in Ophelia's hands against her fingers. "No, I don't think it's a joke."

"Does it mean us?"

Ophelia bit her lip. "No other witches here."

"Yes, but we can't do much, other than pick a lock and squat in a property that's not ours."

Holding the paper made Ophelia feel like maybe they could do anything.

"This house is ours."

"Not officially."

Ophelia shrugged and pointed to the side of the paper. "This is from a notebook. See how the edges are jagged like it was ripped out of the spine."

"You think someone left it behind?"

"No." She cocked her head. "I mean, technically, I guess someone else could have broken in before us, but we would have heard about it. Or seen signs in the house, and it's like a time capsule in here. No one even knows this place exists. That dust on the floor didn't have any footprints until *we* walked around."

"Only you could employ deductive reasoning when moving into a witch's home. Anyone else would be trying not to jump at every creak in the floor." Finola leaned back on her hands, looking up to the blanket of stars shining in the sky, and how low they hung here, where no one but them could see them in the center of Brigid Heron's property. "Well, except for me, of course. I would love a good creaking jump." She flashed a grin, nodded at the letter. "So what then? Where'd it come from?"

"Maybe the house *is* magic?"

"Maybe *the house* sent you the dream," Finola said.

Ophelia looked over her shoulder through the door, waiting for an apparition, waiting, if truth be told, for Brigid herself—for the ghost of the witch of Ireland to appear and usher them inside and tell them how to save Evermore and stop the monsters.

"Maybe," she said, chewing her bottom lip. "It's a good space, though. To store our salt and work on our craft."

"And hide from that creepy coven."

"That too."

"Home," Finola said, with a slow smile, holding out her hand.

"Yes," Ophelia said, taking her hand, squeezing it in gratitude that Finola got what she was thinking without her needing to find the words. "Home."

A clang coming from inside the oven had Ophelia looking up, returning from the past to the present. She ran her fingers over her arms, rubbing the chill away. The memory of that first day was a soothing balm, settling into her marrow. How once she and Fin moved in, they found a way to more deeply access their magic that first week living in the house. How the house seemed to infuse them and fill them up.

Things got better for a while after that, thanks to their ability to innately understand how to blend which herbs to create a lilac balm to soothe the monsters to sleep or how much salt was needed to line the perimeter and keep them back from the village's center. The house was the start of hope and it fueled them . . . until things turned worse. Until the witches of Knight started digging into the lough like a hound into a mole hole. Pulling out more and more, growing in power and reckless with it.

Ophelia didn't believe in happily ever after anymore, but she had never stopped believing in Brigid Heron. She had to believe she would be the person to save them all.

The oven coughed the door open, and as the teakettle began to sing, a chunk of bound pages flew out and landed in Ophelia's waiting hands.

She flipped through them, her eyes widening. "Fin?" she called. "I think we have to get to the lough, *now*."

⸻O

The mist closed in and then shifted away from the lough as the creature that perhaps had once been a woman reached the shoreline and crawled across it. Her hair was tangled with leaves and seaweed, and from where Brigid stood, she could see the wild hunger banked in her eyes. The iced lake shifted back to its inky opaque surface as mist continued to roll out of it, and Brigid kept her eyes trained on the woman as the witches chanted softly in the background.

> *"Bring the power home*
> *Sift it from the marrow in your bones*
> *Grind it with your teeth*
> *It is now ours and ours alone."*

A heady sort of fear moved into Brigid as she thought through the spells in the *Book of the Goddess* and what might prevent this creature from charging her, or worse, charging out of the lough and into Evermore. She drew in a bit of wind and water, biting her lip at the pain of calling in so much power so fast, binding the elements to her, and then pushed, sending the wind after the creature so it was scrambling back into the depths of the water that tugged it down.

The coven let out a guttural growl, and Brigid shifted her posture, arms up and legs braced for whatever they threw at her next.

Leaves rustled, twigs crunched, and Brigid looked over her shoulder, away from the lake. She let out a deep breath she didn't know she'd been holding as Finola and Ophelia hurried toward her, their eyes wide as they took in the coven of witches standing guard around the lough, the cracked ice of the surface, and the mist pouring up from the water.

"Out for a wee walk?" Brigid called, relief flooding her at the sight of them.

"Ah yes," Finola said, her eyes on East. "Needed to stretch my legs a bit. Then decided to come down and see what the latest beasty was, maybe ask if it wanted to go home and braid each other's hair."

"We received a present from the house, including a drawing of the lough and creatures coming from it," Ophelia whispered. Her footsteps fell softer than her friend's, and the gentle nature of her words skittered along Brigid's skin, the sound nestling in. "It seemed a message, and I never look a gifting oven in its grates. I hate to be the one to ask it, but what in the name of the goddess is behind the mist?"

"An ancient born from another time," the witches said, their heads moving together, looking from left to right between the new arrivals.

"That's not creepy," Finola said.

"There goes the butterfly effect," Ophelia added, frowning at the lough.

At Brigid's blank stare, she added, "Small events, those which appear trivial, ultimately have nonlinear impacts on complex systems, like time."

The witches spoke. "You know nothing of magic or how it works."

"Oh yeah?" Finola called, fisting her hands on her hips. "Educate us, you pack of poorly coordinated hyenas."

Brigid went to call them into her circle to keep them safe, and the ground beneath them groaned. It quaked so strongly Brigid had to clamp her jaw to keep her teeth from chattering. She planted her feet hip distance apart, crouching partway down.

Across from her, Ophelia's mouth fell open, and Finola's hands dropped from where she'd fisted them. The water of the lough splashed, and a crack rang out.

"Dear gods," Finola whispered, "what is that?"

The lough was a rage of ripples and tides and breaking ice. Its diminished state still providing enough of a basin for an angry storm beneath the water. The center was remarkably, preternaturally calm. From it a haze of water gathered, until it shifted from mist to smoke.

A bent head rose from beneath the smoke, then came the body. It was a being like no other, one not born of the earth.

It first appeared the being was a man, then the woman from earlier, then a child, but the form would not solidify. Smoke gathered and rippled. The face settled eventually so it presented dark pools for eyes and a mutinous mouth that elongated and kept on growing.

The being emitted a low moan as its jaws unhinged, and Brigid bit back a scream.

"It almost looks like a Sluagh," Ophelia said, her voice a hoarse whisper.

She was not wrong. The creature might have been a Sluagh, except . . . "Sluagh do not have wings, and they are not made

of smoke," Brigid said, steeling her spine as the creature unfurled its expansive wings. The creature rose from the lough
and took flight into the air above their heads. They ducked and
up it flew, before curving through the air and turning back to
face them.

"Chaos is here," the witches said. "You can run, Brigid
Heron, but you cannot escape us or your destiny."

Then they were gone, slipping into the mist and out of sight,
a low hiss following in their wake.

"How do they get to leave?" Finola cried out. "Come back
here, you poor excuses for feminists, and fight!"

"Fin," Ophelia said, her voice a low whisper. "Stop talking."

It circled once, twice, its form shadows and smoke, a bright
contrast against the blue peeking through the gray sky.

"I think that thing wants to eat our souls," Finola said,
backing up.

A memory pushed at Brigid, as she studied the wings. They
were gray wings, made of spirals woven together. They were
also misshapen and made the creature a bit clumsy. She watched
it struggle to adjust its course, and it veered too far right and
flew over them, a predator eyeing its food, looking to play before making the kill strike.

"Sluagh are restless spirits, cast out of the Otherworld and
doomed to snatch souls of those on earth who cross them,"
Brigid said, speaking quickly from the side of her mouth, before
bringing her hands together and forming an upside-down V.
"They do not need wings to fly, and they are said to never miss
their mark."

The sky darkened as Brigid lifted her hands over her head.
Pain dipped into her side as she pulled again from the wind.
The creature swooped down . . . and dove straight for Finola.

Finola screamed and ducked, but the creature latched on to
her. Smoke wrapped itself around her like a snake, cutting off

her air supply. Ophelia dove for her friend and Brigid drew her hands apart, pulling the wind to her and sending it back out before drawing more in. A sharp pain bloomed across her chest, and she ignored it, blasting Ophelia out of the way and yanking the creature from Finola.

Finola fell to the earth, choking as she tried to draw breath. Brigid stepped from her circle, keeping one hand up and using the wind to hold the creature at bay. She nodded to Ophelia, who did not hesitate. She ran to Finola, who gasped, trying to draw air back into her body as Ophelia helped her up. They crossed to Brigid, Ophelia keeping one arm around Finola as she reached for Brigid with the other.

"It didn't take my soul," Finola said in a whimper, patting down her shirt, "but it damn near took my last breath."

Brigid tilted her head, the words hinting at a memory buried.

"We've seen Sluaghs come from the lough before," Ophelia said, her voice clear and strong. "But never *dragon* Sluaghs."

Brigid's eyes narrowed as she watched it struggle.

"It's breaking free," Finola said, her voice shaky around her chattering teeth.

Brigid didn't move to capture the creature for fear the fight could kill it. She couldn't let it hurt her friends, but she didn't want to kill anything. Especially something manipulated by the coven of Knight. Not even if it was called specifically to end her.

She turned to the others. "I can't contain it, but maybe we don't need to. Maybe we can send it back?"

"How?" Ophelia asked, shifting forward to put Finola further behind her.

"Yeah, they don't really want to go into the lough, B. The Damned are desperate to get *out* of it."

"I sent one back; it may have morphed into this, but it went in. Who's to say for sure this isn't a different monster and the other one is now back from where it came?"

"This seems stupid dangerous," Finola said, as the creature zeroed in on her and let out a guttural cry.

"Danger always seems foolish, but it doesn't matter." Brigid turned to her. The creature broke free and dove for Finola. Brigid was faster, putting herself in its path, her arms rising as she shielded them from its snapping jaws.

As Finola and Ophelia screamed for her, Brigid's voice rang out, clear as a ringing bell.

"It's my fault. I'm the reason the seal is broken and I have to send them all back."

The creature bucked against the barrier, buying precious seconds for the two witches to flank Brigid on the east and west side of her before it broke through Brigid's protection spell. Its wings whipped free, and they all brought their hands up, Brigid sending as much amplification to them as she could to build their strength, but the magic she'd pulled had left her in pain and was wearing down. The creature easily pushed past it, swooping down to encage Ophelia with one wing, while the other snatched up Finola. Then it took to the air.

It tossed Fin into the sky the way a chef turns a flapjack, and Ophelia screamed. Brigid pulled the last of the magic into her palms, keeping one eye on the monster. It heated up and down her arms, and she remembered the feel of Knightly's hand clasped in hers and the surge of power from it. She took a breath and prayed this magic did not misfire this time.

She pooled the water from the lake, tugging it up as though it were a rope, swinging it through the air to wrap around the creature. The effort of the spell sent an ache into her bones, but she dug her heels in. She was no longer in pain, but the effort required all of her concentration as the creature seemed to grow in power the longer it was out of the lough.

"I will draw it down," she said, between gritted teeth, as Ophelia, left on the ground, staggered up beside her. "You must catch Finola."

Brigid yanked with all her might, and the water lasso caught the beast, tethering its arms to its sides. Finola plummeted to the earth, Ophelia catching her at the last moment before they knocked back against the hard ground.

The beast dragged Brigid, tugging her up and forward twenty feet, as she fought to hold it. The others righted themselves and climbed to their feet. They ran for Brigid, Ophelia pushing the hair from her forehead with trembling fingers. Her eyes were alight with rage. "I *hate* that thing." Then, calling after Brigid, "And what do you mean *you broke the seal*?"

"I can't *remember*," Brigid called, the monster tugging her aggressively, trying to get her across the shoreline. "We have to get it in the water now. We need something to draw it in."

Brigid's arms weakened as she sought to control it.

"I'll go," Ophelia said, her arm still around Finola.

"It wants me," Fin said on a wheeze. "It should be me."

"I don't think that's a good idea," Brigid said, her arms straining.

"I trust you," Finola said.

Ophelia looked between them, and Finola caught her eye and held the gaze. In the end, Ophelia only nodded at whatever unspoken communication passed between them. Brigid's heart squeezed at the connection, and the trust they had in her.

"There's a bunching of crystals in my bag," she said, her teeth gritted. "Set them at the edge of the water. Do it quickly, Finola, and enclose yourself in it. It will not be able to get past the barrier there, but I don't want anything to disrupt the balance and risk harming you."

"Jump in a tiny circle and snuggle the beastie. Sure, peachy keen."

"Hold your hands out," Brigid told Ophelia, "And listen for the wind."

Ophelia lifted her palms as though cupping the air. "Like this?"

"Can you hear the song, just beneath the sound?"

"I hear . . . whispers, layered over one another?" Her eyes widened.

Brigid gave a grim smile. "Yes, beautiful, isn't it?"

Ophelia nodded.

"The wind always is, for it is the sound of spirits restless on this plane, and their song is too quiet for mortal ears to hear. It is louder here than it used to be, the Damned serving as an amplifier to the voices lost in the wind."

Ophelia's hands shook and she started to lower them.

"Don't," Brigid warned, as the monster fought above them to break free. "The path of magic is a path of truth, Ophelia Gallagher. Hold the line. Open yourself to the song. You control it. It does not control you. Understand? This is the way of the Goddess."

Ophelia nodded as Finola set the crystals for her circle and moved into it.

Brigid groaned. "I cannot hold the creature any longer. On my say, call the song into your palms, and send it toward Finola. It will protect her."

"But—"

"Ancestors of Evermore are in your blood and the wind, you are mine and I am yours, trust in our magic."

Ophelia swallowed hard.

"Ready?"

"As I'll ever be."

Brigid took a breath. She didn't know if it would work, but they had to try. The world around her seemed to draw closer on her inhale. The lough trickled, the wind sang, and Brigid's heart thudded in her chest.

"*Now.*"

Ophelia's hands went up, Brigid's went down, and Finola moved into the circle. The creature swooped after her. Finola closed her eyes. The creature ricocheted off the circle and bounced up into the air. It let out a blood-curdling shriek, smoke billowing out from its mouth around its blackened teeth.

Finola crossed herself and the creature turned toward her.

"I've got you, Fin," Ophelia called, her arms straining, her cheeks red from the effort of channeling spirit and wind.

Brigid ran forward and the creature turned its head slowly toward her. A slow shudder worked its way up Brigid's back, as she focused on its eyes. They were no longer black, but green as moss and deep as a forest.

Brigid knew those eyes.

The creature opened its mouth and two words tumbled out. "*Don't forget.*"

Finola's knees clacked together, and she capitulated forward. Ophelia yelled her name, and Brigid dove for the creature. It slammed across the ice, skidding toward the crack in the water and plummeting in.

—0

OPHELIA: Welcome to *Ever More History*, Evermore's Historic Society's first-ever podcast. We've had a bit of an issue with the Damned eating our *Ever More News* newspapers, so we're taking advantage of modern technology.

I'm Ophelia Gallagher, and as the lough continues to spit out beasties, we thought it important to explore the myths of Evermore with our very own Evermorians. Evermorites. Huh. Whatever you are.

FINOLA: Ever morans?

OPHELIA: Ha-ha, Fin, thanks for that. Today I'm speaking with our very own Finola McEntire, who, as you all know, runs our *Ever More News* and assists me in crafting potions for protection.

FINOLA: Oh, aye, it's not every day you get Rodney Carmichael opening his door and smelling of Smithwick's and slurring about how he'd like a Hogwarts-worthy potion to help him bring the ladies a-runnin' to his bed. I told you, Rodney, you can't get a potion for a new personality.

OPHELIA: [groaning] She's kidding, of course. Fin's not really trying to alienate our audience right out of the gate. Good luck to you, Rodney, please don't hit on the banshees and remember consent is key. Otherwise, we will let the Damned after you.

FINOLA: Oh, aye, good luck, you big ox.

OPHELIA: That leads us into today's story. Farmer Joanie was going to join us but was called away to the church last minute to line the perimeter with black salt and bar the windows after a report that a leprechaun was trying to break in and steal the communal wine.

FINOLA: [snorts]

OPHELIA: As she's unable to be here, we're going to do our best to discuss typical creatures found in loughs. Now we all know Scotland's got dear Nessie, but what many might not realize is that Ireland has its fair share of water beasties, too. In fact, Evermore's healing waters were once reputed to be the crossover point for a way into the Otherworld. It's no wonder, then, that a magical lough would be a place open to magic and able to spit out monsters for a group of powerful magic stealers who give witches a bad name.

FINOLA: We're talking about you, coven of fright.

OPHELIA: Er, yes. Now, I know we all remember the time about ten years back when it was rumored our very own Fin here had fallen in a lough down by the cliffs and had nearly been eaten by a Fomorian.

FINOLA: I was overserved at O'Maggie's and took the long way home. I wasn't nearly eaten by anything, as if I couldn't take a Fomorian. You throw a sheep in its path and run. I just decided it was a good night for a swim. *I did.*

OPHELIA: Hmm. Well, Farmer Joanie found you as naked as the day you were born. Where's the quote—

FINOLA: She gave you a *quote*?

OPHELIA: Here it is. "Finola was half drowned by the time I fished her out. Said she'd seen a flying goat and that something tried to gobble her up foot first. It was right shocking, it was. 'It's all my fault,' she'd cried, she did. Which made me wonder if she'd made a pact with the fae, because you know how tricky they can be. But to be honest I was just grateful she'd not ended up by the lough of dreams."

FINOLA: Oh, for feck's sake.

OPHELIA: A goat? Did you really?

FINOLA: It was one of Joanie's own wee ones. I was sauced—excuse me that I couldn't tell a goat from a sheep. And I told you after, there were fish in the damn lough, nibbling my toes. It was terrifying, thinking if one lough is a magical cauldron for beasties, why can't all the others be?

OPHELIA: And your clothes?

FINOLA: I didn't want to get them wet.

OPHELIA: And the "It's all my fault" bit?

FINOLA: It was right after Quinn caught me stepping out on her with Erin. It was my fault.

OPHELIA: Oh right, that's true [clears throat]. Well then, mystery solved! No Fomorians have been spotted in any lough other than the lough of dreams.

FINOLA: I think you might want to sleep with one eye open after this, Phee. Farmer Joanie, too, telling tall tales when we've enough to deal with.

OPHELIA: Which brings me to next week's topic, when we discuss the scariest Fomorian of all, Balor and his evil eye, and the confusing haunting of the Sluagh that have been lurking around the bookstore in the romance section.

FINOLA: At least they have good taste.

OPHELIA: Until then, I'm Ophelia Gallagher reminding you to stay on the far end of Evermore as the new moon approaches, look after one another, and let us know of any new sightings. After all, the beasties will get you if you don't look out.

SIX

BOOK OF THE GODDESS (P. 253):

How to Call the Past into the Future

Memory and time, never the best of friends, are beholden to the past. To bring one back to you, you must give up something of the other. Your memory, or those of another, may be used to lure time, and time may be used to lure memory. But be careful, because days offered are never returned, and the past, once in the past, is a hard mistress to lure forward.

Fairy Hill was built on a fort but no one in Evermore remembered that. Much like the rest of the world didn't remember Evermore. Knightly, however, remembered it all. He sat on top of the hill that was blanketed in clovers and thick hearty earth, just down from where the cliffs began, and stared at the ring of stones in the center of it. A fairy ring on Fairy Hill, and his penance of a sort. Overhead the sky, which had been a brilliant blue, was shifting into something somber. Gray tinging the edge of the white clouds, the winds blowing in from the east and then calming before shifting to ride in from the west.

Evermore was unsettled. It wasn't the only one.

Knightly's insides were fizzing with energy. Raw, naked, *energy*. Someone else might mistake it for emotion, but he knew it for what it was. He held up his hands, and energy pooled into the tips of his fingers. Lightning crackled across the sky. He shook out his palms and thunder rumbled in the distance, moving fast, drifting closer, morphing the silvery clouds into charcoal.

Knightly had waited for this day to come. He had woven each second of the ticking clock since he first laid eyes on Brigid Heron into the chinks of armor he now wore. Defense from her crooked smile; wide, twinkling eyes; and the pretty blush that rose under her freckles when she was angry.

And, oh, how he made her angry.

There were many stories in the universe, and Knightly knew well the book of powerful, brave, and reckless Brigid Heron. Once upon a time, she was alone but not lonely. She lived in a house she loved, and she performed services for a deity who loved her. Her days were filled but also empty, her life comfortable and, while not safe, predictable.

"It's not the lack of people," she was known to say, "it's the absence of what comes from them. Chasing snowflakes with a thimble of want thinking it's a bucket full. Seeing who can fill theirs first, arguing over who is going to mind the fire or mop the muck from the floors, talking too loud when they think they're right. Not talking at all but creating the loudest of silences if they've been hurt. It's the chaos of what could be that haunts a person."

Brigid's family consisted of a broken mother and bastard of a father, so Knightly thought it was no wonder she only ever longed for something more. He understood because he, too, longed for more.

Brigid Heron wanted something she could not have, or rather, would not go after if it meant being tethered to a man she did not love, beholden to him for something she needed only a moment of his time for. Knightly had needed only a moment of Brigid's time, and so he thought they made fine bedfellows.

Brigid had possession of the *Book of the Goddess.* Inside the book was a treasure trove of proper spell instruction, and if you knew how to read it, the story of how the Goddess worked her magic.

Brigid knew nothing of the true nature of the book. Which was funny, considering how she had a desire to understand rules. When you're raised in chaos, rules can provide a certain kind of refuge, he'd supposed. Still, she proved to be an exemplary pupil and student, and so her mind held the information Knightly needed most: how to unlock the lough blessed by his almost father. In return for Brigid opening her mind to him, he was able to gift her that which she desired most, something simple and complex: *unconditional* love in the form of a child.

It was also funny, he supposed, though he was definitely *not* laughing, how Brigid would be the one to teach him the truth of what love was.

Even if she could not remember it.

He thought of another conversation, one he'd had with a woman with dark hair and sad eyes. "We can't take back the wrongs we've done," Agnes had once told him, "But we can try to make things right moving forward."

Knightly still did not know if he agreed. He was of two minds, as so many gods were. They were, after all, born to be tricky beings. But he had been waiting a long time, and he was determined to try to restore some kind of balance.

Knightly walked to the edge of the ring of stones at the top of his hill and stood outside them. They formed a nearly perfect circle, the smooth stones of varying sides that were peppered

with moss. Mushrooms and white sprigs of flowers grew between them. He'd often thought they looked like pearls strung
on a necklace, dulled yet with enough luster to remind him he
was the one who had softened what should be bright.

The people of Evermore used to love his fairy stones. They
terrified the Goddess so much she'd often sit beside them, like a
child challenging itself to stay in the dark for one minute more.
Her cape flapping in the wind, her legs crossed at the ankle, a
determined glint in her eye.

Like a child, being brave for far longer than they need to be.
Or a parent looking for its most unruly child.

He swallowed a tidal wave of emotion. Knightly *hated* feelings. They were sticky, clinging to his fingertips and the protective covering of his heart. It was inconvenient to have them, and
yet they had been his constant companion these last hundred
years.

He gave his head a shake. In the end, he decided Brigid had
been right to fear him after all.

But that was in the past, and he was in the present about
to leap into the future. He leaned down and whispered to
the grass. The blades grew high, springing up like a fountain
from the ground, shooting up into a wall. Knightly pressed
his thumb to the blades and then slipped a hand between. He
spread the grass apart like pulling back a curtain, and one side
fell away, revealing a veil, and beyond it, rolling hills and a valley
filled with colors so vivid they glowed.

A land under this one, through this one, beyond this one. A
place he could see, but could no longer touch.

Knightly hummed under his breath, as the sound of chaos
erupted in the village of this other world, beyond the fields. He
went to sit and watch, wishing once more that it would show
him beyond this view to that which he really wished to see . . .
when he felt the pinch of fear at the base of his spine. The wind

rushed at him, shoving him back, and the scent of apples tickled under his nose.

Brigid.

He did not hesitate. Knightly looked down at his shadow, which bowed to him, and jumped inside.

🗝

Rain began to fall, pinging across the lough, melting the remaining ice and making it harder than it already was to see into the dark, dank waters. Brigid let out a growl. If she'd had sleeves, she'd have rolled them up. Since she didn't, she threw her hair over her shoulder. Brigid stared at the space where the creature had existed moments before and gave her head a disbelieving shake. It *dove into* the lough. Why? Hadn't it wanted *out* of the lough? She looked back at the others, who appeared as confounded as she was.

"Can you see where it's gone?" Ophelia called.

"No," she said, her eyes on the ice. But she could *feel* it. A tug along her fingertips, as though they wanted to reach out and yank. "But it's in there."

"That's good, right? We wanted it to go back?"

"It's not, though. It's hiding."

"What if we position wards around the lough, try and prevent it from returning?"

"I doubt it will work," Brigid said, thinking of how strong the coven of Knight was, and how uncertain she was at how they were managing to control the lough in the first place. "But it's worth a try."

The rain was a blessing and a curse. It melted the ice but it also provided a way to consecrate the crystals from her bag— the ones Finola had used as a protection circle. Since she could not summon fire in the rain and cleanse the air, Brigid used the rainwater to wash away the baleful magic that permeated the ground.

As she sent out her energy, she caught a whiff of cedar. The very scent that clung to Knightly.

Brigid looked around the lough, searching for him. The land remained empty. Brigid thought of the Goddess and her beneficial magic, how it left when she did. The Goddess's magic was compassion and healing, fairness and love. She ran a hand through the air and drew the rain to her. It soaked the hem of her dress, tugged at her hair even as she felt the pinch between her shoulder blades. Unruly magic filled the land now.

She longed to speak to the Goddess, to ask what had happened to the lough, to her. The Goddess would know how to restore what once was. She knew everything. Brigid missed the deity, her mentor who had over the years become a friend. She needed to fix everything wrong, while living in a time she did not belong to, without memories of where she had been. It felt as easy as spinning gold from straw.

"Brigid?" Ophelia asked, laying a rose quartz along the edge of the shore. "How can the Damned be your fault?"

Brigid rubbed the back of her neck. "That's what East, the leader of the coven of Knight, said. She *thanked* me for unsealing the lough."

"No way," Finola said, setting down her crystal with a loud thunk. "Those witches are saying whatever they can to mess with you. They're evil."

"Did they have any proof?" Ophelia asked, her tone gentle.

"They were too busy attempting to kill me for me to ask," Brigid said, peering along the edge of the perimeter, checking for them.

"Because they're making it up," Fin said. "Like I said, B. Evil as panty hose."

"Panty hose?" Brigid asked, when a strong wind blew across

the lake, and a rumble trampled beneath her feet. The scent of cedar and mint grew stronger, and Brigid knew he was there before she looked up.

A shadow cast across the ground, and Knightly stepped out of it.

The air thickened, the sun cut through a sliver in the sky, and the shadow appeared. An outline of broad shoulders, a narrow waist and hips, flexed hands, and wide set feet. It was an arrogant shadow, the chin raised, the head tilted back as though declaring, "Yes, the sun waits for me."

He stepped up and out of it, leaving it on the ground to trail behind him, the part of him, Brigid thought, that might be the most honest. Brigid straightened, her hands coming up, ready to strike. Knightly's tilted smile caused her stomach to give a delicious twirl, and she huffed in irritation and dropped her hands.

"She's not wrong, you know," he said. "The witches will say anything to antagonize the great Brigid Heron."

"What is that?" Finola asked, as Ophelia surveyed the area and asked, "Did you hear that or are we sharing an audible hallucination?"

Knightly's grin widened and Brigid sighed. "Drop the glamour."

"Make me."

"I don't know how," she gritted out.

"Oh, but you do."

Brigid felt the color leach from her face at his words. First his coven told her she caused the lough to open, now he was telling her she knew how to use his magic. A magic of a god not her own.

And the terrifying part was that Brigid was beginning to believe him.

"Not a communal hallucination, I don't think," Ophelia said, her eyes on Brigid.

"Why are you here?" she asked.

A rock hit Knightly in his chest, and he looked down.

"Ow," he said, not looking the least bit bothered.

"Did I get it?" Finola asked, waving another stone.

"Oh, for *my* sake," he said, and snapped his fingers.

The glamour dropped from Knightly and Finola let out a groan. "That sight is worse than the Sluagh dragon."

"Fin, the beastie wanted to eat you," Ophelia said.

"And he wants to gobble up Brigid," Finola said, waving a hand. "Six of one, half a dozen of the other."

"Why are you here?" Brigid repeated, not taking her eyes off him, and absolutely not giving in to the intensity trying to build in her at the idea of him "gobbling her up." Would he start with her lips or somewhere from below? She swatted the thought away, and he lifted a brow as though he precisely knew the direction of her thoughts.

"It is my lough," he said. "I am often here. The better question might be why *you three* are here."

"We're fighting your terror of witches," Finola said, tossing a rock in the air, catching it, and tossing it again.

"Not doing a terrific job of it," he said, ignoring her implied threat as his eyes shifted to the water. He walked to the shoreline.

"Let's shove him in," Fin whispered loudly to Ophelia. "Maybe the Damned needs to develop a taste for one of its own."

"If only it were that simple," Knightly said, before he walked onto the surface of the lough.

He paused, staring at the shoreline and frost that coated the sand. He waved a hand, and his shadow took a step first. Ice formed with each step he took, as he sauntered across the surface. Knightly following behind him.

"He thinks he's the bloody Christ now," Fin said.

"We could still shove him in," Ophelia said. "Draw the witches' wind and send him toppling. What do you think, Brigid?"

Brigid thought of what Knightly wasn't saying. "Perhaps in a minute." She lifted the skirt of her dress and stepped over to where he'd left a trail of ice. "If he tries to drown me, please do send the winds to him. Otherwise, give me a moment."

Knightly stood at the center of the lough, staring down into it. His expression inscrutable. The wind blew against his back, sending his dark locks of hair forward, covering his face. He sighed against it, as though leaning into a warm embrace.

Brigid walked to him with small, fast steps. She was less worried about the thing (or things) beneath them and more worried about the god-man standing before her. She couldn't seem to control the itch in her palms each time he was near, the urge to run her fingers through his disobedient locks of hair. It was as rebellious as he was, and something about it all left her with an unquenchable desire to taste his lips.

Finola had gotten it wrong, it was Brigid who was fighting a compulsion to gobble him up.

"I had thought with a little time, you might remember more," he said, as she stepped to his back, not turning to face her, but shifting closer in her direction. His fingers coming perilously close to where hers dangled at her side.

"My memories are as opaque as this lough," she said, stretching her fingers out, unable to control the motion.

"Perhaps more is buried there than here," he said, before turning to look at her over her shoulder, his thumb grazing against her palm and sending shivers of want curling up her arm.

"If you know me," she said, her voice growing husky. "Tell me."

"The last time I tried, your eyes rolled back into your head and you broke into convulsions."

Brigid jerked her hand away. "Yet you left me."

"I was about to carry you home when your witches came up the walk."

"You ran away."

"I panicked."

"You are ridiculous." She forced her shoulders to relax, glancing beneath her at the water of the lough, finding it still, and raising her gaze back to his. "I thought you knocked me out somehow with your magic."

"If only I were so powerful."

"Ass."

"Witch."

"Almost god." She narrowed her eyes. "What of my memories?"

"You've been gone for one hundred years." He clenched and unclenched his jaw. "The lough is a pass-through from this land into the one beyond these borders."

"I've heard the tales. The Otherworld."

"Yes."

"My Goddess sealed your lough, because you grew bored with your Otherworld."

"She sealed it because she feared it. Deities like your Brighid make rash decisions, they are not mortal." He crossed his arms over his chest and Brigid forced herself not to notice the corded muscles of his forearms. "Not even a little."

"What has this to do with my memories?"

"The lough is hungry."

"And?"

"It ate them."

"It *ate* my memories?"

"There is always a price to magic."

She glared at him. "Then get them back. It's your lough."

"If I could, I would." He sighed, tapped the toe of his boot against the ice. *Clink clink clink.*

"Why do I get the feeling you know how *I* can get them back."

"Perhaps not *all* of them, but we can make a deal."

Let's make a deal.

A flash of a grin, a tug of hope, a rush of desire. Knightly standing before her with his hand outstretched, the dimple flashing in his cheek, his voice low as velvet and his words as pungent as a glass of whiskey. Echoes of what had been flooded through her.

"Have we been here before?" she asked, a tremble running through her voice.

He hesitated.

"We've been close to here," he said.

Brigid reached a hand toward his and energy burst between them. Gold flakes that hovered between fingertips. Heat, desire, and . . . fear. Because he was a god of mischief who courted chaos like flowers seek rain. She dropped her hand first.

"Why would you help me? I'm going to seal your lough."

"Perhaps I wouldn't help you," he said, slow to lower his hand. "Perhaps I would help myself."

"I don't understand."

"And I don't know if you are yourself enough yet for me to tell you."

She narrowed her eyes. He narrowed his back.

"How can anyone ever trust a deal with a god?"

He didn't respond. Simply held his palm up once more toward hers.

Brigid looked back to the others, then into the water where a handful of bubbles reached the surface.

"No."

He leaned closer, breath by breath, inch by inch, and she did not move away. His lips brushed against the outer shell of her ear, and goose bumps rose across her neck and chest. "I will give up a memory of my own for one of yours to be returned."

"Why would you—"

"After. We make the deal, and I will tell you after."

"When you know if I'm really me?"

He shrugged.

"What happens to *your* memory?"

"I give it to the Damned. They have forgotten who they are. Hungry, starved, they will keep coming until they are satiated. This will give it more food than it could need."

"You're feeding its mind your memory?"

"Memories are life."

Brigid did not trust this deal. She did not trust this god-man.

But she needed to remember.

"Fine."

His hand slipped into hers, and the sky slipped under her feet, the clouds rolled beneath her shoulders. Knightly's shadow knit itself to Brigid, and together they looked back.

Brigid sat in the sunlight beneath the hazelnut tree about ten feet from her house. The sun was high in the sky overhead, the grass soft beneath her, and a friendly spideog a few branches over, with its vibrant red-orange chest and friendly head tilt, periodically burst into song. A girl with dark auburn hair sat beside her, her knees covered in dirt, a smear of fresh blueberry across her lower lip, her face scrunched in concentration as she wove a section of clovers into her flower crown.

"Do you think it's true?" the girl asked, pausing to wipe

her nose with the back of her arm, not taking her eyes off the knot she was tying in her clovers.

Brigid pulled a handkerchief from her dress pocket and handed it to her. "That your nose cleans your arm, no, I'd say rather not."

"Ha-ha," the girl said and rubbed her arm across Brigid's.

Brigid rolled her eyes and wiped her elbow, unable to prevent her own grin.

"No, silly. I mean about the Otherworld?"

Brigid bit back the sigh. For weeks she had been fielding this question. She'd wanted to give her a story of hope. Brigid had grown up learning of the Otherworld from the Goddess, and the tales seemed the best distraction for a curious eleven-year-old who of late had taken to using her magic to turn the neighbor's chocolate pies into mud pies and dyeing the sheep in the shades of the rainbow. Brigid rather liked the improvement of the sheep, but their reputation was already questionable, and she needed to help a curious mind find better distractions. Storytelling had helped Brigid through some of her toughest moments, so why not talk of the Otherworld, regardless of how true it was.

"I've never found a way into the Otherworld and I've been up and down, over and under, every nook and cranny in the field. It's a shut door, locked up tight, no key in sight."

"Yes, but you walk while daydreaming and writing in your journal. I'm surprised you haven't ended up in a lough from not watching where you're going."

Brigid had, in fact, ended up in the water a time or two, but she wasn't about to admit that.

"The Otherworld is a fairy tale," she said instead. But even as she said it, that same vibration that had been thrumming along under her skin, light as the touch of a falling feather, flared to life again.

"You said the sidhe only let in those who believe. You don't believe, so how would you ever know? How would you ever find it?"

"I suppose I wouldn't, as I'm a witch and the fairy king doesn't allow witches like me onto his land," Brigid said, making a joke that was more than a joke. "And that's enough talk about the fairies for today. Maybe when you're older and wiser, you'll find the Otherworld and lead me there."

"Maybe when I'm older and wiser I'll go on my own, and I'll be crowned queen of the fae and you'll have to make my crown of clovers for our Harvest Festival."

"Hmm." Brigid rubbed her cheek, like she was considering. Then she scooped up a handful of clovers and tossed them into the air over the girl. They rained down like confetti falling from the sky and the girl laughed and tried to catch them. "Or you could just wear the one I've made now."

The girl looked at her, eyes bright, cheeks staining a happy pink. "Really? But it's your turn to be the magic maiden."

Brigid laughed. "I'll tell you a secret. All maidens are magical on Evermore. Every day of every year, and that crown was made for you. Besides, it's our festival, the two of us, so we can write the rules."

Then Brigid held out a hand, took the crown from her, and gently set it on the girl's head. Brigid stood and bowed. The girl jumped up and curtseyed so deep she nearly toppled over. Brigid grinned, bowed deeper, then tugged the girl back up, twirled her around, and spun her into a dance. Laughing, she threw her head back.

Everything in her world was settled, complete, and she owed it all to the child before her.

A splash sounded from far away. An angry magpie called. Brigid gasped, and a vibration rolled up her spine. It dipped low over each vertebra as it climbed up her neck until it was so strong she braced her feet against the pulsation.

"Brigid?"

A chime sounded.

"Brigid?"

The deep tones from the voice ricocheted into her palms. She tried to catch the sound.

"Brigid?"

Her eyes flew open.

Knightly stood over her, glowering, something dark and unruly flashing in his half-hooded eyes.

Brigid forced herself to sit up. She was on a patch of ice, in the center of the lough. She tried to draw a breath and realized her chest was heaving, her hands shaking.

The girl.

Brigid remembered her. They had been happy, utterly and blissfully content. How could she have forgotten for even a moment?

She tried to stand and tumbled into Knightly. She knocked the man back a foot, and they both tumbled over across the ice. But Brigid couldn't feel the cold.

"Oh Goddess," she said, rolling up. "I need to find her."

"Who?" he asked, standing up, his eyes wide, expression hard to read.

"The—" Brigid stopped, her hands pressing against her chest, over her heart and the sob building there. "I didn't get her name."

Brigid looked over her shoulder into the water. She tried to find it, but it was gone. The girl was gone. Her throat clogged with tears. She fisted her hands, brought them to her mouth and *screamed* into her closed palms.

Knightly stumbled back, his eyes widening.

Brigid ignored his hysterics—men could be so dramatic—and scrubbed her hands over her face. Tried to stuff her grief in her mouth. She looked back to Knightly, and the way his face contorted into sadness. Was it for her?

She took a breath. Tried to think. She had a memory back, which meant he'd given up one of his. Knightly held out a hand, and Brigid's eyes focused on his fingertips, which were shaking.

"I found her to lose her," she said, the truth pouring from her lips, tinged in sorrow so true they saturated the air between them.

He swallowed, and Brigid fought the urge to press her fingers to the base of his throat.

"You will find her again." He reached for her, and guided her up. She stood and leaned against him.

He looked offshore to where Ophelia and Finola paced, looking for all the world like two jaguars waiting to pounce. Brigid pressed the memory of the girl to her heart, letting the echoes absorb into her bloodstream and wrap around her bones. She took one last shuddering breath and accepted Knightly's arm, curving hers into his. He helped her back to the shoreline, staying beside her and yet somehow following her as well. They stepped off the ice, and once his shadow was safely on the shore the water shifted from frozen to liquid in the blink of an eye.

"I'd say that was impressive, but he doesn't deserve the notice," Ophelia said, placing her hands to her hips.

Brigid rejoined the two women, so they stood together, facing Knightly.

"Now," she said to Knightly, setting aside the memory and pain of it to finish what she had started. "The truth. Why are you helping us?"

SEVEN

BOOK OF THE GODDESS (INTRODUCTION):

The magic of the Goddess is a beneficial magic, of grace and care. Be wary of magic from other lands. The gods and goddesses of old were as tricky as they were wise, and their magic is not always meant for mortal use. What has the power to transform, also has the power to destroy.

Knightly studied Brigid's face, noting how the color was slowly returning to her cheeks. The two witches, her coven, stood sentry at her side. They were formidable in a way the coven of Knight was not. They didn't function as one, but for one another. It was evident in the way they leaned into each other, supportive but not overly so. The witches who used his name wouldn't be far, and once they realized the Damned he had fed was not seeking others to claim in the village, they would return.

"We need to speak somewhere ears can't follow," Knightly said, and ran a finger along his lower lip. "How about your workstation, I assume you left it spelled?"

Brigid jolted. "How do you know of it?"

"Because I know you," he said, the words falling softly between them.

The air thickened and thunder rumbled in the distance. He needed to get his emotions under control, and staring at Brigid Heron with her red hair blowing about her face like flames spreading from a fire was distracting and intoxicating.

She looked to the two other witches. "I have a caravan where I worked my more involved spells." She nodded to him. "It should be spelled tight."

"I will meet you there," he told her. "At sundown. I'll handle the coven when they return, let them know their Damned was damned to get in my way. It won't be the first time I've spun the lie for them or the last."

Brigid gave him a curious look. "Why would you—"

"There is much to say, but I would prefer to say it where it is safer."

She looked as though she wanted to argue, but Finola tugged at her wrist. "I don't know what's going on, but I'm cold and wet and he's not wrong, the ground is vibrating beneath my feet."

"It seems to do that when they are near," Ophelia said.

"The earth does not know whether to greet them or reject them, so it reacts," Brigid said, her eyes on the ground. She flicked a glance to Knightly. "Outside of the caravan, at dusk. If this is a trick and I have to track you down, I won't hesitate to employ the best and worst of magics to bind you."

"It sounds like my kind of an evening," he said, his dimple flashing. "But let's save that for our second date when your bodyguards aren't around."

"You're impossible," Brigid said, but the corner of her mouth gave the slightest twitch.

Knightly nodded. "Yes, I'm that and so many other syllabic words with varied meanings and a few more colorful iterations of language, too."

He didn't say what he was thinking. That he was also, unfortunately, entirely hers.

"Let's go," Brigid said to the others, who shot Knightly scalding looks meant to sizzle the hair from his body, before they swiftly walked from the area.

Knightly stood at the edge of the lough, the water lapping up to the edge of his boots like it was trying to return home to him. This corner of Evermore was sharper, louder, angrier than all other parts of the island. Manannán mac Lír blessed the lough. The legend had it right, in tribute to the Goddess Brighid. He did more than that though, he created a weapon that was fast falling into the worst hands.

The wind blew in from the east, the last dregs of warmth bitten from the air as the four witches he had struck a deal with centuries ago walked across the land. Their feet made no sound, their bodies not fully visible as shadows swam around them, keeping them protected and in many ways, keeping them caged. To their mission and their thirst for power.

"We called the Damned," they sang out to him, the sound coming from above him, below him, swarming all around. Their voices were buried deep in the lough, or born from it—he wasn't sure which, because the ancient power of these deep waters kept as many secrets as he did. He might be the ruler of the lough, but the lough did not seek a leader.

"Yes," he said, "and the Damned served its purpose."

The four witches took to their preferred places around the lough, the four corners of the earth that marked their elements, and stared at him with their blank stares. It was like looking into the faces of shadowed dolls, empty holes for eyes, the light shifting in shades of gray to reveal the dip of a brow, the curve of a lip, the ridge of a cheekbone.

They blinked and the masks they wore dropped from their faces.

Knightly had seen many things in his millennia in and out

of the world. That did not stop him from having to force the neutral expression on his face as the true nature of the witches of Knight gazed back at him.

Eyes black as the holes eating their souls, skin the color of overworked clay, and hair no longer made of anything human, but somehow shifting into a substance more closely related to seaweed. They were of the lough as much as they were born from it, more Damned than any creature on Evermore.

And this, too, was his fault.

"Where has the Damned gone?" they asked.

"To where the Goddess's well rests in near ruins," he said, rocking back on his heels, putting his hands into his pockets, playing the disinterested demigod once more. Unaffected and unconcerned, the boy-god who was meant for mischief and missions.

"You said that seeking the well was a fool's mission," they said, their mouths moving faster than their words, their eyes never shifting away from him.

"That was before Brigid Heron returned."

"We must end the witch," they said. "Before she remembers her daughter and moves to set her free. If she succeeds, she will end us all."

"I agree," he said, looking up to the sky, instead of meeting their gazes. "If she succeeds, she will end everything." He looked beyond them. "Which is why I need you to go into the well now that it is open. The Damned will guard the land around it. You must draw any power of the Goddess out that remains in the well. It will give you the ability to tap into the magic of the Goddess. Then you will be so powerful nothing and no one can stop us."

The four raised their hands, palms up in an offering, out to him. "We serve the master of the Knight. We are the coven of Lugh, guardians of the lough, keepers of the creatures of chaos. We will not fail."

He bowed and fought the shiver pulling at the back of his

neck. He turned from the coven, and keeping his shadow as close as he could, he walked away from the lough.

He did not look back.

＊━０

Back at her home that wasn't quite her home, Brigid surveyed the bedroom that had once been hers, and Ophelia told her had served as a guest room, though no guests had yet to stay in it.

"It was waiting for you," Ophelia said, with that focused look she had. It made Brigid think that somehow everything would be okay. When really, nothing was okay and might never be again.

The room still featured her bed frame, but the mattress was something out of a storybook, soft and somehow sturdy. The comforter was a thick white quilt, the pillows and sheets the same. On the small, dark green side table sat a collection of journals from Agnes, a bowl of crystals, and a soothing rock salt lamp. There was a rug striped like the rainbow on the floor, and a bookshelf against the other wall filled with books on magical properties, healing herbs, and spells of the moon.

She took the borrowed clothing she collected from the women, uncertain if any of it could fit quite right, and headed for the room at the back of the house.

Nothing in the tiny room looked as it should have, and it took Brigid a long time to work out how to use the upgraded facilities, even after being shown by Ophelia. She practiced with the sink, turning the water off and on, on and off, for a good few minutes before she attempted the shower. When she did, she nearly froze, then nearly scalded herself, before she found a tepid temperature that left her skin humming. There was a lot Brigid did not understand about the modern world, but she was most assuredly a fan of the advancements in bathrooms.

As she dressed, Brigid marveled at the softness of the underwear, pants, and shirt she slipped into. Even the little slippers with the rubber soles Finola gave her were comfortable. She braided her hair, fastened it with one of the ties in a bowl by the sink, and headed for the kitchen. A teal teapot sat on the circular wooden kitchen table beside a squat navy book with a familiar crest across it and a hunk of pages to the left of it. Brigid eyed the book split in half, before her gaze drifted to Finola seated at the table, and then to the strange silver appliance behind them with levers and bobs and bits.

The kitchen was cozy, with the walls painted a calm coastal blue and gray. Flowers were arranged in jars on the counters, over the refrigerator, on the stove, and on the windowsill above the sink. It was peaceful and soothing, the room, even as it was filled with strange new objects.

"Does that work as many wonders as the shower and toilet?" she asked, nodding at the machine on the counter.

"Oh!" Finola said, hopping up from the table, knocking her knee against the edge as she went. "Cripes. Yes, it does. Sorry, I'm a bit of a mess." She rubbed her knee, offered a pained smile. "Have you ever had an espresso, then?"

"A what?" Brigid tried to keep up. Finola was a rambler when nerves overtook her, it seemed. Brigid gave her credit for still being upright. It was no small thing, to suffer an attack and battle with baneful magic.

Finola ran to the machine and pulled a few levers, pressed a few buttons. "It's a kind of coffee. It's not as common on the island, but it's life-giving."

"Obsessed is what you are," Ophelia said, coming in from outside carrying a bunching of Solomon's seal. "Much like Fin with her Mary Reilly."

"Hey! I can't help it if I prefer my ladies to be loose rather than loyal," Finola said, and Ophelia snorted. "*Kidding*, of course." Finola flashed a grin. "I rather like them to be both."

Ophelia groaned.

"You lie with women," Brigid said.

Finola looked over at her. "I do."

Brigid nodded, looked down at her shirt and ran a hand over it before doing the same to her pant leg. "Women have the softest skin."

Finola grinned. "They *really* do."

"Do you prefer women," Ophelia asked, leaning against the counter, placing the flowers in a bucket of water, "or was there a man you were longing for?"

Brigid thought of the way Knightly's eyes raked over her and promptly chased that devil from her thoughts. "I've always preferred my own company for the most part," she said, brushing the crumbs from the table onto her plate. "There have been a few interesting lovers, but none who stuck. I'd rather please myself than be let down by someone else."

"Not a bad philosophy," Ophelia said, with a small smile.

"Phee's still nursing a bit of a cracked heart," Finola said, nodding her head in the other woman's direction.

Ophelia blew out a breath. "Thorpe Keogh can drop deader than James McDougal. It's none of my never mind."

Brigid looked up. "I knew a McDougal. We called him Jimmy."

"That'd be James's da," Ophelia said, shifting her chin into her hand. "Old Jim McDougal was ninety and two when he fell dead into his Guinness. Nearly ruined Boxing Day, it did."

"The one time Knightly was useful," Finola said, her eyes taking on a gleam like a lion thinking of a particularly aggravating hyena.

"Knightly?" Brigid asked, her stomach giving an unruly flip.

"Aye," Finola said.

"He can't help but pop up, can he?" Brigid said. "In conversation, while attempting to vanquish monsters. Bloody nuisance."

Finola gave a small laugh, and Brigid turned to her.

"How are you feeling?" she asked Finola. "Truly. You've had a lot of monsters back to back, and been targeted."

Finola walked to the kitchen cabinet and pulled out a glass and filled it with two fingers of whiskey. "That thing tried to eat me."

"You were incredibly brave," Brigid said.

Ophelia set about boiling and stirring the Solomon's seal. "And ridiculously stupid," she added, but with affection. "Brigid, are you sure it's wise to meet with Knightly?"

"No. But he helped me regain a memory, and I need to know if he can help with the rest." She cleared her throat, as tears pressed in. Better to tell them the truth of it fast. "I remembered a young girl. I . . . she . . . she was mine."

"Yours?" Ophelia asked, her hands going still. "We've no records of your having a daughter."

Brigid pressed a hand to her stomach. "I can feel the truth of it. But that's it, the rest is gone." She took a breath and looked to the book on the table. "You've the *Book of the Goddess*, and yet you did not know her. She existed. You might be in the dark from certain truths, but that only makes them the brighter when you bring them into the light."

"We thought the book was yours," Finola said. "And we didn't even have that section until today."

"My Goddess gave it to me . . ." Brigid squinted out the window, trying to yank the memory out like a splinter being pulled. "*Why* can't I recall the rest? I can see up to a point and then there's nothing. You say you got the second half of it today?"

"It showed up. And it sounds like a memory did, too?" Ophelia asked.

"Yes. *My* girl." She rubbed a hand over the pain in her heart. "I am part of this. The Damned, the curse on Evermore. The loss of my child. Knightly knows, too."

"It could all be connected," Ophelia said.

Brigid nodded.

Finola threw back another two fingers of whiskey. "Okay. Then let's gather all the god-killing things we have in the house, and go get your answers."

"Finola—" Brigid started.

"If you're about to tell me we can stay here, safe as houses—an expression that is sorely inappropriate considering that your house has a mind of its own—then you can sod off. We're coming."

"She's right," Ophelia said, handing Brigid a cup of water with a bit of root from the flower in it. "We're family, Brigid. Where you go, we go."

Brigid sat down the tincture for healing and warding off malicious forces on the counter. The tears threatened to pull her under again, so she rubbed at the edge of her eyes, willing them back. When her voice was clear enough to speak without breaking, she reached a hand for each of them. "Together then."

"Together," they repeated, and Finola groaned. "And now we sound like those bloody freaky witches. Let's promise never to speak in unison again, load up on hemlock, and hit the road."

—0

The walk from Brigid's house to her workshop was a short one. It was down the little paved path, over a stream, and through a clearing. The sky was clear and welcoming, the sunlight peeking through the clouds and lighting their way. No shadows chased after them, and the blooming flowers bent toward them as they walked. Magic in the land recognizing its mistress and her like, grateful for their restorative presence.

Brigid's workshop had been atypical in 1922 standards, but she supposed the modern world supported structures of a different sort than the one that sat before them—if the openmouthed, wide-eyed, flushed-cheek stares of the two witches was a correct indication. What was previously unseen revealed itself when Brigid called for that which was unseen to once again be seen, and the glamour fell away.

"It's a bloody caravan," Finola said, clapping her hands together. "Where in the world did it come from and why do you have it?"

Brigid studied the caravan, with its chipped cream paint and peeling frame. It had been kept hidden and safe, but it was in distress, that much was clear, and her heart tugged at the sight.

"It came to me," she said, hefting the basket she carried and stepping forward to better catalog the caravan's frame.

"You're not Romani," Finola said, looking Brigid up and down. "Are you?"

"If only," Brigid said, thinking back to the man with the deepest eyes and nimble fingers, who had taught her a very worthwhile lesson in how tongues were used on various body parts during a wonderful fortnight beneath the stars. His was a potent kind of magic, and she'd been thrilled and surprised when his caravan had turned up on her property. She'd told him of the well's healing waters and invited him to fill a pail for his ailing mother from the well of the Goddess if he were in need, for the Goddess never turned away those in distress.

Brigid had been a bit bruised, feelings-wise, that he hadn't sought her out again after their tumble, but she found the payment of the caravan and note of gratitude charming enough to overlook his rejection of seeking her bed one last time.

"No, I don't have Romani blood, which is a pity. Theirs is a divine magic."

"So how'd you come by the caravan?" Ophelia asked, walking around the base.

"Payment of a sort," Brigid said. "From a friend. Of a sort."

"All kinds and sorts around here, huh?" Finola asked.

"Was he or she as bonny as the ride?" Ophelia asked, giving Brigid a slow smile.

"He was near as big as the caravan, and far more fetching on the outside. While a talented man, I think I got the better deal with this than anything else he could have given me."

"A man gives a woman a caravan, and I'm thinking you must have cast one hell of spell over him—intended or otherwise," Finola said on a low whistle, as she squatted to study where the steps were rolled back into the vehicle.

"'Twasn't me," Brigid said. "He sought help, and I granted it to him in a tonic born from my Goddess's well. His ma was ailing, and he'd exhausted all other options."

"The well was that powerful?"

"It was."

"Did it work?"

"According to his letter, it revived her whole." She bit back the bitter taste of his rejection one last time—it did not suit her—and studied the caravan before her.

Its face was round, with a sharp awning overhang. It had reminded her, when she first laid eyes on it, of the home a curious fox might choose, should it be able to have its pick. Fanciful and deceiving, its aqua and cream exterior with its great slashes of navy made it look like a decorative cake roll. The wheels were cream as well, and she could only imagine the horses that would have pulled her caravan should she have ever met them. In her imagination, they had headdresses, the uncooperative ones with eye blinders and too bright colors because the caravan itself was as bewildering as it was dear.

"I love it," Ophelia said, reaching up to rub a hand along the intricate wood awning, sighing a bit as she did. "How do you work in here, though? Is it not a bit cramped, or uncomfortable?"

"You've never been inside one before?" Brigid asked.

They both shook their heads.

Brigid smiled, reached up, and ran a hand along the side panel where the door was tucked. She blew across the latch and closed her eyes. The caravan rumbled, a low grumble like that of an aging man waking from an afternoon doze to find his favorite grandchild standing at his feet. The door unlocked, Brigid gripped the handle and pulled.

If the exterior of the covered caravan was flamboyant, the inside was downright grandiose. To the immediate right was an upright bench, littered with papers and stacks of books. Beyond it was a circular table, with a shelf above it holding all manner of little vials and tiny boxes. Beyond that was the bed. Assorted cabinets held crystals of various sizes and shapes, more vials full of corked liquids, and a few cabinet cards. To the immediate left of it was another table, which was where Brigid had taken her meals—a clean saucer and plate still set out, with a spoon across the bowl—and in front of it another bench, this one wider with a cushion sewn in and a pillow cushioned on top.

The wood for each of the furnishings was a warm red, a mahogany or another welcoming wood. The mirrored sliding panels opposite either side of the tucked-away desk were trimmed in teal, and wood carving was etched all along the trim. Even the lanterns were painted, a red that had softened; and the large, beautifully detailed drawer knobs were rimmed in cream carvings. It was a sight, one that shouldn't have worked, and yet this was the place that looked the most like Brigid. It felt the most like her—if she were being truthful. She may not have created the caravan, but she had known it was hers the moment she first set foot inside.

"Now *this* is a work space," Finola said, coming to stand beside Brigid, her hands on her hips.

"I've always thought so," Brigid said, reaching out to run her fingers along the little desk.

"Is it spelled?" Ophelia asked, looking about. "There's no dust."

"Yes. It's cloaked from sight and spelled clean. It's lost a bit of luster, though." Her voice dropped to a whisper; she was unable to keep the sadness out. "Time has moved through here, too." She studied the space, a heavy weight pressing against her chest, and heard the snapping of twigs and crunching of grass. She turned and stepped out of the caravan, the two women following.

Knightly strode through the grass. He'd added a black overcoat, and the wind blew it back, revealing his dark pants and boots, and gray shirt. His hair was tousled, his eyes were bright, and Brigid's mouth watered on instinct at the sight.

"I wasn't sure you would come," he said, not taking his eyes off Brigid.

She cleared her throat, telling her hormones to *calm down*. She had to focus, there was too much at stake, too much unclear that needed to be sorted.

"What memory did you give up?" she asked, setting down her basket to give herself an extra moment to gain her composure. "In order for me to regain mine?"

"How would I know?" he asked, stopping by the side of the caravan. "I gave it up, didn't I?"

"Why would you make such a trade?" Ophelia asked, leaning against the side of the caravan, cocking her head like a fighter studying its opponent.

"He's a trickster," Finola said, sizing him up. "He won't tell us the truth. Only a variation on it."

"I'm a god, I have no need to play games with mortals."

"And yet that is precisely what you did," Brigid said. "I know all about you, Knightly. The Goddess was forthcoming with who you were, what you did, and why you were cut off from the magic you so desired."

"Forthright and forthcoming are not the same thing. Your Goddess was sanctimonious and compromised only when it suited her. Where is she now when your people need her?"

Brigid bit her lip.

"No answer for that one, huh?"

"If she isn't here there is a reason."

"But perhaps not a good one."

"You're trying to distract me. I think you would give up a memory you might not want to remember. Or one you might not want me to gain," Brigid said.

He inclined his head and frowned. "I have no desire to play games with *you*."

"Then why did you help us?" Brigid asked, pulling a cord from her basket and passing it to Finola. Ophelia pushed off the caravan and walked to Brigid. She and Ophelia laid the cord on the grass in a circle, before pulling sage from their own bags and lighting the herbs. "You're a trickster, it is your nature, is it not?"

"I'm many things, Brigid Heron. I helped you because I made a . . . miscalculation with the witches who guard the lough."

"You mean the senseless people you bewitched into doing your dirty work?" Ophelia asked.

"They are not bewitched, and they aren't without sense. Or they weren't. They were wise women. Your ilk, with a vision too grand for their abilities. We made a deal. I thought theirs was a noble cause. I was assisting them as they helped me."

"They're real helpful," Finola said.

"I may be part god, but even we can't predict the future."

"How did you 'assist them'?" Ophelia asked, an edge in her voice.

"After centuries of oppression, of being hunted, they sought a divine power to protect them. To help them protect others, and enable them to live free from persecution. I joined with them, gifting them long life, and they in turn amplified my powers. We worked together."

"They are the witches of Knight. They serve you," Brigid said.

"I am made of flesh, but I am no man. I am a demigod, and they serve themselves."

"They are corrupted by the power of the lough," Brigid said, adding a pinch of salt to the cording circle they laid. "Whatever noble means they began with, they no longer serve that cause."

"I did not know what would befall them. I was trying to do them a good turn," he said, his mouth thinning into a determined line even as his eyes flashed. "Now I am trying to prevent them from destroying Evermore."

"You're helping us because you want to stop the evil witches you created?" Ophelia asked, placing crystals along the edge of the circle she and Finola had lain. "How noble."

"They want the lough to break wide open. They want every ounce of chaos power they can leach from the ancient power of the waters and will stop at nothing to achieve their goal," he said, urgency shifting into his voice. "They are closer to it than you know."

"Samhain," Brigid said, nodding and looking up at him. "We have until then to stop them or whatever is at the bottom of that lough will erupt across Evermore. We know."

"It didn't take a god to tell us either," Finola said, leveling Knightly a look.

"Is it ready?" Brigid asked the others, having to drag her gaze from Knightly's.

"Yes," Ophelia said.

"In you go," Brigid said to Knightly, pointing at the circle.

"I do not think so."

"You want us to believe you? To trust you to any degree? Let's make a deal," Brigid said, and grinned. "You let me into your mind."

No sooner had the words left her mouth, than Brigid suffered the strongest sensation of déjà vu she had ever experienced. The world went fuzzy, the light dimmed, and Brigid recalled the feeling of Knightly's hands on her face, his lips crashing against hers, her hands tugging for his belt.

"Stay with me," he said, and the world righted. The shadows receded and Brigid was staring into his deep cinnamon eyes, counting the flecks of gold. Her hands were on his face, and they were standing together inside the circle.

⚷

OPHELIA: Welcome back to the podcast, and thanks for voting on the name. Evermorians, it is! Today we have Iona Doyle with us to talk about the myth surrounding the loughs and the magic of Evermore. Iona, thanks for joining us.

IONA: A pleasure, Ophelia. I'd also like to add that, *Rodney*, whatever was in that bottle of witches' tonic you threw on me, it did not work. I do not want to kiss you, and I hope you're run down by a stampede of Davis Byrne's wandering sheep.

OPHELIA: Well, that went dark faster than I was expecting.

IONA: I know where you live, Rodney, and I have no problems getting all litigious up on your—

OPHELIA: Okay, then! Can you tell me, Iona, how you became an expert on the magic in Evermore?

IONA: [clears throat] I'd say the same as most, my family has been plagued by the Damned and the various things that seep from that lough for the past century. Before that cursed night, Evermore's waters were for healing. Villagers would come from all over to buy water blessed by the clootie well that Brigid Heron tended. One of her tonics was said to cure everything from gout to phobias and could even predict rain.

OPHELIA: A right marvel, our Brigid was.

IONA: Yes, until she disappeared, and everything here went tits up. Thanks, Brigid.

OPHELIA: Right, well. Your family is said to have one of the first written records of the Damned crawling its way from the lough.

IONA: Yes, in nineteen and twenty-two. There's an account of Connor Murphy—

OPHELIA: Of Seamus Murphy or Cian Murphy?

IONA: Of Cathal Murphy.

OPHELIA: Ah.

IONA: And Connor was walking home from the baker's and said that the light outside—it was near on midnight it was—the light in the sky was as black as coal and the stars as bright as the sun's first light. The moon glowed so wide that he thought it was falling from the sky and he was sure he was going to die and all he could think was that he should have punched Paul McGuire for taking the last loaf of cinnamon bread from the bakery after all. Then there was a blast of light and he said, says he, the earth shook and the trees bent forward, as though bowing.

OPHELIA: Where was good Connor when he saw this?

IONA: Down from Brigid Heron's property. He'd cut through the fields outside town. I believe there's some disagreement of whether or not he had stopped into the pub for a pint after the baker's closed.

OPHELIA: Oh, aye, it's hard to turn down one for the road on a cold night. It does make a bit more sense why he'd be near a field at midnight, though.

IONA: To be sure. He was so stunned, he said he lay in the grass to watch the stars and make sure they stayed in the sky. Fell asleep at some point and awoke to find the biscuits he'd bought were gone. Started to walk home, and that's when he noticed it. The water in the lough outside the Heron property had gone way down. All the water in Evermore, it seems, had receded in one night.

OPHELIA: That is wild.

IONA: And that's not even the strangest thing.

OPHELIA: No?

IONA: He stopped by the clootie well, the one it's said Brigid used to pull the water from when she'd make her healing salves and tonics and potions and the like.

OPHELIA: And?

IONA: And he couldn't find it. Said it was like it'd never been there at all.

OPHELIA: Not a trace of it?

IONA: Nope. And after that, they tried to find Brigid and she and her house were gone, too.

OPHELIA: Like they disappeared.

IONA: Just like her.

OPHELIA: I must say, this has been informative, Iona. We appreciate your sharing with us what you've learned.

IONA: Anytime, Ophelia.

OPHELIA: Thanks for tuning in, everyone. We'll be bringing round our weekly drop-offs of salt and tonics, so email or text or call if you need anything. Remember to take care of one another and salt your perimeter. 'Cause the beasties will get you if you don't watch out.

EIGHT

The witch who called herself East remembered the Goddess Brighid. She didn't think many aside from the god named Lugh who called himself Knightly and herself could. She knew the story, how once upon a time, there had been two gods of Evermore, that they had quarreled over the power and the people of this island.

Then Brigid Heron opened the seal on the lough, and the witches of Knight did what they did best. They amplified its power and claimed it for their own. In the process, the balance of power shifted. The Goddess Brighid left the island to tend her eternal flame. And Knightly grew restless.

He left Evermore the day Brigid opened the seal. He was gone for a single day, and when he returned, he was weaker. *They* were stronger. He couldn't explain it, but East thought he must have made a sacrifice for them. He was as eager as they were, after all, to open the lough.

Soon they would be strong enough to open it completely, and once they did, they would be able to bend divine power to their will. They would make sure no one ever had the power to hurt them again, and they would rule Evermore and rewrite the laws of the foolish and weaker humans.

The witches of Knight walked over a hill, moving slowly as was their way. They were in no hurry, with little need to rush. They were the things that went bump in the night, and now, finally, there was nothing for them to fear.

Not even Brigid Heron.

The meadow with the Goddess's well appeared barren as they approached from the south side. Once sheep had roamed freely up and down the land, and now it was an overgrown pasture. Grass grew too high, the cropping of trees was cluttered and filled with fallen limbs and an abundance of sloes and hazelnuts. This spot of land was one of the few the Damned did not overrun when set free, and East knew why.

All of Evermore had a pulse of magic flowing through it, the currents of the lough and Lugh fed the land. Except this spot, and the house where Brigid Heron lived.

Here, the land was quiet. Forgotten.

Lonely.

East paused, and the three others caught up to her. There was a time when they had no names, as they had been written out of history when the man painted the portrait of them and regulated them to caricatures. Witches. Sorceresses. Naked in a circle surrounded by skulls and other misogynistic interpretations of what a witch must be. They had been healers, wise women. Which was bad enough to the men of the fifteenth century. Worse, they had been *powerful*.

Men could turn into demons when it came to desire for power. Greedy, insidious, horrible villains over it. The villains of their life captured them, and enacted torture that left the kind of scars both visible and not.

By a stroke of sheer will and too much blood spilled, the four women with power were able to escape, and in escaping they met a man who was not a man, who had been searching for a power such as theirs to amplify his own.

"Retake your identities, rename yourself. I will help you gain that which you desire most," he told them.

Power to enact their revenge against those who had oppressed them, and to make sure such a feat would never be possible again at the hands of men. They did not trust men, but this one was not only a man, but mostly a god.

"All I need from you, is a little of your power to boost mine," he'd said, his dimple flashing.

They might have trusted him less if he had not been seeking the same thing as they were. Divine power and a brighter future.

If he had not been as hungry as they were, with a look in his eyes that told them they were not the only ones carrying scars so deep it left tears in their souls.

They made a bargain with Lugh and named themselves for their corners of earth that spoke to them, and the elements they represented. North, South, East, and West. With the deal struck, they became the witches of Knight.

Everything was going their way, finally, after centuries of waiting and failing to gain the power from the lough. They were so close to their goal; some mornings East woke with the taste of it on her lips.

It tasted of cherries.

East stopped and took a deep breath, holding her hands out. The others paused beside her, South and West each taking hold of one of her hands, while North took the other hands of West and South. They formed their circle, connected to one another and this time, sent their power out—connecting into the earth.

There. A low hum just inside the overrun canopy of trees. Where the earth trees grew dense, the ground soft, and the air perfumed with fragrant flowers that smelled of roses . . . and ashes. They released hands and walked to the little cove of forest. The closer they drew, the sweeter the air became.

"It's a glamour," they said, their voices rising up and out together as always. All for one, and one for all.

The four witches had traversed this land before. They had walked every square inch of Evermore, for they did not sleep, and they rarely ate and they never could quiet the hunger inside them for power. They had also crossed over the land of Brigid Heron, but it cost them to do so. Their bodies grew heavy, their bones brittle, and the shadows that cloaked them struggled to stay solid. They had never, no matter how many times they tried, been able to locate the well or the house.

Something had changed.

East reached into her bag and pulled from it a needle made of a shard of a mirror. One of the shards of Lugh's, from a magic he had broken long ago. One of only three that remained. It was a small bit of mirror magic she needed to perform. Lugh carried these mirror coins, had once given them to the people of Evermore as passage into other lands, greater ones. Now, though, he did not share them. It did not matter. The shard was enough. It drew magic from their blood, and today they would use it to try and beckon power here, where the old forgotten magic of the Goddess once resided.

They faced one another in their circle formed of their corners, and one by one each of the four witches pricked their thumb, then pressed the tip of the finger and drop of blood to their third eye and then to the bark of the tree closest to them.

The glamour fell away.

A circle of white ash trees stood where the mess of a forest had been. These trees were barren and beautiful, their bark pristine, their bodies long and curving up toward the sky. They appeared to be in movement, or dance.

The women walked between the openings of trees, each entering through their corner of North, South, East, and West. There was magic in ritual, and there was great magic in each of their steps. Calling to the corners, drawing in the power they had cultivated and cloaked themselves in.

In the center of the circle of trees was a well. A clootie well in the form of an ancient ash tree bowed over a small spring. The tree was covered in ribbons wrapped around each slender branch. Prayers for healing, for comfort, for care, from the followers and seekers of the Goddess Brighid. The women crossed to it and looked down. The water of the spring reflected nothing, not the sliver of sun that shone through the tips or the reflections of the witches standing around it. Like the lough the mirrored ability of the spring was diminished. And yet. A glint off the corner, a flash like a shooting star.

"It's not as it appears," they said.

East bent down, scooped up a small brown pebble in the shape of an orb, and tossed it into the spring. They waited, and waited, until at last they heard a plink as the rock plonked in.

"It is deep."

East crouched at the water's edge and pressed her palm to the surface. A pulse of magic met her fingers, and she stumbled back at the power there.

A rush of heat, a blast of joy, and the sucking feeling of sorrow rushed through her in one breath.

"A piece of the Goddess remains."

They smiled at one another, and then, one by one, jumped into the spring, and down

deep,
deep,
deep,
into the well.

—0

Brigid's heart thumped heavy in her chest, as the moments of past and present swirled within her, and for a single breath, she could taste everything that was and would be. Then she was blinking and staring into the face of Knightly, studying the small scar cutting through his lip, the golden flecks in his cinnamon-colored eyes, and the imperfect set of his nearly straight nose.

Knightly's hands rested gently on Brigid's face, his thumb moving across her cheek to brush the top of her mouth. Her skin tingled from the path he traced, heat moving through her and pooling at her core. She tilted her chin back, and his pupils dilated as he leaned in.

"Um, I'm sorry, but what do you two think you are doing?" Finola asked, stamping a foot. "You do not let a demigod put his tongue in your mouth, Brigid Heron! Who knows where that thing has been?"

Brigid let out a groan and tried to step back from him. His grip tightened for the briefest of moments, and his panic flowed from his fingertips into her skin. He released her and dropped his hands to his side.

"We've been there before," Brigid said, her fingers coming to her lips. "How? Have I been through your thoughts?"

"You have owned them," he said, in a near whisper. "I will show you, if you allow it."

Brigid stared deep into his eyes and gave a single nod.

Knightly brought his fingers up to the sides of her face once more and the world around them went dark. Day rolled into night; the stars shifted out from behind sleepy clouds to shine down on them. Winter rolled in around them, the lake icing and the trees filling with frost. The sun's gentle rays heated the earth and the ice melted as buds unfurled. Happy peonies bloomed, the earth heated, and summer wrapped around them with a splash of water and a peal of laughter. Brigid pressed her bare toes into the earth, leaning into the smell of grass and lemonade.

Knightly stood statue still before her. Ophelia and Finola were gone. Brigid looked beyond him to the lough, which had grown twenty times in size and glistened. The sky was reflected in it, the shoreline vibrant and green. She glanced down and saw the brown day dress she always wore, her basket from the kitchen that she used to forage herbs off to the side of the lough. A blanket spread beside it.

She looked back to Knightly, and his face was open. Brigid read the emotion frozen on it as clear as any sunrise. He was looking at her with love.

She swallowed hard, fear suddenly seizing her at what this memory might bring. Brigid had known there was something she needed to do, *to remember*, but she hadn't been able to peel the layers back. She'd grown one step closer with the memory he gave her of the girl, and now she understood this was one more peel of the orange. There was a coin on the blanket, silver and shiny. The urge to pick it up once she locked her eyes on it was a fire under her skin.

Brigid stepped back from Knightly, his arms and hands frozen in the air, reaching for her face. A swell of longing rushed through her, and she bit her lip before looking away from him and crossing to the coin. Brigid picked it up and saw the face of the girl staring back at her. Doe eyes and dimples and a sweet smile on her face.

A throat cleared behind her, and she turned around.

Knightly's hands were relaxed to his side, his eyes pinched in pain. "Dove," he said. "Her name is Dove."

The mirror coin in her hand burned her fingers. This coin was no passage into another world; it was a passage for one traveler, Brigid, into a specific place. Into Knightly's mind. Brigid dropped the coin, letting out a cry as the weight of his memories poured from him into her.

Brigid stood before him, her eyes narrowed, her hand outstretched. She was shaking Knightly's hand, making a deal.

Then she was in his arms, dancing beneath the stars, her eyes locked on his in wonder.

On the banks of the lough, Brigid sat across from him, learning how to call the magic in the water. Knightly guiding her hands through it, so the lough recognized her, knew her.

She was filling up her little blue vase with the water and carrying it to her workshop to pour out into her tinctures as he followed behind.

Knightly lounging on the side chair, telling her stories of the Otherworld and the gods as she threw back her head in laughter.

Knightly stripping her clothes off slowly and laying her down in the soft grass of the meadow, as the sun went down and she opened her arms and her body to him.

Her belly growing round with child while he made dinner.

Winter rolling into spring and spring into summer.

As the fire burned and autumn crept in, Dove sleeping in the bed with both of them in Brigid's home, while Knightly gazed at each of them, not wishing to stir either, unable to move from their sides.

Days blurring into a happy rhythm. Until.

The four witches slinking onto Brigid's land, circling the house, setting fire to the perimeter as they tried to uncloak her home.

Knightly slipping out in the night to find them, to distract them, never to return to Brigid or their child.

Wishing for them every day.

"Stop," she said, her voice breaking. "Please stop. It *hurts*." The sharp of her nails bit into the palm of her hands and drew blood, as loss wracked itself through her, causing her knees to buckle and her stomach to churn.

"I can't take the pain away," he said, his voice as rough as sandpaper. "You need it to save your daughter."

"I don't want this," she said, the tears breaking through. She scrubbed them away. "Let me out of *this*."

Knightly nodded once, and the world spun. The seasons unwound, his memories returned to him, leaving only the echoes to shadow over her. Brigid blinked and she was staring into his eyes, his fingers brushing soft against her temples.

She jerked away and stumbled over and out of the circle. The sob broke free and she fell to the earth. The truth of his memories and the loss of the past and her daughter rolling through her like a knife wielding a killing blow.

"Brigid," he said.

She turned her hands toward him and let out a guttural cry. She pulled magic from deep inside her, from places she didn't even know it had been hiding. The piercing sound sent the lazing swallows in the nearby hazelnut trees tearing into the sky. Sparks flew from her hands. Golden light blast into Knightly. He flew back from the circle and shot straight up and away from Brigid and out of sight.

—0

Finola and Ophelia watched the body of Luc Knightly careen across the sky and heard it with their witches' ears drop off into the lough, about a kilometer away. There was a splash, a crack of thunder, and what could arguably be constituted as the sound of cursing from far off.

"Wish I'd thought to do that," Finola said, before she and Ophelia ran to Brigid.

Brigid let out a cry as she dusted herself off. She stood, fought a sob, and pressed her fisted hands into her abdomen as she let out a scream.

"Brigid," Ophelia said, waiting less than a foot away. "Honey, what do you need from us right now?"

Brigid lifted the hem of her dress to her face and gave one more shriek into it, before she dropped it and met their eyes. "I need you to fish that devil of a god out of the lough. I'm not done with him yet."

Then she turned on her heel and marched back inside her caravan. She curled up on the scuffed wood floor and let go of her will to fight as his memories wracked through her body and mind. It had been too much, too fast. Worse, because these memories weren't her own. These had been his, his version of a past she had lived, and the pain, she realized, that had been his, too.

She was carrying his grief, and it was shifting into her own at what the memories told her, at the truth under it. She didn't think she would be capable of holding it all.

Her child. His child.

Dove.

For long minutes she stayed curled in the past he had shown her, in the mosaic of moments. A deal became more than a deal, a life grew and changed hers, and in the end he left them behind and she still did not know where her daughter was.

When she had finished crying, Brigid went outside and nearly burst into tears again at the tender looks on Ophelia's and Finola's faces. They had lit a bonfire and set out healing crystals and sage. Brigid forced herself to steel her spine and reach for them.

They drew her into a hug and she breathed in their strength, their solid support, and acceptance in her as she was in this moment.

"Did you fish him out?" she finally asked.

"Yes," Ophelia said, "and then Finola punched him."

Brigid snorted and when she realized they weren't joking, leaned back. "What?" Her gaze drifted to Finola's red knuckles.

"He's a head as hard as a besotted sheep, he does, the fucker."

"He fell back into the lough," Ophelia said, pride in her eyes. "Our Fin nearly knocked a god out."

Brigid's lips twitched, and she let out a laugh, grateful to discover she could. It was easier to embrace laughter than sorrow, to remember the layers of the world.

"What did he do to you?" Ophelia asked.

"He showed me some of what I lost," Brigid said, swallowing hard. She told them of the memories from his mind, and their faces paled and then transformed into openmouthed stares, before settling into worried, grim expressions.

"Oh Brigid," Ophelia said. "Your daughter."

"Dove."

"Where is she?" Finola asked.

"He did not show me that, which is why I needed you to fish him free."

They nodded, and the wind picked up speed. The skies overhead darkened, the trees bending to the breeze and the grass rustling.

Brigid sighed as the scent of cedar reached her. "He's here."

She walked by Ophelia, stopping to give her shoulder a gentle squeeze, and stood inside the door of the caravan, where it faced the rolling hills

Knightly, with his hair still wet, stood waiting.

NINE

Knightly stood unencumbered. The wind whipping against his coat, rustling his hair dripping down his cheeks. Still, he did not move a muscle. The green of the grass behind him deepened to a mesmerizing emerald. The sky shifted from dusky gray to near violet. The wind settled around Brigid's shoulders, an arm pulling her close. She could feel every blade of grass bend. Smell every sliver of bark in the tree as it gave way to sap.

"I am not going to play games with you," she said, willing herself not to move, not to react at his presence.

"I am not playing a game," he said. "I am trying to help you."

"You can help me by telling me where my daughter is."

"She is beyond this world, where the lough took her in." He stared hard into her eyes. "Can you still not remember?"

The sky tilted, and Brigid dug her heels into her shoes. "What do you mean beyond this world?"

"I don't think it's wise to let creatures like him in," Finola said, coming to stand at Brigid's side at the door. "He's probably where vampire myths come from. Undead evil and all."

"That is not my legend," he said, and sighed. "Mine is the story of gods and magic."

"And my daughter?" Brigid asked.

"You need your memories back. I can help you regain them."

"Trade me mine for yours?"

"No." He shook his head. "I can only show you what I remember, and we both have too much to lose from that. You have the spells of the Goddess. Your magic is strong but it is faulty because your Goddess is no longer here. My power has been seeking yours, and if we join them, we may be able to recover that which you lost."

"If you know, why not tell her?" Finola asked, before adding, rather loudly, "Jackass."

"Because my memories don't tell me that," he said. "I don't know what *she* knows."

"My daughter is somewhere on the other side of the lough, my Goddess is gone, and you are our only hope to seal the lough," Brigid said, rubbing at the edge of her eyes. She dropped her hands. "Where is my Goddess, Luc Knightly?"

"Dark magic and chaos blanket this land," he said. "Your Goddess would not come here even if she were near. Chaos was never her game, and she has her nineteen to tend. Her everlasting fire is needed in the world, and unlike me, she has never been quite so self-serving."

"Leaving me was rather self-serving," Brigid said, unable to keep the hurt from her voice.

"Even a god can make a mistake."

When Brigid did not reply, he continued. "The Goddess only moves in ways to help," he said, wincing as though admitting such a thing was painful. "If she did leave you, it was because others needed her more."

Brigid stared at Knightly, who had not taken his eyes off hers the entire time he'd been speaking. Which was a little unnerving as he spoke about himself and the Goddess as though he were speaking of a neighbor who was on a recent trip.

If you were a god, what was time? Did you remember everything as though it was the day before or the day before that?

And did he really think she would trust him?

"What of your coven? They won't want you helping us use your lough."

"I'm not worried about them," he said, the earnest look in his eyes shooting straight to her solar plexus. "I am on your side, Brigid Heron. I want to help you regain your memories and stop the leaching of magic from my lough." He drew a ragged breath. "Will you work with me?"

Brigid looked to the others. Finola shook her head and Ophelia frowned. Brigid looked inside herself and the blank spaces in her mind stared back.

"I must seal the lough and get my daughter back," she said. Ophelia nodded and even Finola, who sighed, looked resigned. "But I need you both more than him."

"We're with you," Ophelia said, stepping up and placing a hand on Brigid's back. "We save Evermore and your girl and stop the angry witches."

"And if he gets in the way, we string him by his balls?" Finola asked.

"I'll give you my twine," Brigid said.

Finola turned to Knightly and grinned. "Excellent."

⊶

The next super moon was not due to rise for three days. Knightly believed they would have their best chance pulling from the magic of the lough when the moon was at its closest point to the earth during its orbit. As they waited, Brigid spent her time helping Ophelia and Finola craft satchels full of salt and scentless tonics that stole the sense of smell from those who breathed it in to aid the villagers in better protection from the Damned.

"Are you certain it's a good idea for me to come with you to deliver the salt and potions?" Brigid asked, pouring the bottle of the last potion in her batch as she sat at the kitchen table.

At that exact moment the clear skies shifted to gray and thunder rolled in the distance. A light rain began to fall, the patter of drops a soft, inviting sound. Behind them, the kettle whistled. Brigid's gaze drifted from the comfort of the falling rain to the courage on Finola's dancing brows.

She sighed.

"*Yes,*" Finola said, clapping her hands together. "I promise, you won't regret this."

"What are you doing with your face?" Brigid asked.

"Grinning from ear to ear," Finola said, lifting her chin and flashing her teeth.

"Clearly, but why?"

"Because. This is just like when Marty McFly went back to 1955 and tried to order a Pepsi Free and Lou told him he'd have to pay for it. We can pass out our anti-monster goody bags and I can show you the world."

Finola got up and left the kitchen in a rush.

"Who is Marty? What is free Pepsi?" Brigid asked.

Ophelia bit her lip and studied her shoes, which did little to hide her smile. "It's a movie, a film, one Finola will likely try to make you watch. I'll explain it better on the way, but this is a good reminder that like the new appliances in the house, the town has had its own evolution over the past one hundred years. You know, outside of the monsters and inability to leave and everything being one hundred shades of terrible."

"Of course it has," Brigid said. "I'm not an idiot. I can draw the rain and steal thunder from the sky. Do you really think seeing the new world's order will leave me suffering from the vapors?"

Brigid did not faint, but she might have done were she any-one other than herself. She had always gone back and forth to town by way of walking, it was a journey shy of four miles and pleasant if the weather cooperated, which it rarely did. But she didn't mind the rain, it was a fresh start, washing away worries when one's arms grew too heavy from carrying the regrets they should have set down long ago.

The women did not travel by foot and they did not have a single car, they had *two*. What they drove bore little resem-blance to the cars of Brigid's time. Gone was the box on wheels that wobbled more than a buggy, and in its stead was a metal beast of burden.

Apparently shipping containers still made it to the island, even if people did not. Finola explained the orders went out, the supplies came in, and then those who delivered the materials immediately forgot where they'd been and why.

"Makes the ordering process tiresome, but it's still worth it," she said.

The "car" they climbed in to drive to town was Ophelia's sil-ver tamed beast on wheels. Ophelia called it an SUV, and it was as plush inside as any living room and rode like a floating cloud. Magic was not simply an invention of the elements; technology was a sorcerer, too.

The car had its own radio and it exploded as soon as Ophelia turned on the engine. She had turned the vehicle on by *press-ing her finger* to the dashboard. Brigid may have accidentally screamed at one point, but she felt certain she'd shown the ut-most decorum once the radio was turned off and the windows

were down. Hadn't she stopped slapping away Finola's hands
and allowed her to assist her with the seat belt? Truly, it wasn't
Brigid's fault the contraption felt like something they would use
at an asylum to restrain blunt and strong-willed women.

As a witch whose life work was making the impossible possible, Brigid thought little could surprise her. It turned out she
was wrong. Because even with Ophelia going "so slow the turtles
are lapping us," riding in the automobile was like being on the
back of an adventurous cheetah. The world sped by. Trees and
branches blurred into flashes of emerald and chocolate as the rain
slowed to a drizzle and stopped completely. The hills rolled from
one into the other, a gorgeous patchwork of green and yellow
offset by stunning blue-gray skies touting clouds so fluffy they
could have been painted by an impressionist.

"Where are the Damned when they aren't in the lough?"
Brigid asked, as they traveled down the countryside, marveling
at how this at least had not changed. The land was as it had
always been.

"You'll see," Finola said, wrinkling her nose. "Those who
don't end up in the caves down on the other side of Evermore
get stuck in the barren pastures and Farmer Joanie has to call
Ophelia to drive them out with salt and tonics."

They passed a barren field, and in the middle Brigid spotted
what looked like a group of banshee sleeping with a pack of
sheep. She turned to Fin, her eyes wide.

"Told ya," she said. "Phee, Joanie will be calling you soon."

"Got a text from Father O'Malley," she said, and her eyes
met Finola's in the rearview mirror. "Don't get started."

Fin just snorted.

"It's always been this way?"

"It used to be one or two, over the past decade it's shifted and
in the last year the numbers have really picked up," Ophelia said.

They continued down the road, passing rolling hills and pas-

tures, rock walls dividing the land, sheep roaming, and once thriving farms with cottages now abandoned as the majority of villagers
were driven inland to the center of Evermore to avoid the Damned.

Brigid didn't have knowledge of what a traffic light was,
and made Ophelia stop and go back to the first one they drove
under three more times so she could marvel over how it switched
from green to yellow to red and back again.

"Sweet cheese and crackers," Finola said, as she watched
Brigid gasp and coo. "She's more surprised by the lights than
the monsters."

"The *colors*," Brigid said. "They're so vivid."

Thinking of colors as remarkable as these had her thoughts
shifting to the gold flecks in Knightly's eyes. Then she was seeing the slope of his wide shoulders in the curve of the rocks
along the road, his sable hair in the bark of the passing trees.
He *must* have done something to her mind. He was like a burr,
stuck in and refusing to budge.

"You think these are great? You should see my vibrator,"
Finola said, knocking Brigid with her shoulder so hard the seat
belt jerked her back into place.

"Mother of a hen's egg," Brigid said, yanking on it.

"Quiet back there," Ophelia said, rubbing her temple, "or I
will turn this car around and take both of you home."

Finola snorted. "You have the patience of a barn cat, Phee."

"A barn cat is exceedingly patient," Brigid said. "They have
to be to catch mice." She paused as Ophelia took a curve so
fast her stomach did three somersaults in a row. "Though I am
beginning to fear this journey may well be our last."

"Ha-ha," Ophelia said, and muttered something about them
being worse than a car full of monsters.

Brigid didn't have time to dwell on possibly dying trapped
inside the luxurious metal beast, because they turned again and
everything took on the tilted, woozy quality.

The town of Evermore was tucked in close to the water. If you approached it from the sea, it would rise up to greet you. The row houses were tall and thin, sandwiched together. Cozy stone cottages lined one street, with thatched roofs and doors painted bright cobalt. A road curved to where the shops waited, with the stores on the bottom and lofts for the owners on top. The buildings were mostly unchanged. New signs added, fresh paint, and little upgrades given that made them look far more inviting than they had in Brigid's time.

Finola suggested seeing it now must be like going from black and white to Technicolor, whatever that meant. Brigid marveled at the fresh shutters, lights, streetlamps, and sidewalks. Gaped at the paved roads and colorful hydrangeas of pale pink and indigo—everything was picture-perfect, even the wear and tear that inevitably crept in.

Brigid leaned out the window, drinking in the scent of the sea air. It smelled of brine and promise. It smelled of her past trips leaving the island, of stolen kisses with clever men whose words were pretty and beds were warm. It broke her heart to think Ophelia and Finola hadn't had such adventures. That her sister had returned to this island for her, and never left again. Brigid thought of the lovers from those trips, then she thought of how dead in the grave they too were and let out a groan.

Ophelia pulled onto a side road and parked between an old Volkswagen Beetle and a Volvo. The women exited and Brigid stood on shaky legs as she turned in a circle, studying the world. A few other cars sped past, steel panthers in a hurry. She grew dizzy watching them, so she closed her eyes and listened instead.

Honks and growls and groans and squeaks. That was the first layer of this Evermore. Beneath it was the quiet call of a black guillemot nearby, the soft, rhythmic slapping of feet on the earth, and the splash of fish as they swam upstream from the sea. Warm air ran along her arms, and the whisper of the water brushed against her ear. She thought she heard someone singing.

"Come to where beauty lasts,
where joy never wanes.
Bring us your very best;
the winds here never change."

Brigid lost track of time, until a hand squeezed hers. She opened her eyes and met those of Ophelia.

"Are you all right?" she asked, her smoky voice an anchor. "I know it's a lot, but we're here with you. We won't let anything gobble you up."

"Speaking of gobble," Finola said, rubbing her flat stomach. "After almost dying yesterday, I am in desperate need of a curry."

They walked down Abbey Street, named for the abbey that once resided on the far hillside in town but had fallen to disarray before Brigid's disappearance. The winding street led them uphill, and behind them the sea rose and fell, like a gentleman standing to offer his seat and sitting down again when it proved unnecessary. As waves lapped behind them, Brigid took a deep breath, pulling in the scents of home and shaking off the worry that resolutely clutched at her ankles with every step she took.

She had so many memories of Evermore, and yet only the one of her child. The desperate need to remember scratched at her throat, tugged at her scalp, and itched along her palms.

They turned down a side street, cut through an alley, and turned again, entering the heart of Evermore. Pastel houses lined the street. Their stoops were adorned with potted flowers and dusted with salt. The sound reached them first, flutes and bagpipes, laughter and squeals, followed by the scents of fried batter and baked bread, pastries, and pretzels.

"Oh dear," Ophelia said, surveying the scene before them. "The festival."

"Festival?" Brigid asked, her mind struggling to process the loud chaos before her. Children running across the lawn waving brightly colored ribbons that flapped in the wind, the people dancing at the other end of the street, kicking their feet up and hooking arm over arm as they spun one another around.

"Seasons of Change," Finola said, "I thought we voted to cancel it this year."

"We did," Ophelia said, before turning to Brigid. "The Damned are drawn in by loud noises. Bright colors, anything a toddler would fall to pieces over really."

"Then this festival is going to be like a fresh brew to a thirsty drunkard," Brigid asked.

"We can't make them shut it down," Ophelia said, "much as I'd like. They'll only fight twice as hard and throw another one in a week's time. Obstinate bunch of lovable nuts. Our best bet is to salt the perimeter and then remind them they are playing with fire and how to douse the smoke."

"I can't say as I blame them," Finola said. "It's hard living on edge. We all need a break from these creatures."

"I know," Ophelia said, "but still. It's too risky."

Brigid followed the others up the road, taking in the little changes to the town. Some shops had changed names but not purpose, others offered new services, and the clothing boutique featured the prettiest dresses in the window.

"Look over there," Finola said, pointing to the tents set up on a lush, green lawn.

Brigid's eyes tracked to the squat oak off to the side of a series of tents with merchants giving away food and drinks and selling their own baubles and creations set up along the edge of the road. Beneath the large oak tree sat a large, flat gray stone. Sitting on it was a framed drawing, three candles in jars, and a clumping of rose quartz crystals.

"What . . . is all of that?" Brigid asked, the grouping familiar. She'd always sent her jars of salves with a rose crystal and, if
she had a batch, a new candle to burn for intention.

"It's for you," Ophelia said, her voice soft, her long dark
locks stirring in the wind, and her eyes surveying Brigid's face.

"How can *that* be for *me*?"

"The people of this town celebrate you," Ophelia said, her
words slow and measured.

"No, they don't."

"Um, yeah," Finola said, rolling her bright blue eyes. "They
totally do. You have no idea how often people say, 'May Brigid
this' or 'May Brigid that.' You're not quite to the deity level, but
you are mystical, to be sure."

"I'm neither of those things." She rubbed at her collarbone,
unsettled with the idea.

"You've been gone a hundred years, and you've reappeared
out of thin air," Ophelia said. "You're a wonder."

She was a curse, not a wonder, and dread built as she surveyed the stone beneath the tree, crouching down to study the
paper in the frame. It was a drawing in her likeness, a woman
with auburn hair, its strands woven into the letters of her name.
It was clear the people in the town were celebrating her, prais-
ing her in the manner of a saint or even the Goddess. Brigid
was neither.

"How is this possible?"

"You performed miracles in your time," Ophelia said,
crouching down next to her. "People remember the great healer
Brigid Heron, who could aid in both delivering a babe and increasing fertility and curing the most difficult of ailments. After
you left, the peace went with you, and the Damned came."

"Promising mistakes is what I made," Brigid said. "I'm the
reason the Damned are here."

"You've magic and power, and you're going to seal the
lough," Ophelia said. "You are light for us."

Brigid gave her head a shake and reached a trembling finger, tracing the smooth surface of the portrait.

She, Ophelia, and Finola walked from booth to booth, dropping off the tonics and salt, scolding their friends and neighbors for the festival. There were fiddles playing a warm, radiant melody, a bonfire blazing, pints turned up, and laughter perfuming the air. At the McDougals' booth, a man with bright red hair and dark eyes, looking much in the way of his grandfather, grinned at Brigid and offered her flowers and a dance.

She took the flowers, smelling them deeply and returning the smile, before he turned and waved a new bunch at a girl with copper skin and dark curls.

"He seems lovely, I hope he doesn't follow the path of his grand-da and fall down dead on Boxing Day," Brigid whispered to Finola as they walked away, and Finola laughed so hard she had to stop to catch her breath.

The festival featured a little bit of everything, and "the best Evermore has to offer," as Finola put it. Brigid particularly loved the crowning of the goat queen, in honor of the goats that roamed the hillside and were said to keep the Damned at bay.

"They don't," Finola had told her. "Ophelia is the reason the Damned won't go on that hillside. They ate all the goats last winter, truth be told."

As Brigid perched on a wooden stool in front of a local pub sipping a fresh ale, an elderly woman approached. She had eyes the color of the sea after a storm, clear and azure, and moved like her bones were protesting each step of the way. She waved to Finola and rested on her cane, wincing as she stopped.

"Good morning, Miss Overman," Finola said. "It's good to see you out and about."

"My knees aren't aching as much. The headache's a bit worse, though. Not as bad as the O'Malley twins—they've not been out of bed all week after the Damned came near."

Finola frowned. "Did they not drink the tonic Phee made?"

Miss Overman's brow pinched, and she harrumphed. "Of course they drank it. Swear they weren't touched by those creatures, but something's not right with them." She pointed the cane at Finola's legs, and Finola stepped back. "Now let me pass, lassie. A bit of brown liquid courage and shepherd's pie await."

The old woman pushed past Brigid and she raised her brows at Finola. "The woman and twins she spoke of were touched?"

"Aye, it's rare but from time to time a few will be brushed by the Damned instead of full-on attacked and the symptoms are slow to come."

"How slow?"

Finola looked down at her shoes. Rubbed at her nose. "A year at best so far."

"That's horrible."

"We've been trying to get the tonic dose right, to stop the wasting, but haven't been able to perfect it yet," she said. "They'll grow sicker and sicker and turn. Like the rest before them."

"How many? People turned?"

Finola looked Brigid straight in her eyes. "Twelve? Fifty? Two hundred?"

Brigid sucked in a breath. "All together?"

"We don't know. For most of the twenties people assumed those who went missing had gone off with the fae. Or gotten trapped in stray sod. Agnes started documenting toward the end of the thirties. A few people a year, each year. The Damned didn't start pouring out rapid fast until this past decade, with a serious increase this year."

Brigid closed her eyes. A few people a year for a hundred years on its own was too many people. "Where are they buried?"

"They aren't."

She opened her eyes. "What do you mean?"

"They become the Damned, Brigid."

"They're still out there?"

"Can't say for sure, and we try not to think too hard about it. Logic says yes, or they pass on and go back to the earth like we do after some time. They tried to capture one once, but it went bad and they never tried again."

"Bad how?"

Finola licked her lips. "Just bad."

"Fin."

She sighed. "The reason Agnes's body wore out so fast at the end was she captured a sidhe. She wanted to study it, ask it questions and see if she could get the answers to help them and us. In the end it attacked her, and she wounded it with iron. Then it slunk off and no one could find it again, and Agnes passed before the curse could take her."

"Passed?"

Finola swallowed. "Aye. With help."

Brigid placed a hand to her belly, trying to slow the twisting of the ale inside it.

"We can't save them, and we've been fighting for a long time trying to save ourselves. Agnes was brave, but in the end her bravery proved a fool's errand. We've kept her mission in protecting the town going, waiting for you, waiting for the curse to be broken."

Brigid swallowed around the hard lump of warning in the back of her throat. A town damned and the healer who damned them. A sister who sacrificed everything and a daughter lost in time. That was her story. It was too much to bear.

Ophelia ran over then, her cheeks flushed. "Story hour is about to start. I've told them they have to shut everything down in one hour and after a lot of threatening, they've agreed. Come, Brigid, you have to see this."

Brigid cleared the regret from her throat, set down the ale that had lost all appeal, and forced a smile for her friend.

Story hour, Ophelia explained, was set up for the wee ones and put on by the local bookstore. A man with copper hair dressed as a knight read from a large book about turtles, while a younger man helped the older children construct colored paper hats.

"Her ex," Finola whispered to Brigid, nodding at the knight as they entered a sweet space of oversized pillows and blankets tucked between a row of the brightly constructed booths.

"Ex what?" Brigid whispered back.

"Boyfriend," Finola said, rolling her eyes. They watched Ophelia and the bookseller steal glances from each other until it grew too intimate. That sort of longing was deep, and unforgiving, and—Brigid feared as she thought of Knightly—contagious. She slipped her arm through Finola's and tugged her on.

There was face painting and an archery and a torch-creating station. The last two stations were judged by the townspeople with the spears and torches dispersed to individuals for later home protection measures.

"The Damned don't like pointy things or fire," Finola explained.

They sampled pudding and clapped for the musicians who played a rousing rendition of a song called "Seven Drunken Nights" that left Brigid snorting.

Brigid felt as though she had stepped through a looking glass into an upside-down world. There was charm here and community even amid the chaos. There were stories told about the Damned, and a man named Rodney who apparently tried to kiss one of them. Toasts were offered up to those who had gone before and been gone too long. It was a magic all its own, the comradery of community, and the remembrance the people of

Evermore carried for those who no longer remained, but who still mattered just as much.

The most shocking moment, however, came when Finola deposited Brigid in a chair on the cobblestones in front of a stage.

"Stay here," she told her, fluffing her hair and dusting off her skinny jeans. "I'm going for food and to find Ophelia. I bet she's still making cow eyes at Thorpe. I'll be back in two winks of the eye unless there's a pretty lass who catches my attention. You won't want to miss the show, though. I hear there's juggling this year."

Brigid sat, waiting, watching the people hurry up and down the makeshift aisles to her left and right. A chair creaked behind her. The wind ruffled her hair. A young girl, in her early teens, danced up the steps and across the stage, before she twirled down the other set of steps and ran off into the crowd. Brigid's heart pinched. Would her daughter have been like the girl? Twirling and laughing with flowers in her hair? She'd longed for a festival in the memory, could she have been happy here?

Brigid stiffened in her seat at the sounds of someone sitting behind her. She turned to look and found Knightly sitting in the chair, arms folded across his broad chest.

Night flashed once, the sun shifting behind the moon.

"Breathe, Brigid," he said.

"Why does that happen when you are around?"

"You've the magic of the Goddess. I've the magic of a god. They're conflicting powers coming too close. If we paired them, maybe we could control them."

"Why are you here?"

"Same reason as you, as I said."

"You're here to help the villagers your witches damned. Still seems convenient."

"I'm here to stop the witches, yes, and it's a nice bonus to help the people of Evermore, but mainly, as I've said, I am here to help you." Knightly reached out, a hand brushing her shoulder as he pointed and leaned in. *"Look."*

Brigid jolted at the contact and turned. A man carrying flowers crossed in front of the stage. Golden hair, porcelain skin, and glittering green eyes. He was quite possibly the most beautiful man Brigid had ever seen. The sun hit his face, illuminating deep shadows and purple bruises spreading across his skin. The contusions shifted his beauty into something grotesque and painful. Brigid looked to the right and saw threads of illness working its way under the skin of the group of six others following him. They moved slower than the rest of the people, their steps light but weighted, their arms swinging gracefully and gradually at their sides. A river of ache and loss tethered them one by one to each other.

These were not people of Evermore out for the festival. These were the Damned and they had infiltrated the village without anyone noticing. She dug her nails into her palms, refusing to let the terror cowering in her belly clamber up her chest and face as she tried to tear her eyes away from them, but found herself spellbound by their cruel beauty. There was something familiar to it, like the echoes of a bedtime story sung to her as a child.

"They're of the Aos Sí," she whispered, as recognition clicked.

"They are the Damned," he said, standing and moving to her side as though a shield waiting to shift into position.

Brigid studied the group and how they eyed the children sitting crisscross applesauce on the floor at story hour. Their cheeks pink from the weather, eyes alight with joy at the tale the knight was reading them.

Brigid would pluck the heads from the Damned's bodies if they made an inch of a move toward those innocent babes.

"You look positively murderous," Knightly said, his voice low and filled with a rage she understood.

"I feel it. What do we do?"

"To offend the Aos Sí is to bring their wrath."

"They aren't the old folk," she said, meeting his gaze. "They're a perversion of them. Aren't they?"

Knightly did not look at her, instead he stepped into the walkway. "Perhaps they are both."

A shudder wracked through Brigid, and she stepped after him.

"And my daughter?"

"Is not Damned."

"But if she's on the other side of the lough, is she with these creatures?"

He did not answer, and Brigid's heart gave a painful thump in her chest.

"We will see her again," he said, brushing his hair from his face, his hand dropping to his chest.

She gave a tense nod. "What do we do about them?"

"The only thing we can," he said, surveying the festival and the way the people of Evermore danced and laughed, unaware at what was pressing in toward them. "We give the villagers as much time as we can to get inside before we fight to send them back."

The tall Damned, who minutes before Brigid had thought one of the most beautiful people she'd ever seen, turned and focused on Brigid and Knightly. Recognition shifted across its features, and it let out a low groan. Its eyes turned black, lips pursed as its mouth opened, showing a row of pointed teeth. Then it let out a scream that pierced the air worse than any foghorn Brigid had ever heard.

"Run!" Knightly shouted at the top of his lungs in the direction of the villagers before he charged toward the creature, his feet moving too fast for the nonmagical eye to see as he leaped over a table laden with a punch bowl.

The Damned hesitated for a single heartbeat, before they skittered back from him and took off running toward the story hour—toward the easier, more docile prey. Brigid looked to where the children sat, struggling to understand what was happening and get out of the way.

She clamored over the chairs in her way, her feet catching in the back of one wooden chair and she kicked it free. Her heart raced, sweat puckered along her skin, and she pooled power into her palms as she skidded in front of the children. Brigid threw out her arms as the Damned closed in.

⊷

Ophelia found Finola loaded up with curry and nearly flammable punch, with Brigid nowhere in sight. She'd spent the past half hour watching Thorpe read to children, reminding herself why relationships in Evermore couldn't work. For starters, she was a witch and he was a bookseller who sympathized with the Sluagh who occasionally haunted his romance section. But most important, when they'd gotten serious, he'd begun talking of a family and marriage, and Ophelia could barely keep herself and Finola alive. She certainly didn't have space or the inclination to add more family into the mix. Aside from Brigid. Who it appeared was missing?

"What do you mean *you left her by the stage?*" Ophelia asked Finola, who was precariously holding two plates and an oversized drink.

"Stop panicking and help me, will you?" Finola asked, sighing with what sounded like relief when Ophelia took the drink. She swallowed a deep gulp of the Seasons of Change punch, her mouth puckering at the terrible and marvelous concoction of wine and fruit juice and something unidentifiable that Mari McFee made every festival and should likely have been illegal.

"Brigid needed space. You could tell by one look at her, her eyes were as wide as yours after you spent the night rolling with Maxwell Callahan."

"I truly had no idea someone could do such things with his tongue," Ophelia said, her eyes going soft before she took another sip. "Goddess, that is potent. Brigid is made of granite. Nonporous stuff, impenetrable. Still, she didn't need to be left alone, Fin, particularly not now."

"Do you hear that?' Finola asked, looking up at the heavy gray clouds shifting across the sky.

Screams erupted down from where they stood, and they dropped the plates of food, the punch splattering as it fell at their feet, and they took off in a rush toward the sound. Villagers pushed past them, tearing out of the center of town and running for their doors, their eyes wild as they called to them.

"It's the Damned," Aine Casey said, barely coming to a stop in front of them as she tried to catch her breath. "We rushed the salting this morning, trying to get the festival set up. It had been quiet. We didn't think. Oh gods, I can't find Miss Overman."

"Go," Finola said, grabbing her hands, trying to still the shaking in them. "We'll find Miss Overman. Get inside and usher in anyone you can."

Aine nodded and sped off.

Ophelia and Finola ran on and came to a halt when they found Brigid and Knightly across from the stage, in front of where the children had been holding story hour. They were fighting what looked like a horde of some sort of zombie fae.

Ophelia and Finola slowed to a walk, reaching out to wiggle fingertips with each other. A ritual handshake they adopted early on and a way to beat back fear. They had been facing the monsters for so long, they'd long since learned to face their terror with a smile.

"What are they, do you reckon?" Finola asked, trying to keep her voice light.

"Nightmare fairies."

"Not goblins?"

"Too tall."

"Hmm, good point."

"Are they all male? Could they be cousins of all the males whose hearts you've broken?"

"No, I see a female in the fray. Right there between the two who look like they got lost on the way to a Legolas convention."

"Yeah. There would have to be way more women in there if that were a collective of all our broken hearts. Is it bad that I'm thinking there are a few of my exes who were less attractive than these Damned?" The sun came out and Finola sucked in a breath. "Nope, never mind. I take it right back. They are hideous."

The collective turned toward them, and Finola and Ophelia dropped their banter to make a run for Brigid and Knightly. Ophelia surveyed more closely where story hour had been, relieved to find the children were safely ushered away.

"We're trying to hold them back," Brigid called over the roar of the wind; it blew cold against her cheeks and chilled her fingers.

"They didn't complete the perimeter," Ophelia shouted. "We'll finish salting it if you can push them back to where the bookstore is. They'll be blocked out once we are done."

Brigid nodded, her face pinching in frustration as three more Damned joined the group and Finola and Ophelia ran off.

"Why can't you blink them to the lough?" Brigid asked Knightly, through the clench of her jaw.

"We have a similar power source," he said, "It won't work."

Brigid tried to plant her feet and ended up sliding back a

foot. The ground was rough, uneven, and the wind didn't help. "This is all your fault, you know."

"Bit of yours, too."

She grunted but this time when she planted her feet, they stayed.

Knightly circled the south side of the group, trying to block the Damned working to go another direction. They weren't the brightest bunch of monsters, and Brigid wondered if there wasn't a better way to beat them back, when Miss Overman tottered past them, weaving on her cane.

One of the Damned, beautiful with jet-black hair and haunting blue eyes, turned to her. It smelled of dead roses, sweet and acrid. It grinned, and grabbed her hand.

"No!" Brigid called, before Miss Overman reached out with her cane and started to whack it in the head.

It stumbled back and she crawled out of the way. Brigid took a step in her direction, but the old woman held up a hand. "Stay back and keep doing what you're doing. It was already too late for me, I've been turning for a week, just didn't want to let down the two lasses. They've tried so hard." She climbed to her feet and picked up her dusty cane. "If I'm going down, I'll go down with vengeance in my hands."

Then she stumbled from the group and into the center of the fray, her cane swinging wildly as the Damned pushed back to where the bookstore began.

The air thickened with mist and screams for a small forever, and then there was nothing. No sound. Not a whisper, not a shout.

"They've set the perimeter," Brigid said to Knightly. "We're inside it."

He nodded once, lifted his hand, and yanked at the air. The Damned that were gathered around Miss Overman were tossed like bowling balls down the lane.

But they were too late.

Miss Overman turned to face them, dusting off her navy coat and shaking out the end of her gray slacks. She looked down at her cane and flung it aside like it was twig. Her skin had transformed into a color as pale as freshly spun silk, her short hair had grown shiny and long. The years rolled off her as they watched, and she looked up to them and smiled.

"There are many forms of the sidhe," Brigid said, her words coming out in a rush. "Aren't there?"

"In the Otherworld, there are no limits to what power can become. What creatures can thrive."

"So when they are touched by the Damned, they can become any of these creatures?"

"Aye."

"Brilliant." She narrowed her eyes at the once kindly grandmother whose smile now featured teeth as sharp as fresh razors. "Are any parts of them human?"

Miss Overman snapped her teeth at them, and tried to break through the barrier, letting out a fierce scream when she failed.

"Not enough."

A piercing yell came from far off, in the direction the Damned had gone, and Miss Overman turned from them and sprinted down the path, leaving her pain and age and past behind.

Brigid and Knightly looked on as the perimeter held and the Damned moved away. Behind them the bonfire blazed, the tents lay crumpled on the ground, flapping forlornly in the wind. The town of Evermore was toppled and broken.

TEN

Finola and Ophelia met up with Knightly and Brigid at the perimeter. It smelled of decayed roses and ash, and the air was thick with a fog that would not dissipate. They guarded it for the rest of the day, taking turns walking up and down the line, the grass bending beneath their feet, the blue sky mocking them as it shifted into a mesmerizing burnt orange and pink sunset that looked like peace but brought none of the respite. The Damned did not return. The atmosphere, which that morning had started off so cheerful and uplifting, was plunged into tears of sorrow. The loss of Miss Overman was monumental, and a reminder of fatalities yet to come.

Brigid checked on the O'Malley boys before she returned home. Looking at their pink tongues, feeling their slightly swollen glands, and whispering spells of protection into their ears. She provided new tonics and after they gave her hugs and ran off to see if there was any cake left anywhere, declared them well enough, all things considered. What she did not say was that there was a thinness to their skin that left her fingers vibrating when she touched it through the gloves their mother provided. Brigid didn't have the heart to explain to her that as a witch, they couldn't affect her, curse her, in the same way. It didn't seem fair, and it served as yet another reminder she was responsible for their condition. She was responsible for it all.

Brigid promised to return the following day with new salves, and, she hoped, better news. She would search the *Book of the Goddess* and Agnes's journal for some hope that she might find a way to slow or stop the change.

Once Brigid, Ophelia, and Finola had finished checking on all the villagers, they headed to the pub and Knightly went to locate the Damned and make sure they weren't wandering too close to any stragglers still out in the pastures. He planned to barricade them as far off as he could.

The three witches toasted to Miss Overman with Jameson until they wobbled in their chairs, their heads grew light, and the hour of dawn approached. Once Ophelia was sober enough to drive, they returned home to sleep and build the courage to face the coming days.

The next afternoon they awoke sore and tired but determined. Breakfast was a quiet affair around the kitchen table. Ophelia's thick brown bread with blackberry jam and espressos for all, before they showered, changed, and headed for the lough.

Knightly was already there, standing by the edge, his hands in his pockets looking far too much like a hero lost on his way to the moors. Brigid had to remind herself this was a god who could bend the truth and always had a plan, and the plan historically was for his success and his alone. Otherwise, she was tempted to cross to him, run her fingers through his thick black locks, and see if he tasted as good as his memories.

"So?" she asked, walking up to stand beside him, looking out at the stillness of the opaque lake and marveling at how it could hide such horrors. "What's the plan today?"

"One and the same," he said. "We get your memories so you

can remember what it was that opened the lough and we learn how we close it."

"We get my memories, and then I remember how to get to Dove. Dove is my priority." Brigid blew out a breath, rubbing her hands together. She glanced to Ophelia and Finola who stood in black leggings and running shoes and oversized cream and charcoal shirts, their hair piled on both their heads, their hands on their fists like they were ready for battle. "And saving Evermore of course."

She looked back to Knightly. "I was hoping you had something more concrete than my memories as your plan."

"I'm a god who is good with wind and rain and lightning, and you are a witch who has the power of Goddess. What more do we need?"

"For starters," Finola said, brushing imaginary dirt from her shoulder, "you need to speak to all of us here involved in this conversation, you wanker. And second, I recall a tale that our Agnes wrote. One of you having a cauldron that can transmute materials."

Knightly took in Finola, and inclined his head. "Apologies. I did not mean to discount your presence, and Agnes is correct. I have a cauldron blessed by the Dagda."

"How do you have a cauldron of the Dagda?" Ophelia asked.

Knightly's smile was soft at the edges when he replied. "He was a generous god, and sovereign over life and death. He gifted me one of the *coire ansic*."

"Wasn't his cauldron meant to feed his followers?" Ophelia asked. "To provide a boundless feast?"

"His does," Knightly said, crossing his arms over his chest. "Mine provides something else."

"It turns the water it touches into yours?" Brigid asked, shivering against a cool breeze.

"It might. It never worked well for me. This cauldron will give the rightful user whatever they need."

"What do you mean it never works for you?" Finola asked, sitting down on the plush grass by the shore, running her fingers gently through the blades. "Did the Dagda give you a faulty cauldron?"

"No. He gave me just what he believed I needed. Such is the way of gods."

"What happened when it 'never worked' for you?" Ophelia asked.

"It burned the skin off my hands and left boils that took weeks to heal."

"Nope," Finola said. "Hard pass. Unyielding, impenetrable pass."

"It can't hurt you by holding it or being near it," he said, his dimple flashing.

"But it can hurt *you*," Ophelia said. "A god. What makes you think it won't, I don't know, fillet all of Brigid's skin from her body if she tries to use it to get her memories back?"

"Because," Knightly said, setting the cauldron on the sandy part of the shore of the lough so the water lapped over it and receded back, leaving tiny grains inside the basin of the cauldron. "She's used it before."

The water in the lough lapped lazily against the side of the shoreline. The sun bit through the graying sky but did little to warm the chill from Brigid's bones. The world was too bright, even with the clouds overhead trying to offer shade, as Knightly's words ricocheted around and around in her head. "She's used it before." Brigid looked to the emerald grass, dragging her gaze out to the dark lough, and back to the being before her. His fingers flexed, long and tanned, and she licked her lips before turning back to study the cauldron half sunken into the clumping sand.

Knightly refused to say more than he had, or he simply didn't have more to say. It was hard to tell with the trickster god. Brigid didn't know for sure if he was telling the truth, but he was fighting with them, and they needed his protection from the witches of Knight—and his assistance if they were going to attempt and access the magic of the lough.

Brigid walked over to the cauldron and ran the edges of her fingers across its rim, dragging a nail across the gold, listening. The cauldron was silent, still in the shore. Barely an echo remained inside.

Knightly had told her their magics were reacting to each other. She had wanted him to be wrong. This time, it seemed, he was correct.

"I'll need a bit of your magic," she said, standing, "if I'm to access my past, combine yours and mine, twin magics—one born from the god who created the lough and the other from the goddess it was gifted to."

She would give of her magic with her wise women—Ophelia and Finola—flanking her, doing this together. She knew, without a doubt, she was stronger with her coven.

Before they could begin, they would need a proper circle. For this spell, Brigid led Ophelia and Finola through the methodical and arbitrary steps of using a besom, one she collected from her caravan, to sweep the negative energy from around the lough. She had to quiet Finola after she got a bit excited circling the lough and began shaking her fist, shouting in a deep voice, "Out, damn evil witches. Out, I say!"

Ophelia chose which crystals to set out, picking black tourmaline for grounding and selenite for protection and clarity. Brigid was adamant about casting in the daylight, when shadows would be closer to this world seeking a way in. It would give them shades of magic to bend, and there was great power in that.

Together, with Knightly watching, they cast the circle with

a ring of salt and a perimeter of candles. "We will move deasil, clockwise, around our circle first," Brigid said. "There is luck and protection in going sun-wise." She passed a small bottle of white powder to Ophelia and Finola. "This is cascarilla, banishing powder, in case you need to use it."

Ophelia's gaze widened. "For?"

"If something goes wrong, try and use this to send back anything that comes over."

"Do you think it will work?"

Brigid shrugged. "Mayhap, but it's a hope, and that is a thing with feathers."

"If only we all had souls for it to perch in," Knightly said, from where he stood watching, drawing gusts of wind into his hands and sending them down into the worn earth and back up again, like a child bouncing a ball.

Brigid walked to the crescent moon circle Ophelia had created with her crystals. She took a breath and stepped inside, tasting magic in the air, saturating it. A hint of cherries and apple. The apple reminded her of the Goddess, the scent that had clung to her, along with smoke of a fire. The cherries reminded her of waking in her cellar and she whispered to herself, "Don't forget."

Knightly joined the two women at the edge of the circle, and kneeled between them, directly behind Brigid. One by one the three passed a match back and forth until each crimson candle at the edges and center of the moon was burning bright. The air warmed, a melodic whistle cut through the trees on the far side of the bank, and the wind grew still and quiet.

Peace shifted over Brigid, raining down on her, little droplets of calm sinking into her forearms and cheeks, brushing across her brow and chest. She cupped her hands, and pulled the peace inward, toward the center of her circle. A bliss, an equanimity, born of the elements coming together settled inside her.

Brigid held out her left hand first, palm up. "The ritual guides us. It's sacred, and so we welcome it. With our left hand, we open to the universe." She then held up her right hand, palm down, the pale pink paint on her fingernails shining in the sun. "With our right hand, we open to the earth so that it may ground us."

She spoke to the women as Brighid the Goddess had spoken to her, teaching them the old ways so they might blend them with their new. Instructing with gentle tones and compassion, letting Knightly in on the secrets of her power, without giving away anything she held too dear.

"We draw the energy in with every inhale," Brigid said, tilting her chin up, inhaling the sweet sap of the trees, and the grittiness of the sand and earth. "We send it out with each exhale. We share energy, and it will move between us, and follow us."

The lough before them shifted, the water rippling as it moved from deep blue to black. The wind, which had been nonexistent, blew a cold blast across her shoulders.

"Brigid," Knightly said, "now would be the time to hurry."

"A hurried mind means hasty hands," she said, her eyes shifting to the ripples undulating across the water. "Speaking of, Finola and Ophelia, raise your hands and bring them palm to palm. Hold this space, for it is blessed. You are protected, and you are safe. Hold space for me, and in doing so, you keep me protected. You keep me safe. You are my anchors."

Brigid looked down at the cauldron in the center of her circle. Rounded and gold, indeterminable of age. She took a breath and nodded to the others. They began to move deasil, and Brigid's shaking fingers closed around the cauldron, the rough edge digging into her palms. A vibration burst to life at the touch, and she tilted it forward into the lough, pulling the cool water in as it slipped over her fingers and rushed into the cauldron.

A splash of cold against her hands, a catch of breath, and Brigid was no longer looking down at the golden cauldron and the dark water of the lough, but looking through the world. The fabric and essence of it. Brigid was on the sandy shore standing within her circle by the lough in one moment, in front of her coven and Knightly, with her toes pressing into the soft give of the earth . . . and then she wasn't.

The world around Brigid expanded. She watched a single drop of water swell out like an inkblot from the center of the cauldron and into the lough around her. A whirlpool of water spun from the edge of the lough, once, twice. The inkblot sank into the center of the water, light pooling around it. Brigid felt the space between her conscious self and beyond it flip upside down.

She blinked and she was no longer staring down at the cauldron, but standing before the Goddess, seated by the well.

⊷O

Ophelia and Finola stood holding the edge of the circle, their eyes on Brigid, who had gone as still as a frozen lake. Magic pulsed from her, golden sparks dusting across her skin, a vibration rumbling beneath her feet out toward them. Her skin, which was as pale as a fresh snowfall, had a faint glow spread across it. Almost as though someone had lit her from within.

Knightly kept his eyes on Brigid as well, coming to stand in front of her, facing the water of the lough as though prepared to fight anything that rose from it.

As the minutes ticked by, sweat broke out along Ophelia's brow. Ophelia's own magic pulsed in and out of her palms. It started like a tickling of a feather, brushing against her skin, and grew into a pinch and then a tug. There was a cost to even the most practical of magics. She knew this, but she had not realized the price of tapping into the power of the lough. They were using two magics, light and dark. Brigid's and Knightly's. Judging by the way Finola's upper teeth dug into her bottom lip, she was not the only one suffering. Only Brigid appeared unaffected, Knightly was as still as the lough he watched.

Ophelia shifted her weight, debating whether she could speak or if the sound of her voice might break the spell; and a crack echoed in the forest behind them.

Her eyes moved to Finola, who was standing across from her. She watched her sister release her lip as her mouth dropped into the shape of a large O. Finola's eyes moved from the woods to Ophelia.

"Fin?" Ophelia mouthed, her brows lifting.

A snap from behind; a creak and then, low and menacing, a growl.

Every hair on the back of Ophelia's neck rose. Goose bumps broke out along her skin.

Finola gulped, her arms shaking, but she did not lower them or break the spell. She looked from Ophelia to Brigid's frozen form, and back to the forest. She swallowed again and met Ophelia's eyes. She mouthed one word.

Monster.

⊷

Brigid watched the Goddess tending to her well, her long cloak on the ground beside her, her dress a navy material that twinkled as if she had sewn stars into the very fabric. Her fiery hair was braided down her back, her crown glimmering in the light. She was humming, and running her bejeweled fingers along the ribbons in the clootie tree. The ribbons always appeared overnight, they were wishes and prayers for healing in the village. The Goddess would send a bit of healing into each strand, then Brigid would bring the little bottle over and tie a string to its top before she lowered it into the steady stream that ran beneath the tree. Once the bottles were filled, Brigid added the proper herbs into them and would deliver them to those in need, and set aside what she did not need for another time when it could be of use.

It was a familiar scene, one she had witnessed hundreds of times, but on this day, a certain electricity clung to Brigid, as she stepped toward her Goddess.

The Goddess stood, dusted her dress, and turned to face her, flashing a beautiful smile that reached her eyes for a moment before dropping away.

"What's wrong?" Brigid asked. "Why does your smile flee?"

"I was thinking of Lugh and his coven."

"Are they leaving?"

The Goddess shook her head. "The coven of Knight wants the power to bring the chaos that has grown in the Otherworld here."

"Why do they need its power? They have their god."

"They want more than he can give. They must pay a great cost to stay alive. Their souls do not age but they do."

"They look the same age as I am."

"Illusion is a convincing lie. If they can access the power of the Otherworld, the ancient power of the lough, they will truly become immortal. They will be revived physically, but the wear and tear on their souls is too deep. They have lost their spark of love, of empathy."

"But they can't open the lough."

"No, they cannot."

"Do you know how it can be opened?"

"Through the thing they have lost. Love, and sacrifice."

"So they are doomed to guard it?"

"They are damned to the fate they chose, yes."

"That's terribly sad."

"Free will is not meant to be upended."

Brigid nodded. *"I guess I just wish there was a way to help everyone."*

The Goddess smiled again, and this time it stayed. She turned back to her well. "There is always a way, Brigid Heron."

⌐O

A mist rolled in like smoke billowing up and over the land. It brushed against Brigid's ankles and calves, as she walked forward to a grouping of trees just down the path from where the Goddess tended her well. She did not remember seeing these trees before and was careful not to touch the trunks that shimmered. When she grew close enough, she leaned in for a better look. The trees appeared to have turned to dazzling stone. Petrified wood in a petrified forest.

She turned and looked back, and the world faded from gray into a golden haze, the Goddess disappearing from sight. Brigid looked south, for where to go next, and the earth shifted from dark sod into green grass, flat land into rolling hills. She stepped deeper into the forest, the sounds of her footfalls echoing. Here shadows moved across the ground, snaking out in various directions.

She thought of Dove, pulling up the face from her only memory of her daughter into her mind. Dove's almond-shaped eyes and pert nose, her generous smiling mouth. She needed another memory of her daughter. She needed *all* of the memories and a way back to her.

The mist billowed out around her. Brigid took a breath, and the vapor tickled the back of her throat even though her mind knew her body was standing in her crescent moon circle and the mist was a product of the astral plane caught between worlds and time. She walked on and the shadows that skirted her feet and swam in and out of the pathway she walked shifted into forms. Hazy creatures, they hovered before her, their vibrations not quite right. Brigid thought it was like seeing radio waves come to life. Static and mass, and something more, real or that had once been alive.

These shadows were made of smoke and something else, and their voice came out with a hiss and a growl. "What do you want, witch?"

Brigid turned, tried to find a face in the shadows, but all she saw, as far as her eyes could see, was the smoke and the trees and the shadow undulating across the land like sound waves.

"I am looking for Dove," she said, remembering a missive in the *Book of the Goddess* that if you were to encounter shadow creatures to appear as nonthreatening as possible, for they were trapped and liable to react to any wrong move. She held up her hands, lowering her shoulders.

"What will you trade us for this information?" the voices asked as one.

Brigid grew still. She *knew* those voices, though they sounded different here among the shadows, softer and more human.

The coven of Knight.

"You do not have the information I seek," she said, as a hint of rosemary brushed under her nose.

"About that, you are wrong," they said.

"Even if I am, why would you give me information and how could I ever trust it?"

The shadows in the forest deepened, the light shrank into tiny rays that illuminated the trees, and nothing else. Brigid's pulse jumped in her neck and she forced her breath to stay slow and steady. The dark, here with these witches, would not work to her advantage if they realized she carried not only her power, but that of Knightly's as well.

"We are trapped, and we need help. You are the only one who has traveled near this well, and perhaps the only one who can."

"I thought I was in my memories," Brigid said, her tone deadpan.

"You were *open*, and heard our call."

"Open?"

"To travel as you are, you must open yourself to all the elements, all the paths. We reached you here."

"And you pulled me from my memories?"

"We called. *You* chose to answer."

Brigid's knees were shaking, so she reached out, and brushed the petrified bark. It was solid beneath her hands, warm and safe.

"What do you know?" she asked them.

"We know *we* were the last to see your goddess after she came to your aid. You disappeared from the lough after making a bargain with her. After you nearly killed one of ours."

Brigid let go of the tree. "Why would I hurt you? We stayed away from each other until I showed up here and found you all pulling *monsters* from the lough."

"You want what we want."

"I want my daughter."

"You want what you lost returned."

Brigid stepped over a root in the forest, the dried branches scratching at her ankle. "You saw the Goddess after I left?"

"We did."

"Did you do something to her?"

"We do not have that kind of power."

"Did she speak to you?"

"She sent you through time and then she left. Perhaps she did not expect you to return."

Brigid's stomach tightened at their words. "What does this have to do with my daughter?"

"Is it not obvious? Are you not the wise and noble Brigid Heron?" Derision dripped from their voices, it slithered along the ground and circled her.

"Apparently not," she said, a bite to her own voice as she stepped out of the circle they tried to wrap her in. "Perhaps if I were really smart, I wouldn't waste a single second in the forest with you and your baneful magic."

Brigid turned to leave, and they spoke, their words in a rush, need coating each syllable.

"She sent you after your daughter. Wherever she is, you were."

Brigid looked over her shoulder and tried to see the faces in the smoke. "You don't know that for certain."

"No, but *you* can. Ask our king."

"You think he would tell me?"

"We cannot know his ways. His nature is born from gods and the gods do not understand when they are helping or hurting. When they are playing or tricking. He watches you, so maybe he likes playing with Brigid Heron. Or maybe it's all a trick."

"What do you want for this trade in information?"

"You have already given it to us."

Brigid swallowed as they shifted in closer to her. "I haven't given you anything."

"That is where you are wrong, Brigid Heron." Then they were surrounding her. Four witches in a circle, standing tall as they closed her in. For a moment, she could almost see who they had been. Beautiful, powerful, broken. "We'll be seeing you."

Then their shadows receded, like water pooling backward. The trees of stone and petrified wood, which had been hard and un-forgiving when she entered the forest, swayed. They creaked and cracked, bending.

Brigid tried to call out, but her voice was a squeak of air. She looked down, and she was nothing but ash and wind and sand.

And then, she was gone too. Spinning. Upside down, sideways, right side up.

She was on the cellar floor in her home. She knew the room, the darkness of it, and heard the skittering of little mice feet trampling over dirt and dust. Her heartbeat sped up; her skin grew clammy.

The cellar was ice-cold. Drenched in the sweet scent of raw cherries, and something beneath it, tart and bitter.

Brigid looked for the broken leg of the chair from her childhood and saw it rotting in the corner. Covered in dark moss. The wood decayed in rapid speed like an apple core turning into dust. Brigid looked to the other corner and saw herself, decaying in the same manner, her skin flecking off, her hair falling in clumps from her head. Her eyes frozen in her skull.

She bit back a scream. A rattle came from the hands of her corpse, and Brigid looked down to see her own hands holding the golden cauldron. It was filled with a liquid, gurgling and bubbling over the edge, steaming as it dripped toward her fingers.

A light grew around her, soft and bright. Urgent in warning. The thrum of a thousand drumbeats rose around her, the notes of a hundred guitars plucked to life.

Invisible hands came around her waist and throat and tried to draw her under.

She tried to tug herself back but couldn't move. She was frozen, her breath leaving her body. If she didn't get her spirit back into her body, she would be lost forever.

She mentally called for the Goddess, for Knightly, and the wind picked up, blew her up and out of the room into the ether. Suddenly she was over the lough, hovering just above it. She tried to catch her breath, to remind herself it was not her breath at all, but the memory of it. Fragments, the past pulling at the threads of her and splintering something there. Her memory, already cracked, breaking apart.

She screamed inside her head, and a sharp cry of her name came from below her. The sound unstuck something in her.

Brigid blasted out and back into her own body. The force of it knocking the fire from the candles, dispersed her circle, and sent the cauldron careening into the lough.

ELEVEN

*I*t started with a flicker of light that grew into an ember that exploded into a flaming fire. The heat blasted through Finola and Ophelia, knocking them to the earth. They broke the circle and the barriers, and as they crawled to their knees they saw Brigid curled on the ground.

They jumped up and ran to Brigid, forming a protective barrier around her as they crouched nearly back-to-back, arms up, ready to fight. Standing in front of the lough and looking at the perimeter of mist that had formed around it. Knightly pulled the rain, dousing the fire as he hurried to where Brigid lay.

Brigid sat up slowly, her hand coming to the base of her neck, and she rubbed the back of her head. "That was unexpected," she managed.

"Are you okay?" Knightly asked, bending over her, and helping her all the way up.

"I think so."

"Good," Finola said. "We can't wait to hear all about it, but we've got a fairly large problem made larger by the fact that your protective circle has been blown to smithereens."

"The circle?" Brigid asked, as Ophelia stepped closer. Brigid looked to her left and took an involuntary step.

"Wait," Ophelia whispered. "I think it doesn't like it when we move."

"What doesn't?" Brigid asked, her words trailing off as her eyes took in the mist and the fog, not unlike that of the petrified forest, now coating the land surrounding the lough and the broken circle.

Two shadows slithered along the ground. They growled and hissed, pressing in, inch by inch. Fear, the slumbering beast, came to life inside Brigid's rib cage, knocking on the door to her heart and sending it galloping.

⊶θ

Magic isn't emotion. It isn't bones or blood or ligament or breath. Magic is energy. It is older than time. Magic is the stone beneath time, that first step in the winding staircase. While magic may not have what humans call feelings, it would be foolhardy to say it is without passion. Magic is the essence of desire, the DNA of craving. It's unwieldy in nature.

The power facing the women, it wasn't unwieldy. It was wicked.

The shadows pooled and separated, slithering into the edge of the mist before turning and crossing back through. The first stood at the edge of the mist, her voice melodic and gentle.

"Finola," the voice whispered from where it waited. "Finola, why do you turn from me?"

Finola let out a gurgled cry, and a tall woman wearing a cloak the color of midnight stepped from the mist.

"Opheliaaaaaaa," another voice called, soft and insistent. "She will leave you, too."

Brigid's heart raced in her chest; a chill wracked her body. The voices.

Dove strode through the mist, her eyes too wide and bright, her hair knotted and her clothing in tatters. She circled them, diminutive and fierce, wearing flowers in her hair, her bare feet caked in mud.

"No," Brigid said, her legs giving out as she dropped to her knees. "It cannot be."

"She's no druid of the forest," Dove said, her voice a harsh gong banging in Brigid's mind. "No green witch or wise woman. She's in the wrong place. The wrong time. Wrong, wrong, *wrong*."

"It's not her," Knightly said, his voice cracking even as he strode forward as though he had not a care in the world. He crouched beside Brigid and wrapped an arm around her. "That is not your daughter."

The sky darkened as the woman in the cloak threw back her hood. The Goddess, cloaked and powerful, with her hands on her hips, glided closer to Finola and Ophelia. Brigid registered her presence, but she could not take her eyes off her Dove. The way her hair, even matted as it was, curled at the ends. How the left side coiled just a bit more than the right, how her cheeks flushed with life. Dove stared hard into Brigid's eyes, through her head, and laughed so loudly the ground shook, then turned and walked to the edge of trees. She raised a hand, parted them, and slipped through.

"Wait!" Brigid called, climbing to her knees.

"Monsters," Knightly said, his voice hoarse as he tightened his grip on Brigid. "They're the Damned."

Brigid's eyes filled, but she nodded, telling herself the words out loud so it might sink in better. So she might resist the need to wrap her arms around the creature wearing her daughter's face. "Not real."

"No."

By the edge of the water the Goddess circled Finola, tilting her head one way and the other, her lips a deep red, her eyes flashing with ire.

"Her cape," Ophelia whispered, tracking her movements. "It's *bleeding*."

The Goddess stood with her shoulders thrown back, her midnight cape dripping black along the ground as it trailed after her like a dying slug.

Laughter slipped into the circle of mist, high and reedy. Ophelia backed into Finola, blindly grasping her hand, and Brigid tried to clear the sorrow from her heart enough to think.

"How did they get out of the lough?" She turned to Knightly. "The coven isn't here, are they?"

"It managed to call them without being near the water," Knightly said. "I don't understand it."

Brigid swallowed, thinking of how she'd opened to them, spoken with them. Traded information.

Could she have provided them a door, giving them a new path here?

A giggle broke through the air, coming from the Goddess. Brigid cocked her head. The *laugh*. She did not know it. It was a gurgling, choking noise, no chortle or guffaw. She did not know that laugh, but she knew every sound of the Goddess.

This goddess smiled and spun in a circle, her red hair streaming behind her, no crown sitting atop her head. Brigid held up her hands. She pressed her thumbs together and then her index fingers, making a triangle. She looked through it, and her eyes narrowed.

"You are no god," Brigid said to the creature who, when viewed through her magical keyhole, had no face.

The not-Goddess grinned. "You see nothing, child. You are as blind as the rest of the people on this decaying island. From the depths of chaos the truth will rise. It will free us, and we will rule you all." She turned, and Brigid's eyes tracked her cape to where it left an inky stain, not blood, but camouflage.

"We need light," she said to the others, and no sooner had the words left her lips than a gale force wind blew through.

"I'm thinking that the Damned doesn't want any candles lit," Knightly said, pulling the wind toward him, opening his coat and drawing the breeze into the inside pockets like he was storing candies or sweets instead of the elements.

"She has no shadow," Brigid said as she looked up at the trees. "The mist is cloaking the light. The Goddess does not hide from her shadow, but this being does."

"What does it mean?" Finola called.

"It means she is no goddess," Brigid said. "On my say, Fin and Ophelia, throw your cascarilla at it. Knightly, can you call your wind to clear the mist and help drive it forward?"

He opened his coat, and a cold breeze blew fiercely over them, tugging their tresses up and knocking them forward so they had to put their arms out.

"Okay then," Brigid said. "One, two, *now*," she called, before she stalked to the goddess.

The witches let fly the powder Brigid had given them, and it coated the goddess. She growled, looked down at her cape, and dusted it off.

"Whoops," Fin said, her voice a squeak.

"Let's see who she really is." Brigid said, reaching for the edge of the cape and yanking it free. The creature pretending to be the Goddess tried to cover its face, but Brigid lifted a hand and sparks flew, catching in its hair.

The goddess ran to the lough to put the sparks out, and as soon as it had, Knightly snapped the fingers on his left hand. The water frosted. Clean and clear. The reflection of the creature stared back at itself from the now mirrorlike surface of the lough.

The creature screamed at what it saw, slammed a foot down

into the ice. It smoldered the flames out, turned, and began to advance on the women.

"So this is a real fight, and not a magic fight then?" Finola asked, reaching down to pick up a large hunk of rock. "Okay then." She took off running and threw the rock as hard as she could at the goddess's head.

"Oh my," Ophelia said as the rock missed. She scooped up more stones at the far edge of the lough and hurled them at the creature, this time hitting it in the stomach.

The two witches began hurling rocks and sticks and anything else they could find. Finola threw a shoe and missed Brigid by an inch.

"Really, Finola?" Brigid called, looking over her shoulder. "You only need to bind it. See if we have any cord left."

She turned and looked over her shoulder and froze.

Dove slipped out of the mist. She no longer wore flowers in her hair and a smile. Her flesh had gone from golden to pale green, her hair falling off in patches, purple circles marring the tender skin beneath eyes and covering her arms. "They're *next*," she said, and as she walked forward, she shrank in stature. Her nose elongating, her eyes deepening and darkening into two empty black holes.

"A *far darrig*," Knightly said, relief coating his voice.

Brigid's eyes widened as she took it in.

"I can take care of it," he said. "You work to send the other one back into the water."

She glanced back to the goddess, its hands at its side and face fully visible. Large ears, a beak for a nose, and red eyes stared back. Their glamours could not hold, and were fading fast.

"Pooka," she whispered, backing to the lough where she saw the cauldron sitting by the shore where it had flown from her hands.

"Tricksters," Knightly said.

"We are *yours*," the Pooka said to Knightly,

"You are your own," Knightly said, as the creature flashed its sharp teeth and ran full speed for him.

They grappled on the shore, the illusion falling away from the not-Goddess to reveal a small but agile creature that flipped Knightly over his shoulder before diving on him. Knightly struggled, too far from his lough to call to the water and pull the Pooka into its depths.

Brigid reached down and spoke the words from one of the spells in the *Book of the Goddess*.

*"The earth bends to me
And brings every creature to its knees."*

The trickster flew from Knightly, careening through the trees on the left side of the lough, sending branches flying before it crashed to the earth, where it struggled and failed to get up.

"Not bad," Knightly called. "Thanks."

"You only need to—" Brigid called out, and the *far darrig* wearing Dove's features jumped to where she was.

"You only need to what, Brigid Heron? Bind us? You really think you can?" it asked, giggling. The sound so high and reedy it bore its way into her skull, and she feared she would never get it out again. She pressed her hands to her ears and looked around for Finola and Ophelia, who she had been certain were binding it five seconds before.

"They're not here," it said, before cackling again. "Little witches like to fly."

Then it reached out and wrapped Brigid in a bear hug. Brigid fought to kick herself free but it held her high in the air, and then it brought her lower, inch by inch, so that they were eye to eye.

Brigid saw in its eyes a reflection. Of a pond and a cavern of trees and a land that did not exist in Evermore, and beyond them she saw a girl with flowers in her hair spinning and laughing before she ran down a hill. The girl paused and turned at the bottom of the hill to look up. Her eyes growing wide.

"*Dove.*"

"Ah, yes," it growled, before it spun Brigid in a circle. "I have a message for you. But I don't think *you* deserve it. Nevertheless: the fairy queen waits for no man."

Then it released its fingers one by one, and Brigid from its grip, and sent her careening up into the air and deep into the mist.

⚷

OPHELIA: Welcome back to *Ever More Monsters*, the new name of our podcast as voted on by those of you listening. I am gobsmacked by your enthusiasm, I tell you. Today's topic ventures into the tricksters of the monsters, like the Pooka, leprechaun, and *far darrig*. I have Jack Donnelly to tell us about his experience with one of these devious creatures some years back. Thanks so much for joining us, Jack.

JACK: Thanks for inviting me to pass along this warning. It's been giving me nightmares for years, having tangled with the Damned like I have.

OPHELIA: How much tangling would you say you've been caught up in, Jack?

JACK: I had three run-ins with one of the Damned leprechauns—as they tend to do things in threes, sevens, and thirteens—and a few with a particularly aggressive Damned Pooka on Sundays and late at night when the moon is hidden from the sky and ground is ridden with dew.

OPHELIA: That is quite Damned specific.

JACK: I know. The Pooka hate salt and don't like it when you make fun of 'em. They're also partial to song. I've distracted quite a few singing "Molly Malone."

OPHELIA: You seem to know a lot about them.

JACK: I learn everything I can about my opponents. It's how I prepare to face them.

OPHELIA: Sound advice, that. Will you walk our listener through your run-ins with that particular creature?

JACK: The first one happened some forty years ago. I had been out at Sherry Bannon's house, studying, and time got away from me. I was hurrying home so as not to worry me ma and then, suddenly, there she stood on the street. My ma, in the same exact dress she'd been in when I left that morn.

OPHELIA: Was she looking for you?

JACK: She said she was, and then she raised her left hand and I saw she had a rolling pin clutched in it. She chased me down the road, swinging it, until I jumped the fence between Pat Teagan's and Cormac McGee's. As soon as I landed and stood up, she was gone.

OPHELIA: Ooh, and then what happened?

JACK: Then I walked home. Went to bed and avoided her for the rest of the week.

OPHELIA: Erm, how do you know then that she was a monster?

JACK: Because when I got home she was in her room, the door open, and she was snoring and wearing *a completely different dress.*

OPHELIA: Right. Then when did you see the creature the other two times?

JACK: Once when I was stuck in a storm out on Pat's field. I walked home during a thunderstorm, and there she was, my ma in the same dress as on the night I'd left Sherry's.

OPHELIA: I know the Damned are deceptive, but did she simply happen to like the outfit, Jack? Certain people have favorite outfits, do you know?

JACK: She might have done, but it was a good ten years later and she hadn't aged and neither had the dress. Which she had donated to the village fundraiser five years earlier.

OPHELIA: That is alarming.

JACK: Fecking A.

OPHELIA: And the third time?

JACK: The third time I was coming home from Killian's again.

OPHELIA: Of course you were.

JACK: And it was near midnight, no more than a week or two ago. I was near the stone wall out by the Heron land and I heard it. My ma, who has been dead and gone in Father O'Malley's cemetery for these past seven years, singing. She sang my name over and over, and when I got close, she switched to singing about how a kingdom needs its ruler. Then when I got near enough to toss my holy water on her, she jumped up and ran away.

OPHELIA: You carry holy water on you?

JACK: Of a sort.

OPHELIA: What kind of sort?

JACK: It's a good bit of Jameson in my flask with the cross on its front, which is holy to be sure and as good as water in a pinch.

OPHELIA: I can't argue that.

JACK: I switched to carrying the herby stuff you gave me, but sometimes I forget it and I rarely forget my Jameson.

OPHELIA: I wonder why that is, Jack.

JACK: Oh, it's on account of how it helps with headaches, bowel issues, my nerves, even puts me in the mood when I'm not feeling sprightly and the lady is.

OPHELIA: Well. I'm not sure what to say now.

JACK: I think this is where we close.

OPHELIA: Right. Sorry about that. You heard it here first, listeners. Jameson may just cure what ails you. But if it's a Damned you're trying to keep out, please start with a salt perimeter and any one of our "herby waters," as Jack calls them. This is Ophelia Gallagher, reminding you to be kind and look out for one another, and beware any mothers wearing outdated clothing singing off-key on your way home from the pub. Remember, the beasties will get you if you don't watch out.

TWELVE

BOOK OF THE GODDESS (P. 54):

How to Turn a Spell

There are spells in this world that cannot be done, and there are others that are like a bit of spilled milk. They only need sopping up. To undo a fear spell, face the thing that terrifies you. To slack a lust spell, hold the object of your affection until the desire falls away. If you find you have been bewitched by a fairy, and your mind turned inside out, turn your clothes wrong side out. There is always a counter, if you're courageous enough to walk toward the fire.

For the first time since breaking up with Thorpe, Ophelia no longer felt the devastation she'd sewn into her soul at finding and losing true love. Instead, she felt . . . nothing. She studied the road she was walking on, how it sloped down and away from her feet with every step she took. She had been heading home, hadn't she? She looked to her left, at the rolling green and yellow fields and then to her right, and the stone wall. She walked on, not recognizing the road, but knowing it must be the path home. The sky overhead was gray, the wind smelled of freshly tended grass and something sweet, hibiscus blooming perhaps.

She wondered where Fin was, and reached for her phone, but it was not in her pocket. She tapped her other pocket, and then her chin. Strange. Ophelia was a witch, not a scientist, but she understood the brain could grow tired and overworked, and it could lose its way.

Panic attacks could cause a lapse, couldn't they? Didn't she read about them online after losing sleep the first week three Damned came out of the lough in a row, six months ago?

Ophelia liked to read. Her house knew that. That's why it would bake her stories and letters. She would go to open the oven to clean it, and instead find a waiting missive from Agnes to her journal, the edges curling as the heat prepared to singe it whole. Or they would open the pantry door and find a spell written by Brigid, one for a cream to cure eczema, resting on the counter.

Brigid.

Brigid Heron.

Ophelia stopped walking and looked around. Brigid had returned. She was her family and her friend. But . . . where was she?

Where was Fin?

Ophelia turned back to the road with its tumbled stones and picked up her pace, her feet slapping hard against the pavement as she hurried on.

Brigid and Finola.

They had been fighting.

She broke into a jog.

How had she ended up here?

Where *was* here?

It didn't matter. She would find them. They were hers, and she was theirs.

Ophelia wiped sweat from her upper lip as it dripped down her face, thinking of Brigid's lost memories. Was that why she couldn't remember why she was running down the road she was on? Was it connected? Could it be catching?

Ophelia needed to get to them. They could be hurt or lost, too. She would find them both, no matter the cost.

She only had to remember where she was, and how to get home.

—0

There were things Knightly knew for certain. One being it was easier to breathe at night, when the world was asleep and his lough was quiet. When he could walk the fields he had claimed since he first came to Evermore. He loved how he knew the white sheep were ornery on Tuesdays, the green and yellow weeds sprung up from the ground if he looked at the earth wrong, and how when he walked under the hazelnut trees they occasionally pelted him like a spoiled child having a temper tantrum.

His deep and unruly lough, however, had been his constant. Until the monsters came out of it, the witches he had partnered with turned their hearts to coal, and Brigid and Dove Heron disappeared.

Now half of the equation was where she belonged, fighting at his side, and the other half still missing. Dove was an ache in his chest, a rip in his gut. The bright and beautiful girl that was more powerful than all of the monsters from the lough combined.

Knightly would have to tell Brigid now. The truth. Which was as dangerous as the Pooka that currently had him pinned to the ground.

Well, that wasn't quite right.

Knightly punched a fist out and connected with its side. Then he reached out behind him and clutched at the air, gave it a tug. A tidal wave rose from the lough and swooped down over him, sucking the Pooka up into its cyclone.

"It's time for you to go," he said, rolling onto his stomach and crawling to his knees. "And don't forget who gave you everything."

The Pooka tried to call out, but the water sucked him back into the lough. Knightly turned to where Brigid had been fighting the other Damned, the nasty *far darrig*, but she was nowhere to be seen.

"Where is she?" he asked the creature with its elongated beak and beady black eyes, stalking toward it.

"Lugh of the Otherworld and king of no world, you think I'm afraid of you? You abandoned those beyond this realm."

"I set you free."

"You grew bored, and when the Otherworld was no longer enough you came for this one and left us with untended borders."

"I was locked out," he said.

"And then your priorities changed. We know who it is that could claim sovereignty over us now."

"Yet you choose to align yourselves with a coven who only seeks to claim power from you."

"They can make us stronger."

"No." He shook his head. "They will make you dead."

Then he tugged the wave again, pulling it forth and catching the creature before he sent the water dragging him down. Knightly closed his eyes as the waves receded and the lough returned to the eerie stillness it normally possessed. He listened to the heartbeats thumping around him. He did not hear the one he sought . . . and then he heard it one pasture over. This heart beat a little faster, and as he listened to it, everything inside him settled.

There she was.

He looked up at the sky and moved his hand to the left, shifting the clouds enough for a ray of light to break through. His shadow spread across the ground, and Knightly stepped into it.

—0

Finola's journey was not going the way she had hoped. She lost Ophelia, lost Brigid, and while she wasn't all that sorry she'd lost Knightly, she was standing down from the emerald cliffs by the fairy ring—and she was tired and irritated. Brigid had gotten a memory back, Fin knew it, and for a moment, before the monsters came out of the lough, the water had shifted from navy into a soft blue. The same color as the loughs and springs around Evermore.

They'd been on the right track.

Then the Damned arrived, and they'd fought those horribly terrifying monsters, and Ophelia—her lovely, clever, and wonderful best friend and sister—had been tossed by one of them, and then when she stood up she took off running in the opposite direction. *From* Finola.

Finola called after her and tried to follow her, but once she crested the hill that led to the fairy ring, she was turned around. She still didn't even understand how she ended up on the damn hill. Finola was not a geographical expert. She did not understand how cartography was a hobby or a vocation, how people could spend hours savoring the different roads and byways and viaducts and paths each town and city and county and country and fecking world could have. Understanding where one was in the world should be as simple as walking out of one's door, no more and no less. And yet she knew she was somewhere she should not be.

Finola was standing by the fairy ring, a ten-minute walk up the hill from Brigid's house, and a ten-minute walk from the lough, and she had no bloody clue how she came to be there. Or where her friends were or how to get back to them. So she did what she did best. She stamped her foot and let out a scream that shocked the robins perching on a hawthorn tree ten feet over.

To top it off, each time she tried to walk down the hill, and back to the path that would lead her to Brigid's house, she ended up circling back to the top of the hill. She went the other way, then sideways, then across and down. Each time she tried; each time she was returned to where she began. All roads led to the fecking fairy ring.

It was bloody maddening.

Finola was not a patient woman to begin with; living a life where you are born and stuck on one island and far too often hunted by monsters did that to a being. She lived life in a state of constant reaction. It meant she had a solid gut she trusted, and she surrounded herself with only the most trustworthy of people. She trusted Ophelia, and she trusted Brigid.

If only they were here. She stamped her other foot and then kicked the stone closest to her. It felt good, fighting *something*, so she kicked it again, then groaned as she stubbed her toe. Hopping on one foot, she wracked her brain.

If only she could do *more*. Help Brigid, help Evermore, stop the freaky witches and close the lough.

She hated feeling so helpless.

Finola, pissed at the boulder for having the audacity to fight back, kicked the rock yet again. As she did, the sun came out from behind the clouds. The stone she kicked hissed and sunk farther into the earth. Finola halted, one foot in the air, and peered down.

The air shimmered around the rock and for a moment she

could see through it into a world beyond this one. Then a book flew out from the center of the fairy ring, smacking Finola in the shoulder and falling to the ground. The rock returned to being just a rock, and she bent over and picked up the book. Turned it over. It didn't look like much, with its faded brown leather cover. But it was smooth and soothing somehow as she gripped it in her hands.

She turned it over and read the inscription scrawled across the top of the back cover.

This book belongs to Dove Heron

Finola let out an excited yelp and tried to open the book. It hugged its pages tight. She shook it and yanked at it, but the book remained closed.

She looked back to the fairy ring and crossed to it, peering inside. It looked like an ordinary fairy ring. Of course, the book looked ordinary, too. The stupid fighting rock even appeared usual and boring.

But she had seen something there, beneath it.

She leaned into the center of the fairy ring and waved a hand through, and the air rippled.

Finola took a deep breath for courage, jumped into the ring . . . and nothing happened. She looked around it, nudged at the earth with her toe, got down on her knees and pressed an ear to the earth to see if she could hear anything. The grass tickled her cheek. It was just a fairy ring. No more or less. She stood and walked out of it, holding the book tight to her chest.

With a renewed drive, she hurried down the hill to find Brigid and Finola. She didn't know what the book meant, but it had Dove's name on it.

Surely it was a good omen. A sign of better things to come.

—0

One moment Brigid was caught in the snare of the Damned, and the next she was flying through the air, her arms pinwheeling, legs kicking as the creature dropped Brigid two fields over. She landed on a bed of hazelnuts, sending them flying as she careened into them. Her breath was knocked from her chest, and she lay there gasping until it returned. She rolled to her side, her eyes tracking the nuts and noticing that not a single hazelnut had smashed its way open. They were as cursed as the island.

"Bloody evil you are," she told them, before rolling up into a seated position. A nut that refused to open was unnatural. But then so was Evermore. She looked for the Damned, but it was gone. She checked herself all over, finding a number of tender spots along the side of her head and backside where she'd careened into the earth, and rolled out her neck and shoulders.

She closed her eyes and took a long, slow breath, tasting the tartness in the air and feeling the cold earth beneath her knees as it seeped in, damping the borrowed pants she had gotten from Ophelia, having rolled them up a number of times at the bottom so they fit. Brigid stood and tottered forward, ignoring how her stomach curled into a knot at what the creature had said before it took off with her.

The fairy queen.

The sun came out and the shadow before her stretched long, and Knightly walked out of it.

"Are you hurt?" he asked, stepping to her, his long legs covering the ground to reach her in seconds.

"Only my pride," she said, pulling twigs and leaves from her hair. "Where are the others?"

"We got separated when the Damned attacked."

"Mine told me it had a message for me," she told Knightly.

"It's a trickster. It would say whatever it needed to keep you from attacking."

"It spoke of the fairy queen."

"There is no queen of the Otherworld. You cannot trust a Damned."

Brigid nodded, but she wasn't so sure. She thought of seeing Dove reflected in its eyes, but was it only an illusion?

She longed for the Goddess and wished to remember all that she could not. To see how to fix it all. The air around her thickened. A tingle, cool and soothing, started at the base of Brigid's spine and worked its way up along her vertebrae, a shiver growing in its urgency to clamor to the top of her head—and settled down into the dark matter of her mind.

A *memory*. A true, thriving memory. Waking up cranky as any toddler arising mid-nap. This memory zapped her skull with a pain that had her doubling over before it jerked her up and resewed into her mind.

Brigid saw herself training with the Goddess. Bent over a notebook, making notes by a low-burning fire. Working tirelessly to memorize incantations from the *Book of the Goddess*, saying them until her words ran together and her eyelids grew too heavy to see. Sitting alone by the fire, a plate of barely touched food, a cup of tea grown cold. Then her hand in Knightly's and an unfailing sense of purpose, of destiny.

"Brigid?"

"I remember," she said, holding out her hand to him as though to make another deal. "We made a deal."

"Yes." He reached out and took her hand. Then dipped his chin, took a deep breath. "We did—"

The ground beneath them rumbled, dozens of sloes and hazelnuts fell from the trees, and a terrifying roar filled the air, then another, then what sounded like ten more.

"What is that?" Brigid asked.

"The Damned," Knightly said. "More have broken through or are being released from where the witches keep them."

"Keep them? In the caves?"

"Aye, it would seem so."

"You *let* them harbor those creatures?"

He lifted his brows. "No one and nothing can leave the island, Brigid. Not even the Damned. They're safely away from the townspeople."

"At times I forget what you are," she said, her lip curling. "Then you say things like that."

"A god?"

"A villain."

"I wouldn't go casting stones just yet."

"The Damned wouldn't be here if you hadn't stopped and let them through."

"*I* didn't pull them through or teach them how to do it. They did it when . . ."

"When what?"

Another roar cut through the trees; this time drawing closer.

"We need to find the others," he said, looking off into the distance.

Brigid glared at him. "This conversation isn't over."

"I'm sure it isn't."

"What does that mean?"

"You like to argue." He gave a slow smile. "I like to listen."

She gaped at him and let out an aggravated cry. "You are insufferable."

"I've been called worse."

She counted down from five. "Give me your hand."

He held it out.

"You aren't going to ask why I need it?"

"No."

She took his hand and examined it. The long fingers were

distracting, his palm calloused but firm, like he could crush bones in it, and yet when he touched her it was as though he were cradling glass.

She shook the thought away and looked at his open hand. "I don't have my bag. Do you have anything sharp?"

He pulled a sliver of a mirror from his pocket and handed it over.

"You carry bits of looking glass?"

"Mirror magic is potent magic, but when it's splintered it's less troublesome."

She raised the sliver, and before Knightly could so much as flinch, she jabbed his palm.

"*Hey,*" he bellowed as blood pooled in his palm.

"It was a tiny jab," Brigid said, rolling her eyes. "You claimed this land as your own, yes? Sovereign over the lough and Evermore. Which means your blood knows it and can map it."

She raised her hands over his, hovering them in the air.

"What are you doing?"

"Shh, no talking."

He growled and she shot him a look that silenced him.

She cleared her throat and held his hand up.

"I ask the blood
to hear my spell
and help me where it may.
Present to me a path
to the lost witches.
Please do not delay."

She lowered his hand, his wrist warm and lax with her fingers clasped around it. Together they watched the blood splinter from where it was gathered, spreading out into lines across Knightly's palm. A small circle beneath his thumb showed the lough, the longer lines drew the paths back to Brigid's, to the pasture where they stood, and beyond Brigid's house, to the cliffs.

"This is no simple spell," he said, watching the way she bit back a grimace.

"It's one the Goddess taught," Brigid said. "The cost for blood spells is always unruly."

Brigid lifted the shard and flipped it, and using the opposite end from what she had used to prick Knightly's palm, she cut her own thumb.

She let two tiny droplets fall onto his palm where no blood had pooled.

"They are mine, claimed by me, one by blood and one by love. This should show us the way to them."

The two droplets slid together, forming one larger drop, before it split apart. This time into three droplets. One rolled to where the fairy ring was marked, the other to the land in front of Brigid's home, and a third to the lough.

Brigid stared at his palm.

"Why are there three?" Knightly asked.

"I don't know," she said.

The ground rumbled beneath them again and Knightly studied his hand. "Well then, let's go find out before whatever that is charges in, and you have to save me from it."

"Again," Brigid added.

"Yes," he said, his dimple flashing. "Again."

⚬—O

Following the map on Knightly's hand, Brigid and Knightly walked up the dusty trail that ran alongside the hazelnuts, and then down to where there was a fork in the path splintering three ways. Overhead the sky shifted from gray to blue and the air was as crisp as newly printed paper. One way led back to Brigid's house, the other to the fairy ring at the cliffs, the third to the lough.

"The cauldron," Brigid said as they walked. "It can return that which we most need, can't it?"

"For those worthy of it, I think it might."

Brigid nodded, studying the dark clouds building at the far end of the horizon.

"That circle looks like it's heading up the other side of the hill, and there's still one there," he said, showing her his palm.

"Then up we go."

As they crested the top of the hill, they found Finola walking in a circle, holding something against her chest, muttering to herself, "You only walk north on Wednesdays if the tide is low, and who the bloody hell can tell where the tide is when you're not on the beach?"

"Fin?" Brigid called, rushing forward, placing a hand on her shoulder.

Finola paused. "Brigid?"

Brigid stood in front of her, but Finola blankly stared beyond her. She muttered again to herself about the wind, and holy ghosts, and shook Brigid's hand free before she started to walk down the hill, before circling it up and then doing a smaller circle by the ring. Brigid followed the path with her, while Knightly eyed the fairy ring with a curious purse of his lips.

The mutters, the confusion, the way she strode over the sod back and forth . . . Brigid thought back to waking in the cellar. Wearing the tattered dress, the one she'd worn inside out, and the warning to herself. "Don't forget." She gave her head a shake.

"Stray sod," she whispered. The coven of Knight had told her when they pulled her from her memories that the Goddess had sent her after her daughter. Perhaps they had not been lying. Perhaps Brigid had been in the Otherworld and taken every precaution to make it home. Stray sod is the worst of the fairy traps. You could be walking in a place you'd tread a hundred times before but come upon a patch of stray sod. It was near impossible to know sod had gone astray, the sod having slipped out of fairy and not wearing any signs of being different. It could be a patch of green grass, a rolling slip of a hill, or a gathering of stones. Those who stepped on stray sod would find themselves nowhere . . . and yet somewhere entirely new. Walking down a road they once knew that now led to a village they could never reach or walking across a well-tended field that refused to end.

Brigid whispered Finola's name. Her head shot up, as though she heard her, but she went back to wearing a path in the earth. Brigid stepped closer, and as Finola passed the second time, Brigid whispered loudly in her ear,

"Turn your clothes inside out, Finola McEntire, to right yourself once more."

Fin stopped, looked up. She blinked down at the book she cradled and then turned to face the path that led on up to the fairy ring and the cliffs. She set down the book and Brigid turned to Knightly.

"Give a lady some privacy, please."

He snorted, but walked to the other side of the ring, facing the cliffs.

Finola proceeded to rip off her charcoal shirt, turning it inside out, and plunking it back over her head. Her eyes narrowed, lost focus, and found it again. She blinked and turned.

"Bloody hell!" she yelled seeing Brigid, and threw her arms around her.

Brigid laughed, and once they had broken apart, Finola gave a short rant about "walking in circles and going nowhere for hours, which is pretty fecking traumatic. And who knows where our Phee is, probably stuck on the opposite side of the property, conversing with one of Farmer Joanie's stray sheep, or being intercepted by Father O'Malley as he tries to sneak in Joanie's far window," Finola said, as Ophelia came walking up the path, her clothes already inside out, and a line of irritation between her brows as she spotted them.

"Took you both long enough," Ophelia said when they turned to her, before she burst into tears.

Ophelia wrapped her arms around Brigid and Finola in a hug so tight Brigid lost her breath.

"Of course you figured it out," Finola said, pouting, as Ophelia wiped the tears from her eyes after releasing her friends.

"Can I turn now?" Knightly asked.

"No," Finola called. "You're fine as you are."

"Fin," Brigid said, shaking her head. "We're mostly decent, come back on over."

"What happened with the Damned once we were sodded by the creatures?" Ophelia asked, rubbing her arms with her palms.

"Which, by the by, is also a new thing," Finola said. "I've never heard of them carting stray sod out of the lough."

"They're growing stronger," Knightly said. "Their boundaries are evolving faster than I thought they could."

"We need to seal it," Brigid said, "and fast."

"We have until Samhain," Finola said.

"Unless we don't," Ophelia said. "Agnes wasn't certain of the time. The runes they cast, the dates they scried, all pointed to this year. They thought autumn, so they assumed when the veil was thinnest between worlds, but what if they were off. What if it was when the harvest comes on Lughnasa?"

The three witches turned to look to Knightly, who shrugged. "Don't look at it."

"It's your holiday."

"No more than Imbolc is hers," he said, flashing a grin Brigid's way.

"I'm too tired for his subtext," Finola grumbled.

"I think we assume the date is Lughnasa," Ophelia said.

"Then we hurry," Brigid said. "And we figure out how to close it now."

The earth shook, and the shadows deepened around them. The sound of a drum beating somewhere far off filled the air. Lightning slashed through the sky and thunder bellowed.

Up along the ridge of the cliffs, their cloaks floating back from them, the four witches of Knight appeared.

"We would not do that if we were you," they called, their voice riding the wind, swirling around Brigid, Ophelia, and Finola as they stood with Knightly in front of the fairy ring.

The coven moved like smoke, their shadows shifting from one to the other, interchangeable as though they were not four beings but one split into four quarters. Power crackled off of them, charring the air with the taste of smoke. When they stood before them, Brigid felt the color drain from her face at the flowers they each wore woven atop their hair. Made of fire and flame, their crowns were in the style of the Goddess Brighid.

"You mock my Goddess?" Brigid asked, anger flooding through her. It pooled in her fingertips, sending sparks, traveled up to the tip of her head, filling her whole body with a glow of barely coiled power.

"When you sent us into that well," they said, turning to speak to Knightly. "We thought at first it was a mistake. We realized, once inside it, we could not leave. The well was spelled by the Goddess and could only be opened by one of her own. Then we thought it was not a mistake at all, and we were doomed to rot in the bottom of a well. Until we realized it was filled with lady's mantle. We ingested the herb, which had been blessed by

Brighid, and its healing powers took root. Then we heard it, the whispers of a lost witch in between worlds calling to the magic of the lough. Pulling from it."

They turned to Brigid. "You opened yourself up to your memories, and in the astral plane you opened yourself to us and to the lough. We knew how to get out of the well, then. We told you that you gave us what we needed."

The roar of the Damned echoed over the land, thudding across the cliffs. Drums beating, feet running, snickers and gleeful laughter pilling into the air.

"We called more than we've ever called before," they said. "For we are stronger now than we have ever been."

"You draw power from me," Knightly said, fisting his hands at his sides.

Their shadows bled out from them, circling around and enclosing him in a circle. "You do not serve our cause. You have turned your back on us. We are no longer the witches of Knight. We serve ourselves and we will be queen of the Oherworld and this one. We have no need for you."

"The fairy queen," Brigid whispered softly to Knightly. Then she raised her voice. "We will close the lough and return the Damned. You will not stop us."

"No," they turned as one, in a single, painstakingly slow movement. "You will not interfere."

"Sure, because you asked nicely," Ophelia said, glaring at the witches.

"Huntress," they said, turning to her. "You should not trust Lugh the knight, warrior king of the Otherworld." They looked from her to Finola. "Nor you, seer of truths." They looked back to Brigid.

"*We* do not trust *you*," Brigid said.

"Then trust this," they said, "as your Goddess was clear on what will befall you if you do not listen."

They brought their hands to their faces and, using their fingers, hooked them into the corners of their mouths and manipulated their lips upward into gruesome, decaying smiles. "If you close the lough, you seal your daughter in, and all hope is lost for you and her."

THIRTEEN

BOOK OF THE GODDESS (P. 125):

How to Speak to the Forest of Old

The trees and stones of the forest are the oldest beings remaining. Guard your mind when near to them for both have been known to entrap those creatures they become bewitched by, going so far as to enclose a few lost souls inside their trunks or on the underside of the world.

The only sound Brigid could hear was the laboring of her breath as the words of the witches sank into Brigid like a poisonous snakebite. *"If you close the lough, you seal your daughter in, and all hope is lost for you and her."* A sharp pinch in her heart as their venomous words rushed through her veins. Fear and pain spread across her joints and embedded themselves into her bones.

"What do you mean if she closes the lough her daughter is lost?" Ophelia asked.

"We mean the war between the Goddess and Lugh dammed the lough he so desperately wanted and turned his back on.

The lough is incapable of being anything other than what it was made to be. A portal to chaos, a way to seal the Otherworld from this one and keep the evolving power there out of here. Your Goddess is shortsighted, and now you see the truth. You need it open as much as we do."

"Only until I get her out," Brigid said, barely able to hear her own words against the echoing beat of her racing heart.

"You think you can?" One of the two witches in the middle stepped forward. She pulled the cloak of shadows from her face like a child removes their hoodie after the rain. East Knight looked Brigid in the eyes.

She slipped one hand into her cloak made of shadows and pulled an hourglass the size of her fist from her robe. It was filled with water the color of the night sky, tiny flickering lights inside it like stars.

"You have until the hourglass runs out. Then all the magic of the lough will be free and none of this will matter because all power of the Otherworld and those trapped in it will be ours."

"If you can pull monsters from the lough," Finola said, looking from the witches to Knightly, "why not pull Dove from it?"

"I don't have that ability," Knightly said.

"Why not?" Brigid asked, turning to him. "You helped send the Damned back through it. You are the powerful king of the Otherworld, are you not?"

"He cannot take from the Otherworld because the Goddess spelled it to protect you," the witches said.

"What?" Brigid looked at Knightly. "Is that true?"

He did not respond.

"Knightly."

He lifted a hand, dropped it. "It is true, everything your Goddess has done is to protect you."

"You can pull monsters, why not pull a non-Damned and get Dove out?" Finola asked the coven.

"Then you would stop interfering?"

"No," Ophelia said, stepping closer. "We won't stop until you are gone, and the lough is sealed. Until our town is safe."

"You don't want to free Dove," Brigid said. "You would have done so in the first place if you thought I would leave you alone. If you had any power to gain me to your side, you would have made a move from the beginning."

"We did make a move," they said. "You simply don't remember."

The witches locked hands and began to chant, their words flowing together, one after another as the ground shook and the rocks in the fairy ring vibrated. The air snapped with electricity. A circling mist, then a fog of smoke and lightning pressed in, circling the hill.

"Into the fairy ring," Knightly said to Brigid. "This fight is mine."

"I don't think so, big boy," Finola said, moving up to stand beside Brigid. "Evermore is our home."

Knightly clapped his hands together and a loud boom sounded off into the cliffs. Thunder shook the ground and lightning splintered from the sky. Frigid rain came pouring down in sheets, dissolving the mist and pushing the fog clear of the hill. When the last of the fog rolled free, the witches were gone.

"I guess it's true, evil witches really do melt in the rain," Finola said, soaking wet and tucking her hands under her arms, her teeth chattering.

"What?" Brigid asked, wringing her hair out, barely able to feel the cold with how angry she was.

"Pop culture reference," Ophelia said. "We better get home and dry off before we catch pneumonia."

"Can you even catch pneumonia?" Finola asked Brigid.

"I'm not supernatural," Brigid said. She turned to Knightly. "Did you know what would happen if we sealed the lough?"

"No." He shot her an incredulous look. "I didn't speak to the Goddess. You think I would let our—"

Brigid's eyes narrowed. "*Our*? Our what?"

Finola and Ophelia exchanged a look. "We'll see you at home."

"You aren't going anywhere either," she snapped out, not taking her eyes off Knightly. "Use the flame dry spell in the *Book of the Goddess* and dry yourselves."

"*Brigid*," Knightly said, his voice insistent, his eyes pleading.

She was suddenly panicked at what he was about to say and didn't want to be alone.

But Brigid Heron was not a coward.

"Sorry," she said to Finola and Ophelia. "Go on. I'll be right there."

"If you kill him," Finola shouted over her shoulder as they walked down the hill, "we'll help you bury the body."

"If you get lost in stray sod again, I'll help you remember yours," Brigid called back.

"Fair enough," she heard Ophelia say as the two witches disappeared from sight.

She turned back to Knightly and took a deep breath. "Tell me quick before I blast you into the sea."

"I think it's better if you remember it yourself."

"I only have some of my memories back."

He squatted down and picked up the book that Finola had dropped after Brigid and Knightly first found her by the fairy ring.

He held it up to Brigid.

"What is that?"

He tried to open it, but it wouldn't budge. He turned it over and held the inscription up for her to read.

This book belongs to Dove Heron

The words were scrawled in looping handwriting, a bit

wobbly on the *g*'s and *n*'s. As she stared at it, a cold flush washed up her spine and neck and spread across the crown of her head. The memory settled in slowly. The hint of a laugh and then a groan, and then Brigid was sitting in front of the fire as her eight-year-old daughter held a pencil between her teeth instead of practicing her handwriting. Giggling at the sentence Brigid suggested (stinky Peter the pup likes to roll in poo) and groaning when she failed to get specific letters right.

"She loves to laugh," Brigid said on a teary breath, the memory returning to where it belonged, settling between her mind and heart. "Dove does. She's a juvenile sense of humor, but that's okay, because *I love* making her laugh."

She took the book in her hands, and a shimmer of heat rolled over her fingers, singeing the tips. The cover fell open, and the pages turned.

Brigid sat, drawing her knees to her chest. Knightly wove the clouds back from the setting sun, and shifted a drying spell around them both. As the wet pooled from her, Brigid was reminded of another memory. Of the first time she had stirred the air, and her days learning magic when she was Dove's age.

Brigid had hidden her magic from her mother. She'd been content to work secreted in the woods beyond her home. It was easy enough to store her items in her sack and hide them inside the hawthorn tree with the hole at its base. Her mother, as far as she knew, was no believer in magic any more than she believed the stories she told Brigid. When she thought of her mother now, she thought mostly of her laughter; her feet splashing as they danced bare in the rain; and her tears, followed by unforgiving silence, when she spent weeks in bed turning Brigid and the world away.

Brigid had tried every tonic, spell, and tincture she could to save her. Nothing was ever enough. Brigid was never enough.

Not until she'd had Dove.

Brigid flipped through the book, and as she did the air grew warm, the wind gentled, and the earth between her feet softened. Evermore was opening to Brigid as her memories opened back up to her.

"Do you hear that?" she asked Knightly.

She stood and followed the sound of a flute playing. She walked around the center of the fairy ring and squatted beside it. She peered closer into it and watched as in the span of two breaths, up from the center grew two fully mature hawthorn trees. They were bent toward each other, as though mid-conversation. Brigid stepped into the circle and walked beneath the trees.

"What a curiosity," Brigid said and pressed her palm to the nearest branch. She bowed her head, listening, Knightly and the outside world forgotten.

The trees trembled and shook, the wind pushing through them and over the grass at their base. She dug her fingers into the ancient bark, finding it surprisingly soft. She gave it a light pat and took a single step forward.

As she moved, the light flickered. Gold and green and red.

After five long, slow steps, her foot brushed against something soft instead of the fairy ring she'd expected to find. Brigid took one more step and light cut between the trees, illuminating the area. Before her stood a solitary ash tree, three feet wide and as squat as a cumbersome toad. Its limbs were thick and spread like fingers on an outstretched hand. Brigid looked up. Overhead the sky was a rich violet, the ground beneath her the texture of crushed velvet. A glow of light illuminated the world around her.

She slowly made her way to standing and turned in a circle. She was no longer in the safety of the fairy ring, but in a darkened forest with trees so wide it would require the span of at least five humans to wrap their arms around one of its bases. She looked up and blinked. The large tree's limbs were extended down, like wings folding inward. She huffed, and the branches rose, up and out, dropping tiny balls of phosphorescent light onto her. They burned as they fell, and Brigid jumped out of the way.

"That one doesn't like to be bothered."

Brigid turned. "Knightly?"

He stepped out of the shadows. "Thought to travel without me, did you?"

"Where are we?"

"Interesting story. You went inside a memory, and I followed you. Side note, please don't walk into a fairy ring emitting the kind of magic that would bewitch a half dozen men if you aren't wanting the unexpected to happen."

"We're in a memory? My own?"

"Apparently."

Brigid looked up to the sky and the stars that were sinking closer and closer to them. She bit her bottom lip. Stars should not be in reaching distance. Trees should not glow. Time should not sputter. They, neither of them, should be, well, wherever it is they were.

"What is this place?"

He surveyed the forest around them. "There's a bush over beyond that tree that grows water droplets the size of my head for flowers. Once I stepped into a small creek after I fell and for about fifteen minutes, I talked in sonnets that would make most poets weep."

"The Grove of Mischief," Brigid whispered. A story of her youth waking up at the back of her mind. She looked at the roots along the ground, how thick and wild they were. "This is the Otherworld. *Your* world."

"Yes."

"Where the fairy king waits and bars the gate."

"I haven't been barring any gates for a long time."

She took a step toward the tree behind her; this one was slender and curved. She looked at the roots and followed them forward. The little tree swayed as though beneath a strong breeze, though the air was calm and still, as though it could hear a song only sung for its leaves.

"My mother told me tales of the Otherworld as a child." She rubbed her cheek, as though she could find a trace of her mother's fingertips there. "I told them to Dove."

"Why was it important for her to know?" he asked, his voice tempered, as though he was holding emotion back.

He scrubbed the stubble on his face with the back of his knuckles, and Brigid told herself she was seeing things. Surely he could not make such a simple act look as erotic as his removing her garter belt with his teeth would.

Brigid's heart gave a thump inside her chest. She turned a slow circle, thinking of the folklore of the sidhe and the stories of old.

"I don't know . . . yet."

"Don't know or don't want to admit the truth?"

She held his gaze. "Maybe both."

The edge of his mouth curled down like the tip of an apostrophe. "Then let's walk a little deeper." He looked up at the hanging stars. "It's a beautiful trap, this world."

"You really think that?" She looked up and reached out a hand, tracing a rune for protection in the sky, watching as it fizzled, lighting for one brief moment. "It seems so real, it's hard to believe this is a memory." She glanced down at her feet. "Look at the size of that candied flower. We could eat of it for days."

"And fall dead laughing."

Brigid squinted at the flower. "Quite the price to pay."

"There always is."

"Of all the people to be stuck in the Otherworld with," Brigid joked.

He stepped over a small stream that had sprung up out of nowhere. He skirted a blooming bush of strange, bright fuchsia fruit that smelled of a rainstorm. Brigid hopped over a rock and stopped. The rock below her was in a familiar shape. Almost like . . . a four-leaf clover. Heat rushed over her. She crouched down.

"What are you doing?"

She didn't speak, barely heard him. Brigid lifted the rock, finding it fuzzy like moss, softer than a baby's blanket.

A photograph rested beneath it. Of a smiling, mischievous young woman. A blast of heat rocked through Brigid, followed by a wash of cold.

The sound of vibrant and brilliant laughter floated through her. She clutched the photo and stood up. The air around her thickened and sweetened. Her toes tingled. A vibration worked its way up her spine. A new memory coming in, one that wanted to pull her whole body under with it.

She looked around the garden they stood in, and it warbled, the air heavy with mist and rain. Suddenly Brigid was looking at twenty different versions of the man who stood to her side.

Knightly held out a peony to Brigid. He offered a hand to her and helped her over a rock bed. He lounged in the creek, floating on his back, his hair slicked away from his face. Brigid stood on the bank, reading to him from a book, her belly growing with her child. A spring storm coming after the baby was born and they sat on a blanket in front of her house. He pulled a cloud down into the garden and held it over them, keeping both the baby and Brigid dry, uncaring if he got wet.

"You'll not track that in the house," Brigid said to him, rocking Dove in her arms and laughing.

"It's just a little water," he said, leaning over to place a kiss first on Brigid's lips, then the sleeping baby's forehead, lingering for a long moment. "I could suffer far worse for my girls."

Brigid took a deep breath, found herself dizzy and nauseated, and someone pressed her forward, her head dipping between her knees.

"You really do like to do things the hard way." Knightly. There at her side, a hand softly pressing against her back. Brigid tried to respond, but another memory pushed in, blanketing her consciousness.

Brigid stood in the center of the grove, her hand clasped in Dove's.

"I'm not so sure this is a good idea," she said, squeezing her hand.

"You're not sure of a lot of things, Mom, but thankfully I'm here."

"This has been the longest day ever." She blew out a breath. "We've tried every spell from the *Book of the Goddess* and a variety of variations on those I knew."

"I still don't think you should jump into that river. Every monster that has charged into that river has disappeared."

"I've told you, there is a lough on the other side of all of this. It's been guarded for centuries by a faction of witches who have been trying to unlock it. What if they are trying to unlock a portal here? What if the river leads me there?"

"Then you can get me out once your Goddess is with you."

"Exactly."

"And my father?"

Brigid smiled and ran a hand over Dove's head. "Saved you. He may have also tried to claim you for this world, but you are not only a child of Lugh, you are also a daughter of Brigid."

She squeezed her hands and they stepped forward toward the river that ran through this section of the Otherworld. It was white and misty, impossible to see beneath, and smelled of cherries.

"On the count of three then?" Dove asked.

"On three," Brigid said.

"Mom?"

"Yes?"

"Don't forget. Whatever you do, don't fall in love with a god again. They appear to make horrible boyfriends."

"I love you, Dove Heron."

"I love you, Mom."

Brigid brushed the tears from her eyes before her daughter could see them fall, and squared her shoulders. "I'll see you soon, baby girl."

Dove nodded, her cheeks pink, her bow and arrow slung across her shoulder and her crown of flowers perched in her hair.

"One."

"Two."

"Three," Brigid said, and dove into the river.

—0

Brigid's vision was slow to clear. The taste of salt water coating her tongue, the burning of her eyes, and the determination to get home, get to the Goddess, and get Dove back lit like a flame inside her.

"There you are," Knightly said, crouching down so they were eye to eye. "I was worried when I couldn't follow you into the next memory."

Behind him were the stones that bordered the fairy ring, and beyond that the cliffs. Brigid turned on her heel, the past and present colliding as she faced the being who was the reason her daughter was gone.

She looked into his dark, concerned eyes, lifted her hand, and slapped him. *Hard.* Then again. He reached up and caught her wrist, and she yanked it free.

She curled her fingers into a fist and reared back, and he waved his hand. She let the punch fly and it bounced off the air, spinning her around. She stumbled and righted herself, turning back to face him.

"You *coward*, you erected a barrier? You can't even take what you deserve?"

"What have you remembered?" he asked, as dark storm clouds shifted overhead.

She looked up at them and back to him. "You're angry, are you? Think I'm afraid of a little weather?" Brigid reached down into the earth, calling for the roots of the land, and gave a sharp yank with both hands. The roots broke free, upending dirt and sediment, raining it down on Knightly as he nearly missed being pummeled by a tree.

"I can encase you in its trunk," she said, her tone shifting into something dark and seductive. "Leave you locked away for one hundred years to watch the world go by. That's how long I was there. That's the cost, isn't it? A single day in the Otherworld is equal to one hundred years in the mortal world. But I didn't ask for this. I didn't ask you . . ."

She stopped speaking as a new memory nudged free from the locked box where it had been stored in her mind. Of the relief when Knightly made the deal with her. Of how badly she wanted a child. Of how much she had wanted him the moment she laid eyes on him, before she knew she would have not only his body, but his line.

There was always a hidden cost to magic, especially the magic of a god.

"You did though," he said, the disinterested stare he'd affected falling from his face. The furrow of his brow, the pinch of his lips. "You asked me for that which the Goddess refused, and I agreed. I didn't know, Brigid." He closed his eyes, pain wracking across his face as he brought a fist to his chest. "I didn't know what it would cost me. That I would fall in love with you, that I would have to give you up to keep you safe from the coven so they would never suspect Dove for what she is, that I would lose her and you again for *one hundred years.* That I would be unable to get to you in the Otherworld and have to remain here waiting all this time for you to come home."

His voice cracked on the last word. *Home.* This wasn't home. Nowhere could be home without Dove.

"What is she?"

Bits and pieces of the past were clicking together like a jigsaw puzzle. Brigid and Dove fighting the Damned inside the Otherworld as they were called from the safety of the forest. How they went insane, their eyes turning white, their hands curling into claws, before they dove into the river and disappeared. Brigid and Dove using the herbs and stones of the Otherworld, helping those who were affected but not lost to the call of the coven to refuse it. Dove hugging those who cried and were terrified, Brigid healing those who harmed themselves in attempts to get free of the curse. Dove's power growing, the land responding to her every thought and request. Trees growing books born from her mind, creating stories just for her. The creatures of the Otherworld seeking them both out for help the way those in Evermore sought Brigid for healing or the Goddess for miracles.

Dove knowing what they needed instinctually, in a way Brigid never could.

"You already know."

"She's like you," Brigid said, as Knightly's tears began to fall. "She's a goddess stuck in a godless world."

She bit back a sob, marched away from him, stopped, turned, and walked back.

"Does the coven know?"

He drew in a breath. "Before today I would say no, but now? I think they have figured it out and they can't decide if they should be terrified of her or find a way to make her theirs."

"If I seal the lough, they won't be able to use her."

"If you don't and they pull her through . . ." He swallowed. "She might not be affected like the others."

"Or she could be worse than lost."

Brigid took in a shuttering breath. She could still feel the echo of Dove's hand in hers, smell the sweetness of her skin.

"I'm going to stop them and get my daughter back. I *will* find a way." In the distance a chorus of screeches sounded, and Brigid looked beyond the horizon toward it. "And I'm going to help Ophelia and Finola save this town." She looked at him. "Maybe then, when I've done all that, I'll feel a little less like killing you."

Brigid turned on her heel and walked away from Knightly and the fairy ring, with her memories and the break in her heart following her home.

FOURTEEN

The following morning, Brigid awoke after a restless night of sleep. She had dreamed of being trapped in between two worlds: one made of stone and rules and witches trying to overrun it, the other bending to the will of a diminutive sprite who had more grace than gods deserved. In the dream, whether in the first world or the second, Brigid was slowly turning into one of the Damned.

She couldn't shake the dredges of either image, and got out of bed, dressed quickly, pausing to peek at herself in the mirror and wincing at the wild tangles in her hair and puffiness to her eyes, and walked out the front door, down the steps, and into the front yard. She thought she might meditate in the garden, see if she could find her center before Ophelia and Finola woke.

Instead, Knightly stepped out of his shadow, emerging from beside the hawthorn tree, his face as stormy as any thundercloud, and everything tilted farther off its axis.

"You do not get to kick my ass and then leave," he said, stomping toward her. "I've been waiting for you for *one hundred years.*"

Brigid's eyes narrowed. She was tired, unkempt, and raw. If he was looking for a fight, she had no problem delivering. "And I spent a hundred years in your prison of a palace trying to escape."

He shook his head. "You still don't understand. You're the lock and I'm the key, but nothing fits, because it's all broken."

"Broken? You want to see *broken*?" Brigid's eyes flashed, her hands curled, and she reached out to pull pain from the air and throw it at him, and light burst from her. It poured from within, filling her up, glowing across her skin. Knightly's hand came over hers. "That's grove Otherworld magic you're playing with, Brigid. Have a care."

She looked down at her hands, flexing her fingers.

"Fae magic in an Evermore witch." He dropped his hand, then ran his fingers through his hair, pain rippling across his features. "Dove was sick because of it. Because of the blend of magic. That's what did it to her, Brigid. She needed a power more ancient than mine."

Brigid looked up at him. "The cauldron?"

"It can only be used by those who have noble intentions, who have the blood of a god."

"But I picked it up, not Dove."

"You carry the magic of a goddess. You are worthy. It's why you're also able to hold the magic of the Otherworld now."

"Then why did she get sucked into the lough, was that your plan all along?"

"No. I only planned for it to heal her." He shook his head. "I've spent the past one hundred years trying to understand it. I tried to break the spell on the lough for centuries. When you let me look in your mind, I tried to glean how the Goddess's magic worked, how I could manipulate it. I didn't understand then and I don't know now, but I never meant for anything to happen to Dove."

"You're Lugh the demigod. Ruler of the Otherworld. How do you not know?"

"I am not all-knowing. I am a ruler of a forgotten world, who was banished from a kingdom that I thought had forgotten me."

"Your shadow is unruly," Brigid said. "Your magic is unruly. You bring chaos with you whether you want to or not."

"And?"

"And you're my daughter's father."

"I am."

"I don't remember time with you, with us, beyond a few flashes."

He winced but forced a smile. "Perhaps it wasn't worth remembering. Here." He held out the book of Dove's that Brigid left in her haste to get as far from him as quickly as possible.

"Open it."

Brigid turned the pages and found drawings—endless sketches of herself, Dove, the Otherworld . . . and Knightly. Interspersed with poems and stories, tales that Brigid had told Dove of her father.

Brigid let out a watery laugh at the lines and lines of handwriting so familiar and yet so distant. There, staring up at her on the page, was a drawing of the Sluagh. A page of the Pooka, one of the *far darrig*, merrows, banshee, and everything in between.

"She's keeping a log," Brigid said. On the opposite pages were facts and tips for dealing with the monsters, and below that, notes of herbs and potion recipes Dove had tried or was planning to try.

"What?" He leaned over her shoulder. Flipped the book ahead a few pages. "She really is a talent, isn't she?"

Brigid looked up at the angles of his face and got caught in the dark stubble and the curve of his lips. Forced herself to focus. "She's trying to help them."

He nodded. "Like her mother."

"I have not been helping monsters."

"You helped me."

Brigid closed the book, looked down at it.

"Until I showed up again, you'd been working with your witches. Trying to get ahead of the game."

He paused, sighed, and rubbed his shoulder. "You still don't get it."

"Get what?"

"Those creatures?"

Brigid lifted her head.

"I've been battling them for a century."

"What?"

Knightly brought his hand to his chest and pressed it to his heart. "I have been waiting for you, and I have been fighting for you, for Evermore. For one hundred years, Brigid." He waited for his words to sink in. "Nothing will ever change that."

Then he turned, and left, not by way of his shadow, but by walking slowly up the path and down the lane, giving her ample time to watch him go.

—O

Over the next week, Ophelia, Finola, and Brigid recovered from their battles with the creatures, as more and more of Brigid's memories returned. She told the others each and every detail of her fight with Knightly and the truths she had uncovered. About him, about her, about Dove. When she was done, they cried together, Brigid tried to answer what she could, and even thought long and hard about letting Finola put the curse on Knightly she said she was so keen to try.

"Just a wee one, have him lose the function of his left hand, cause his balls to droop so far he has to move them out of the way to sit. Wait, you can answer this. Do gods have balls? Nope, I don't want to know."

But in the end, Brigid found as hard as the truth was to process, she could not stay angry with Knightly. She was drawn to him, and in her dreams she reached out for him. Far too many nights that week were spent with her waking with his name on her lips, or tears in her eyes when she'd dream of dancing in the groves of the Otherworld with Dove.

Once the week was done, and most of their strength had returned, the three witches shifted into making tonics for those in town and packing new parcels of salt. Ophelia and Finola recorded a podcast warning of the increase in the Damned, and the unruly weather of late. Brigid read and reread the family archives and journals trying to find a clue for how to both seal the lough and save her daughter, and she learned more than she felt necessary when it comes to Finola's favorite topic: pop culture.

Though she loved observing the ease of Finola—how her friend could read a magazine and paint her toenails while curled up in kitchen chair and still talk five hundred miles a minute. Or the quiet soothing ways of Ophelia, and all her many talents. How she could measure flour and bake a loaf of fresh bread, before moving on to sorting herbs for a new tonic, and then running out to salt somewhere new or check on someone feeling poorly without losing an ounce of her boundless, quiet energy. Her house felt more like a home, which brought an unsettling comfort. Because until Dove was returned, nothing should feel right.

Only the witches were able to touch the Damned, but the tonics seemed to help the few villagers who were faring poorly after run-ins, and that was a small comfort. Brigid and Ophelia worked together trying different variations, consulting together and making notes, using Dove's book as inspiration from her liner notes for new herbs to mix in.

Under the full moon precisely one week after they had faced the coven and Brigid learned the truth of Dove and Knightly and the sacrifices they had all made, Brigid sat reading the *Book of the Goddess*. As she flipped through it, she came to a page tucked in the back, one she had not seen before.

"What is this?" she asked Ophelia.

"Another treasure from the house," Ophelia said, peeking over at it. "Maybe a pep talk for a lowly witch? Half of what came from that coven is New Age self-help, and I'm here for it."

At Brigid's raised brows, Ophelia explained. "It's a kind of spiritual belief of the modern world combined with self-improvement."

"Oh."

She looked down at the entry and began to read.

Every witch is as strong as the power she claims. These spells serve as guides. They enable the caster a ritual to call forward what they need. The deepest magics are inside you. When you claim your power, you may find you are limitless. When facing any problem that feels insurmountable, remind yourself of who you are. Know you are as powerful as you believe, and when you believe you are worthy, you can turn the tides, conquer the kingdom, and change the world.

"Ophelia?" Brigid called. "You said that the house delivered you this?"

"Yes, amid all manner of other things. The recipes for removing wrinkles so far are my favorite find."

Brigid stared at the page with the words which were not silent in her mind when she read them. They were alive, with a specific cadence and voice. Of the Goddess.

Brigid stared at the letter and stood. She read the page one more time, and the idea and certainty of what she needed to do rooted.

She had been going about this all wrong. She had been focused on getting back her memories to find the way to seal the lough. When the answer was here. Subtle but clear and well-timed.

Brigid didn't need to figure out how to seal the lough. She needed to channel its power. If she could gain control of it, then she could get Dove out and seal it herself. She walked into the kitchen where the others sat at the table covered in the family archives, Finola drinking an espresso and Ophelia starting a new loaf of sourdough.

"I know what we have to do," Brigid said. "The letter from the *Book of the Goddess* talks about how we are infinite in power if we claim it."

"The pep talk entry the house gave us?" Fin asked.

"Does this mean you want to do a power summoning spell?" Ophelia said.

"It's not an encouraging missive. It's instruction. I think the Goddess knew we'd need help and entrusted the house to get it to us. I'm going to do more than perform a call to power, I plan to take the power of the lough, open the portal, get Dove out, and return the Damned."

Finola sat her black-and-white-speckled mug that read *Witches' Brew* on the hard wooden table with a thwack. "Sounds like some pep talk."

"Isn't the power in there Knightly's father's, so if we find a way to get it, we're stealing from a pretty powerful god?" Ophelia asked.

"It was gifted to the Goddess by his foster father, and she is the one who gave the portal to Knightly. It's none of theirs and all of theirs, and since the Goddess sealed it, the lough must still answer to her call. I have the magic of my Goddess in me. This feels right."

Finola picked her mug back up, toasting the air. "How do we call it?"

"There wasn't instruction, so we create our own ritual."

"Isn't this a little like what the freaky witches have been doing this whole time?" Finola asked, tugging her bottom lip. "Trying to take power that isn't theirs for their own reasons."

"We don't want to claim the ancient power and use it to take over Evermore, we want to channel it and guide it to restore the balance and then release it back. Once the lough is sealed that power is safely in the Otherworld where it belongs."

"Creating chaos," Ophelia said. "I've done a lot of reading on this and thinking about it, and what if the reason the lough was so unruly is because there's no king to the kingdom there? The Otherworld in all the stories we've ever been told needs a ruler. A king or the fairy queen."

"The Goddess sealed it for a reason," Brigid said, a little shiver running through her at the Pooka's warning of the fairy queen and the idea of the witches of Knight taking the place of one. What horrors could they unleash if they made it to the other side?

"But we don't know your goddess," Ophelia said.

"Yes, you do," Brigid said, holding up the *Book of the Goddess*. "You've been learning from her all along. She's a part of me and you. She is all that is fair and good."

Finola and Ophelia exchanged a look.

"You absolutely think this is the way?" Ophelia asked Brigid. She gave a single, firm nod.

"How do we create this ritual then?"

Brigid sighed in relief to have their support. "The Goddess taught me three is the number of harmony, wisdom, and understanding. We use that as the basis for our ritual."

She turned and looked out the window leading to the garden, and beyond that to a path that would take her to the cliffs.

"Can you gather bark from any birch, oak, or rowan trees, as well as dandelions, flax seeds, cedarwood, heather, lemon verbena, rosemary, and shamrock? Oils will do if we don't have any of the fresh herbs. Add in amber, citrine, fire agate, garnet, ruby, and sunstone crystals, as well as any gold."

"Is this for a spell or . . . ?" Ophelia asked, getting a basket out from a kitchen cabinet, and beginning to gather supplies.

"An altar," Brigid said. "We'll set them up in town as well as by the lough and even if she isn't physically here, we call our Goddess home."

—0

Once the witches collected the supplies and loaded them in the car, they headed into town. The sun was out, the skies were clear, and the ride went much quicker this time to Brigid's thinking. There were Damned out in the fields, hardly any sheep grazing, and with Ophelia's foot leaded with intent they reached the edge of Evermore in record time. It only took a few minutes for Brigid's knees to stop shaking so hard that her whole body rattled after climbing out of the vehicle.

They walked over to Orchard Street, the side thoroughfare in town beside the large rocks that bordered the sea. They passed two fisherwomen, who bid good day to the group and paused to ask Ophelia for an assortment of healing balms and salves, tinctures, and potions. They accepted their salt and tried to press the fresh catches on Finola and Ophelia, who waved them off.

"You always give us more than enough," Ophelia said.

"You two lasses have been looking out for us and for a long time, it's never enough," the first fisherwoman said, but Fin gave her a quick hug and shooed her on her way.

Once they continued on their way, Finola turned to Ophelia and Brigid.

"When this is over," she said, "and we close the lough, I'm going to dive off that dock and swim my way to the mainland. Just because I can."

Ophelia smiled. "I'm going to travel everywhere. Break as many hearts as I can and have mine broken a hundred times. Then I'm going to fall in love."

"Without Thorpe?" Fin asked.

Ophelia shot her a look that made even Brigid wince.

"Well, I've been in a dry spell, that's for sure." Finola said, with a wistful sigh. "It's not easy dating while constantly having to fight monsters."

"Has there been no one special?" Brigid asked.

"Once or twice, but the connection wasn't there. Not beyond the lust." Finola shrugged. "I enjoy the lust, thank the gods of naked time for the lust, but shouldn't there be more?"

"There can be," Ophelia said, with a wistful smile. "But that doesn't always last either. Sometimes obstacles can be too big for love."

Brigid reached out and squeezed her hand.

"I think when it matters, there's a bit of both, and maybe when the timing is right the obstacles sort themselves out of the way," Brigid said, and as soon as the words left her lips, a memory worked its way free.

Knightly with his hands in her hair, dragging her down into the grass and taking his time to worship every ounce of skin on her body. Then carrying her home, singing a song about open fields and undying love, washing her hair in the kitchen sink when she complained it was filled with knots and weeds after their tumble. His touch a light caress, his dimple dug deep into his cheek, his heart in his eyes, and her happiness in the palms of his hands.

She took a shuddering breath in and looked down to where her hand still held Ophelia's. She met her friend's eyes. "But what do I know of true love?"

FIFTEEN

BOOK OF THE GODDESS (P. 221):

Spell for Energy Work (Shadow Pinning)

A vengeance spell, shadow magic, can draw the attention of unwanted witches. It's a potent spell and should be used only if you find yourself in need of providing ruination or showing a powerful witch you are not to be crossed.

The center of town was as charming and inviting as ever with its sweet, pebbled roads, row houses in lively colors, and the scents of the sea drifting in. There weren't any Damned on the loose that they could see, but there was another matter that made itself known to Brigid once they took off down Orchard Street.

It took Brigid two minutes to realize Knightly's shadow was following her. It took her four to convince the others to let her meet them at the occult shop up the road, thirty seconds to lure him into a side alley, then under a single millisecond to pin his shadow to the wall.

She stared at it, tapping her foot, as it wiggled from where she'd stuck it. She held her hands up like a seamstress preparing to thread a needle.

"Why are you following me, god?"

There was a long grunt, and Knightly slipped out of the shadow, finding himself trapped to it and the wall.

"I can't believe you have frozen me like an ice pop. You are a vile woman, terrible creature. I like today's dress color, it's rather fetching against the shade of your eyes."

Brigid's lips twitched against her will, but she refused to smile. She looked up at the sky and counted clouds for the sake of gaining patience.

"How did you know," he asked, "that I was following you?"

"I am finding I know you well after all."

She looped the thread through the needle, gave a tug, and he let out a grunt. "Energy work is a marvel, isn't it?" Brigid asked and pursed her lips, studying the droplets of sweat dotting his brow. "You just focus on the area and pull . . . or pinch."

He gave a grunt, then blew out a long, slow breath. With every hiss of his inhale, Brigid found her spell coming undone. Knightly slipped his hand around the invisible thread she'd used to bind him, gave it a tug, pulled it to him, and wrapped it around his arm. Over and over, until the needle was yanked from her hand and flew into his.

Brigid's hands shifted to her hips.

He flashed his teeth in what a scorpion would call a smile.

"I could bind you again," Brigid said.

"And I could do this all day," he said, his face red from the effort of unbinding the spell.

She closed her eyes for a moment to gather patience and resistance. "Why are you following me?"

He groaned. "I was keeping an eye on you, you infernal woman. To guarantee you stay safe."

She gave as unladylike a snort as she could muster. "I do not need you to keep me safe."

Knightly took two steps to her, the heat of him invading her senses. "I have only ever tried to keep you safe."

Brigid let out a low laugh. "You could have gotten us out."

"I got you out."

"No—"

"I had one hundred years here, lost and alone. The very things I needed most in this world were trapped in the one world I created." He stared down at her, the pain on his face honest and startling. "I have hated the very depths of my being for losing you both. I did not teach or aid the witches in how to call the Damned. But I used their power to call you. I do not know what you experienced on your side of things with Dove. But here, I splintered magic to pull you out, giving you my power. I did not know the lough would claim your memories, that there would be a price for what I had done."

"I went into the river," Brigid said, shaking her head. "Dove figured it out."

"My child, with my power and magic. She followed the source I created."

"The Damned."

"Yes. They are mine, evolved mortals and elves and creatures, and you were right. They don't deserve their fate."

Brigid stared, the loss on both their sides soaking her in agony. She was so irritated with him for being who he was, a fool of a god, and yet she understood his drive to reclaim that which he had lost. She carried her own to get her daughter back. She wanted to say all of it, and that none of it was right or fair, but instead she said the thing she'd been reliving in her quiet moments. "You . . . you washed my hair."

"I—" He paused. Looked at her long, auburn locks, and lifted a hand to twirl around a strand. A tingle worked its way down her scalp and spine. She wanted to purr like a cat. "Many times."

"I only remember the once."

"I would do it again for you. Anytime you like. Haven't you realized yet, Brigid Heron? I serve *you*. I waited for you, and I am yours."

They stared into each other's eyes, Brigid losing herself in the cinnamon and gold. The air grew so charged Brigid had to force herself to look away from him before she did something reckless, like throw herself into his arms, back him up to the brick wall where she had pinned his shadow, and rediscover every inch of his body that she had forgotten.

She cleared her throat. "I have to go."

Knightly tilted his head. "What are you doing about the lough and Dove?"

"I have a plan," she said, rolling her shoulders back.

"Great. I'm in."

"I don't need your help." Knightly's presence distracted her, lured her into wanting things she should not.

"You do."

"I do not."

"If you don't have me on your team, you're liable to misstep."

"*Misstep?*"

"It's the Brigid Heron way."

"You can be such an *ass*." She lifted a hand in the air, prepared to pull lightning from the sky and strike the crown of his head.

Sensing the attack, he backed out of the alley, pausing to pick up her basket of assorted stones, herbs, and oils for the altar. "Perhaps, but I'm yours."

Brigid's fingers curled into her palm. "Stop saying that."

"Why? Because it's the truth or because you like hearing it too much?"

"Put that down. You don't know where it goes. I don't think you even have a clue what you are doing."

"Oh yeah?" He winked. "I'm not the only one."

Then he sat the basket down, turned, and strode out of the alley, ignoring the bolts of lightning dancing at his feet.

⚷

The town's occult shop where Brigid was due to meet Ophelia and Finola was in the heart of things, in a stone building Brigid once knew well when it was a market run by beefy men with waxed mustaches. She found the shop and looked up at the new name hung over the door: FASCINATIONS. The front window display was whimsical and featured a small selection of books on a white table beside a dressmaker's mannequin wearing a pair of feathered wings. A few oval mirrors hung from the ceiling with twinkling lights woven around the edges of the mirrors on display. A painted sign rested between the table and mannequin and advertised VINTAGE MAGIC.

It was charming, and a bit of a shock to imagine an occult shop in Evermore.

"You'd look right at home in the display," Finola said, "a witch in the window."

Brigid shook her head. "It doesn't need me; it's already enchanting enough. I am hoping they have something to drink inside this shop of curious things."

"Whiskey?" Finola asked, a hopeful note creeping into her voice.

Brigid laughed. "I doubt shops that aren't pubs pass that out to its patrons. I was hoping more for a glass of water."

Finola let out a little laugh but nodded. Inside, the store featured an organized display of delightful clutter. Along the wall to the immediate left were cream shelves stocked with an array of candles in every shade of every color, assorted crystals, and wrapped sage and rosemary for smudging. Against the center wall was a gorgeous navy linen daybed, with crisp sheets and beautiful pale yellow pillows. To the right of the bed was a rack of clothes: luxurious flowing dresses and butter-soft shirts in rainbow print. The next wall over offered an assortment of tables and shelving featuring aged glass, perfume bottles, masks of varying styles, old clocks, postcards in a box, pottery, and even an ancient barber's chair. None of the items made a bit of sense, and yet Brigid found herself wishing to run her fingers over everything.

Finola picked up an amethyst the size of a deck of cards and set it in Brigid's hand. Brigid pressed the stone to her cheek, savoring the warmth it kicked into her system, and continued studying the objects. It was startling to see magic-based supplies lazing out in the open. Stranger yet to see the altar with a drawing of her by the front door.

"We can put the first altar here," Finola said. "What do you think?"

"Won't the owner mind?"

"Nah," Fin said. "I don't mind a bit."

Brigid's eyes widened. "This is yours?"

"The news doesn't turn a profit like it used to," Fin said. "We needed a place for supplies in town, and it's proven a decent way to get in extra money on the island. Shipping is hit or miss since half the time the post can't go out, and when it does the postal folks end up baffled at where they've got the goods from. The curse makes it tricky, but it's worked well enough for us to get by, and as you've gathered, getting by is all we do here on Evermore."

"For now," Brigid said, staring at the shop with new eyes. "Do you love it? Having your own business like this, in the open?"

"I mean, mortgage and overhead are rather annoying in general, but yes, I have loved it. Aside from the villagers like Rodney, who want love tonics to blind the maidens to his bad breath and greedy hands, or those who want me to tell them how to conjure genies or portals back in time so they can marry a ruggedly attractive ginger Scotsman and have his babies. There's rather a lot of the latter."

Brigid frowned. "Rodney needs a dose of manners and a binding to his hands. Genies are deceivers, and Scotsmen speak their own language. You know, I had a confusing weekend with one once. Couldn't understand half of what he said, but he taught me fascinating things while naked, under the full moon." She cocked her head. "I suppose I can understand the requests for portals to the Scots of the past, after all."

"Have you met a genie? Was it blue? Did it sing to you?"

"Definitely not."

"That's a shame."

"I suppose it would depend on the song." Brigid looked out the wide windows of the shop. "Where'd Ophelia get off to?"

"Placing an altar in the center of town, she should be back any moment."

Brigid nodded, and took her basket that Knightly had nearly gotten off with to the door and went to laying her birch bark, heather, and gold out along with a drawing she had done of her Goddess, praying for a miracle of her own.

⚹

Twenty minutes later, as Brigid had finished the altar and was standing, stretching her arms over head and shaking the fatigue from her legs, the bells over the shop door chimed. Finola straightened as two women entered. The duo were dressed in shades of gray, nickel, and slate. Finola's eyes narrowed at the low hum of magic rolling from them. She had never seen these two strangers before a day in her life. Which meant . . .

"We're not open today," Finola said, looking around for her salt. She hadn't laid any across the door; she rarely did as the Damned specifically avoided this shop. She'd assumed they had no desire finding themselves face-to-face with all the objects that could possibly hurt them, but now she was cursing herself for such an oversight.

The girl in front of her had olive skin and a cascade of silky black hair. She grinned at Finola, and Finola felt a ping of envy for how such a brilliant smile transformed an already attractive face. "You're not? But—oh look, you have moonstone. We just got here and this one"—she pointed to the young woman with hair so blond it was almost silver, who was looking around the shop—"forgot our moonstone. I told her, 'How can you visualize a cone without the moonstone to direct the knowledge?' But she was all, 'I am the cone,' and then I had to throw my bag at her."

"Moonstone, huh?" Finola asked, walking back to her counter, before mouthing a single word to Brigid.

Damned.

Brigid inclined her head as she studied the alchemist symbol of an upside-down triangle the other woman wore as a necklace, a twitch starting in Brigid's calf and working its way down to her ankle.

The symbol was for water.

"You sure you're not looking for a genie?" Finola asked them, thinking fast on what to do. Trap them, throw holy water on them, stab them?

"There's no such thing as a genie," the young woman said.

"Are you calling down the moon, then?" Brigid asked, her eyes staying on the woman with skin so white it was nearly translucent and her pale blond hair.

They had unusual accents Finola couldn't place, and their eyes glittered like new copper pennies as they drank in the items in the store. As the blond, quiet one moved, Finola picked up the chattering whisper of banked power.

"We *are* calling the moon," the first woman with the delicious smile said, taking a step deeper into the store. She hesitated, smoothed a hand over her long, black hair. "We need it to help us find her."

"Her?" Finola asked.

The quiet one with such hidden power spoke, and her voice was melodic. "Brigid Heron. The Lost Witch of Ireland."

Finola and Brigid exchanged a quick look. Finola's said *Huh?* while Brigid's was tuned to the key of *Oh bloody hell.*

"Haven't you heard?" the quiet one said. "Brigid Heron was prophesied to return and bring healing and miracles. It's too bad she's failing at every turn."

Brigid's eyes drifted to the mirrors in the display. One had swiveled around when the door the two women entered opened. Her eyes narrowed at what she saw, and she bit back an irritated growl. Of all the obnoxious, sneaky manipulations to attempt.

"I suppose," Brigid said. "It depends on how you quantify failure."

"This is your last chance," the pale-haired woman said, and Brigid studied the once true features of East Knight. How young she appeared, how cold her beauty. "Join us."

"I will not join you or your coven, and I will not fail."

East pulled the time glass she had shown Brigid on the hill beside the fairy ring and sat it on the counter. It glowed with a liquid now the shade of amber, golden lights glittering inside it.

"We will see."

Then the two witches walked from the store, the first witch shooting Finola an almost smile as if in apology or longing, while East paused to brush the altar from the table to the floor.

When they were gone, Brigid let out a string of curse words that made Finola blush.

"I didn't know you had that in you," Finola said, letting out a low whistle.

"I don't tolerate intimidation," Brigid said, shaking back her hair, "and I *really* do not like those witches."

"That first one didn't seem quite as evil. But maybe it's an act. Good witch, bad witch." Fin walked to where the hourglass sat. "It looks as though time is running out," she said. "Do you think this is real?"

"I think they are scared and so they are doing everything to frighten us."

"You didn't answer my question though."

Brigid looked at the hourglass, huffed an irritated sigh. "Don't touch that timepiece. Bring me your favorite scarf."

Finola brought her a soft blue one hung behind the counter.

"Spells have two parts, one for calling power and one for releasing it. We will call power for protection into our hands and release it into the scarf. Then cover the object so regardless of its intent, it will not affect us."

Standing over the hourglass, Brigid and Finola grasped hands. Brigid used a simple spell from the *Book of the Goddess.*

"Take from me that which we need.
Protect us and keep us safe,
So mote it be."

They picked up the scarf together, a warm rush, like water pouring from their palms shifted over it. They laid it on top of the hourglass and stepped away from it.

"Now we pick up the altar, add a few more flowers and stones for elegance, and go find Ophelia," Brigid said. "The sooner we get started the better."

They walked outside and found Ophelia turning up the main road. As dark storm clouds crept in, black iron streetlamps kicked on. Brigid jumped at the flames lighting in unison, and Finola laughed.

"Marvels of modern technology," Ophelia called.

Brigid nodded and studied Evermore under the amber glow of the light. "Why flames when you have the false light?"

Finola shrugged. "Homage to simpler times?"

"Times are never simple. War, small minds, power-hungry fools, Mother Nature's will—I do not think it is ever easy, no matter the year."

"You're like an ambient beam of joy, aren't you? Spreading all that sunshine."

"The truth is not always rosy."

"Speaking of," Finola said, hooking her arm through Ophelia's as she reached them. "We had a visit with two of the freaky witches. Only this time they looked like goth witches and spoke on their own. It was the leader and a cute one who had lips to rival a goddess. Do we have any chocolate or wine at home? I think we're going to need both."

SIXTEEN

On the return drive home, Finola and Brigid filled Ophelia in on their run-in at the shop with the two witches who slipped into the store carrying barely veiled threats, and marveled at how this time they were operating at a slightly more human level. "You really think it was two of the coven?"

"Yes, I don't know how or why they were able to present as . . ."

"Less smoky messes?" Finola supplied.

"More human, and I don't think they want my help like East said. I think they want to know what we're planning."

"They were gorgeous," Finola said. "And still a little bit terrifying without their shadow masks on. It's sad to think that's who they were before, who they should have been."

"How did their voices sound?" Ophelia asked.

"Still the same," Finola said, affecting a low ethereal voice with a singsong style, "just not at the same time."

"Do you think their power is stronger because we're moving toward Lughnasa?"

"Perhaps. I think regardless of the why, we keep to our

course and plan. They can't do anything until Lughnasa so we have a short window to get this right."

"Well then," Ophelia said. "What are we waiting for? Let's get to work."

Over the next six weeks the witches labored to create the right ritual to summon the power of the lough, while trying to keep the Damned from overrunning the town, and out of the coven's way. It was arduous and tedious, and they stopped only to eat and rest, and help those in the village who called to them.

They set out weekly altars on Sundays, refreshing the ones in town and bringing small and carefully curated versions to set in the waters of the lough, infusing these altars with their love of the Goddess . . . and as a reminder to the lough who it was created for. As a bonus, they knew it would needle the coven should they come across them.

On the days they weren't battling monsters, the witches were laying out a circle by the shore, offering items in threes so they might open a door into the Otherworld—and to Dove.

It was slow going with any progress, and they tried hard not to let it derail their drive. But the waters barely rippled at their in-cantations, and at certain times the earth would sink under their feet while other times it would freeze beneath them. Brigid sim-ply marked the variables in their notebook and tried a different sort of offering. Flowers the Goddess had once gifted Brigid that never aged or lost their divine fragrance, shavings from a page in Dove's journal about the lough, a snip of Brigid's hair. She al-tered the combinations, rotating secrets of Ophelia's she trapped in a bottle, whiskey from Finola's favorite stash, even gifts from the town that had been given to the women in gratitude for their protection.

Nothing worked.

On the seventh week, dead crows showed up across Brigid's

yard. A warning or omen. She was certain where it had come from. The coven of the lough, the former witches of Knight.

"Are they taunting us or is there a message here?" Ophelia asked, starting out into the yard with her chin tucked in her palm.

"It's a murder of crows," Brigid said, bringing her teacup to her lips.

"I take it we're the crows."

Brigid sat down the teacup and marched out of the kitchen. She went into her bedroom and quietly shut the door.

"She's rattled," Ophelia murmured.

"Near two months and we've gotten nowhere," Finola said. "Wouldn't you be?"

Ophelia didn't respond, just turned her face back to the window and watched as another crow crashed to its death on their lawn.

⊶0

Later that afternoon Brigid found Ophelia in the kitchen, flipping tarot cards as the sun set. She grabbed a mug from the counter and filled it with the orange chamomile Ophelia preferred for this time of day, the sweet citrus scent soothing her as she pulled out a chair and took a seat opposite her friend. Brigid watched as Ophelia flipped tarot cards with the flick of her hand one after the other. A clock in the room ticked patiently, a gentle metronome to their beat of life. The countertops gleamed and the floors shined with polish, no doubt the product of Fin's or Ophelia's energy and nerves. Brigid spared a brief glance to Ophelia's so-called chore chart and smiled at the revisions Finola had added. Instead of sweep, mop, and dishes, it read: dance topless, sing off-key, and love (or make love to, your call!) yourself.

"The house is too quiet," Ophelia said, her head bent as she studied the card before her. "When Fin's not talking at us, it's filled with an aching silence."

"I am failing," Brigid said, her hands going to her mug, squeezing tight.

Ophelia looked up. "No, you aren't." She looked back at the cards. "You're working out how to do the most complicated spell you've attempted. Do you know how many times it took me to bake a loaf of bread that wasn't overcooked, underproofed, with too much or too little yeast? I spent years perfecting my baking skills and I'm still nowhere near close to where I want to be. And don't get me started on how far I've come as a witch and how much I have learned from you and have yet to learn. We're getting closer. Each failure is a step to success."

In the short time Brigid had gotten to know Ophelia, she had learned how clever this witch of quiet patience was. She found herself on the verge of tears with gratitude for her friend, her family.

"Now," Ophelia said, as though she sensed Brigid's riot of emotions. She flashed her a devious grin. "Let's try something new to see what window we might crack open. May I have your palm, please?"

Ophelia waggled her fingers, and Brigid bit her lip. Gingerly, she placed her hand in Ophelia's. The moment they touched, Brigid's breath grew deeper. The bunched muscles in her shoulders relaxed, and her other hand, which she'd taken to clenching at her side, uncurled.

"Interesting," Ophelia murmured, staring at the open hand she held.

She walked a finger over Brigid's palm, lightly tracing the lines there. "You have two fate lines."

Brigid looked down. "Surprise, surprise."

Ophelia's light laugh danced over Brigid's skin. "Brigid of

two worlds, with two fates and timelines." She pressed down Brigid's thumb, tilted her hand.

"What do you see in my fates, then?"

"I see a long life and a beautiful reunion. For how we get there, I think we might ask the cards for a little help."

Tarot cards were *not* Brigid's medium. She almost bought a deck once, when she'd been in Dublin and stumbled into a magician's shop. The shop was hidden along a back street and disguised as a butcher's. It had been empty when she'd come upon it, and she had not stayed long. The feel of being inside the magician's room was like accidentally walking into seaweed: it wrapped around her midsection and calves, and she struggled to kick it free. In the short minutes she'd been there, she had seen a deck sitting on the counter. In each card she turned over, she saw her own face staring back. Wide, slight gap in her two front teeth, and worst of all—small *b*'s woven as the curls of her auburn hair. She'd blinked, and the face had changed, but she never forgot the trick of those cards. They had a feel to them, like they hadn't belonged in this world.

Magic was always connected. From one realm to the next. It was like people in that way, though humans often forgot that was the true way of things.

"Have you always been a reader?" Brigid asked Ophelia.

"Ever since I received the cards."

"You didn't buy them?"

Ophelia shook her head.

"It's better that way, isn't it?" Brigid asked. "Being given cards, instead of choosing your deck."

"I've only had the one deck, so I couldn't say. Fin got them for me for my eighteenth birthday. I tend to stick to what works well, and these have always shown me true."

Brigid shifted her weight, crossed her ankles, leaned back and then forward.

Ophelia smiled. "Nervous?

"I don't get nervous." Brigid cleared her throat.

Ophelia flashed a knowing grin.

"I might get a bit . . . uncertain, but never nervous. I put my faith in you."

Ophelia's smile warmed any lingering resistance Brigid had. "I do readings every day. Mostly for myself but also for those I care about and want to help. I pull a card for Finola every morning, to see if it can guide me in how I might show up for her. Sometimes I pull them for the people of the town, hoping to know who might be targeted by the Damned next."

"Does it work?"

"Sometimes. The Damned don't know their minds, so it's tricky." She sat up straighter, leaned in. "It's important to re-member the cards merely show the roads in your path, so you can decide what you want to do before your future manifests itself."

Brigid stared at the deck on the table. "Have you ever pulled the cards for Dove?"

Ophelia's hand stilled on her deck. "No."

Brigid reached over, brushed her hands across the teal and white cover of the cards. "Maybe we should ask the cards how to help her."

Outside the evening moon rose higher in the sky, the sun, its counter, on the opposite side. A lazy breeze drifted in, bringing the salty smell of the sea and blooming jasmine. The blueberry bush in the little garden Ophelia worked would be glistening, and tomorrow morning Finola would run outside to pick a handful for her almond butter toast, while Ophelia swatted her with a dish towel for tracking in dirt and the inevitable smear of violet blueberry since Finola could never seem to bring any-thing in from the garden without dropping and then dragging it around by the heel of her boot.

On this day, though, Ophelia picked up the deck and began to shuffle

⌐0

Finola had never doubted who she was. Not for a single moment of her life. She was the daughter of two rather unhappy people, who had suffered from a rather unremarkable existence. Her parents did not teach her kindness; that she learned from Ophelia when her family took her in, and on her own from television sitcoms and novels. When you don't have a good example living before you, Finola knew you had two choices for how to carve out your life. You can emulate the behavior of your so-called role models, or you could define the terms of life on your own. She chose to build her own foundation, and she chose to do so based off the values she most admired in her favorite characters.

She learned to be brazen from Elizabeth Bennet, to be comfortable making a mistake while having impeccably groomed eyebrows from Beth Harmon, to speak her mind with humor like the Marvelous Mrs. Maisel, and to own her sexuality like the witches and vampires in Anne Rice's novels. She found models for good parenting on reruns from American sitcoms in the sixties and the later Disney movies. Finola knew that her role models were not based in reality, but then she was a witch who fought monsters on a day-to-day basis. What was reality?

As Finola walked the cliffs of Evermore with its vibrantly green grass and oversized stones beneath her feet, she thought of the lough and the spells and how they kept failing. She was growing more and more afraid that they would fail entirely. That not only might they not be able to summon the power of the lough and she would lose Dove, but that none of it might matter. Not when whatever was waiting to release from the lough was upended and chaos took over Evermore permanently come August first, on Lugh's holiday.

Finola sighed, but walked on, cresting one cliff and following it down into the next. There she came to a stumbling halt.

The two Knight witches from her shop stood waiting, their hands on their hips, wearing grins that did not match their faces.

"Hello, little witch," they said, their voices blending together once more. "How would you like to make a deal?"

⚷

Knightly woke with a craving for twilight. He walked his fields thinking of Brigid, and his mind drifted to his first day in Evermore after she was taken from him. That first morning he had tottered along the docks, staring into the endless sea and trying not to fall in the frigid water, before he had come across a statuesque Black woman with piercing hazel eyes. "Hello there," she'd said, sitting down on the bench right before the edge of the dock began.

His face was ruddy from the sun, his eyes, he knew, too bright. "Where am I?" he'd asked, not quite sure if she was an apparition, not quite sure if anything was real anymore.

"You're in Evermore," she had said, peering at him as though she thought him a bit blotto. Or mad. He recalled thinking she'd be half right. "There's a fine hostel up the road if you need an affordable place to stay."

"Evermore," he'd said, nodding as the word and its meaning registering. *Home*. Brigid. Dove. "What day is today?"

"February the second."

"And yesterday was the?"

"February first in the year of 1923."

The ground beneath his shoes tilted. He'd been gone one day and a year. "Do you know where I can find Brigid Heron?"

Her eyebrows shot up. "Brigid?"

He nodded.

"You don't know, then?"

"Know?"

"She's still missing. Has been for the better part of a year."

He sat down, hard, on the bench.

The woman studied him. "I was going to buy a basket of fish and chips. Can I tempt you?"

Knightly didn't remember nodding, but no sooner had he blinked than the woman had returned with the food and an offer. She needed help. Could he do anything, and if so, might he be interested in cleaning her office? She was a solicitor and recently returned to town. He said he did a little of a lot, and they'd made an accord to meet the following day at lunchtime, at her office.

She'd left then, walking with the sort of confidence Knightly had only seen once before. She moved like the very road was rising up to meet her. Like Brigid.

He had gone back to eating his fish and chips, the sun warming his face. After that, he'd cloaked himself and gone to Brigid's house, then her lough, then all over her property.

Brigid was nowhere to be found, and he did not know what to do.

He returned to his lough, just as the water began to bubble, before an Abhartach, a bloodthirsty demon that enjoyed living off the trees in the Otherworld and wept blood, crawled growling from the water onto the shore. Knightly, still cloaked from sight, had watched the witches who had been his slide over the land and claim the creature before setting it free to go into town and claim whatever villagers it might find.

It had taken Knightly nearly the last of his strength to trap and defeat the creature. He'd stumbled back to town the next morning to bathe in the water, only to find he couldn't go beyond the dock.

"It's no use," the woman who had been so kind to him the day before said. "Whatever you are, you're stuck here now like the rest of us."

"It's not my blood," he said. "It's one of theirs. They are Damned."

Then he fell apart, sobbing on the dock, while the calm-eyed woman consoled him and led him back to her office to clean him up.

Later, he would realize the beautiful woman with clever eyes had given him back a purpose for life. She fed him that day, and for many after, and gave him a menial job to keep his mind busy as he regained his strength and began to wait for Brigid.

He owed that stranger more than he could ever repay, and as he crossed his field to the edge of the meadow, he turned and entered the gated way. Walked with the same confidence the woman had once carried in her step.

He strode with focus, one foot purposefully in front of the other, until he came to stand before her.

"Dear Agnes," he said, with a sad smile, as he looked down upon her grave. "The clock is ticking, and I fear time, finally, may be running out."

SEVENTEEN

BOOK OF THE GODDESS (P. 1):

There is no greater magic than giving of yourself to another.

Once upon a time, Brigid Heron was alone and lonely. She lived in a house she loved, and she performed services for a deity who loved her. Her days were filled, her life comfortable . . . and it was awful.

Brigid had been by herself long before the loss of her mother, and all of her days she had only ever longed for something more. Family. Community. Love. At first, the something more came by way of the Goddess. Hope. A spark of magic.

But magic is not love, and Brigid soon began to long for more than even the great deity could provide. So she made a deal for love, from a god who did not believe in it, until he fell for the woman he struck the deal with, with her hair the color of fire and a face as honest as the stars. Brigid was lucky, for a while at least, to have found love not once, but twice.

As Ophelia flipped over the last card in her three-deck draw, revealing the Lovers, Brigid sighed. She should have known it would come back to him. "This is the spread you pull for Dove?"

"This is what the cards show me."

"Knightly," she said.

"It is rumored," Ophelia said, tapping her thumb on the kitchen table, "that the tarot cards were once pages of a book. Lost perhaps in the fire in Alexandria. Some people believe they're actually doors, or a copy of the spokes on a divination wheel. My favorite theory is they are the surviving remnant of a lost magical system, and we're all trying to work out how to use the pieces to rebuild it today."

"So it's given us the pieces Dove needs, or we need?"

"Maybe a bit of both?"

The deck sat on the table and before Brigid could touch it to choose the next card, a breeze came through the house, from the open window in the kitchen, stirring the cards and flipping not one, but three over. The wind died immediately, and the other cards on the table remained undisturbed.

"Maybe you're right," Brigid said, her tone light as they looked at the cards scattered across the table before them, the vibration of magic fluttering through the air, tasting of sweetly spun sugar.

The Empress, Queen of Swords, and the Queen of Wands stared up at her.

"What do these mean?" she asked.

"The Queen of Wands is fiery, magnetic, and fair. She channels ideas into action to change the world. The Queen of Swords is wisdom and strength and unapologetically herself, and the Empress is the ultimate goddess. Lover, mother, creator, she is all-powerful." Ophelia ran her fingers over the edges of the card. "The cards, I would think, are showing us who we need to be. If we are to summon the power of the lough and save Dove, we have to become who we're meant to be."

"And reminding us of who we already are." She stood and ran her fingers through her hair. "It's that first card that gives me pause."

"Because you understand what it means?"

"Yes." Brigid sighed. "I really do need Knightly's help."

She leaned down to give Ophelia a kiss, walked over to the side table to pick up her basket, and strode out the kitchen door.

⚷

Brigid knew she wouldn't have to go far to find Knightly. He wasn't hiding, and he wasn't hard to track. He had been staying in her caravan for weeks, attempting to keep an eye on her or, as he'd said, keep her safe.

She wondered if he knew the reason he slept so well each night was because she'd been weaving protection spells around him and placing mugwort on the windowsill beside the caravan's bed. He was safe because *she* had made sure of it. Just as his cauldron was safe, because she had gone back to the lough to retrieve it and protect it.

She walked up to the door and raised a fist to knock and then yanked her own hand back down. This was her caravan, not *his*. How was it he could fill her mind and dominate her thoughts and her space? Her eyes drifted to a green curling vine peeking out from the side of the cream and teal caravan, and she crossed to inspect it. Weeds knew better than to grow here, and yet this one . . . Brigid reached out to touch it and it flowered. Fairy trumpets. White and red and blooming all along the vine. The laugh erupted from her as the memory awoke.

Knightly planting the vines around the caravan when she was fairly far into her pregnancy, as she ambled up, her back aching and her stomach gurgling from a hunger that never seemed to wane. "What are you doing?"

"Thought you might like something pretty, and these grow around some of the other homes in the village."

Brigid had burst out laughing then. "Sure, and it does. It's fairy trumpets, meant to bar the entrance to keep witches from entering."

Knightly looked at the vine in his hand and then at Brigid. "Is that so?"

"It is."

He picked up a strand of vine and wove it into a lopsided crown and placed it on her head. "Why would anyone try and keep this witch out?" Then he drew her in for a kiss that made her toes curl and her mouth greedy with need, and the vines and their meaning were forgotten.

She sighed as the memory settled. It was coming clear why she was unable to resist him. What had she told Fin? That something more than lust could exist. The echo of it still flowing through her veins from the memory was impossible to name.

Perhaps it was hope.

Maybe love was always hope.

Brigid stepped up to the door and pushed it open. Knightly stood organizing her supplies, writing tiny labels on slips of sticky paper that he stuck to the bottles in her cabinet.

"We've had quite a number of ingenious inventions in the mortal world this past century," he said, like she'd been there all morning. "I find adhesives one of my favorites."

Brigid peered closer. "You organized and named all my herbs."

"And put them in alphabetical order. See what an asset I am to have around?"

She let out a groan. "I suppose I'm beginning to."

She took the card of the Lovers she'd borrowed from Ophelia's pack and placed it in his hand.

"Is this an invitation?" he asked, a smile crooking across his face.

"I think it's instruction."

He stepped so close Brigid was breathing in the mint of his breath and the cedar that always clung to his skin. "That wasn't what I meant."

"No?" He reached out and tucked a strand of hair behind her ear, his fingers lingering on her neck, dragging down across her collarbone. "Are you sure?"

Brigid wanted to say yes, she was sure. She was always in control, and he needed to take a step back. But she was tired of fighting the pull to him, the craving to taste him again. She hadn't come here for this, and yet now that she was here, it felt like this was where she was always meant to be.

She dropped her bag, reached a hand out, and yanked him to her. Her hands were in his hair, her mouth crushed to his, and for a few glorious seconds she gave herself over to the tidal wave of lust as it rolled through her. Then she took a ragged breath and leaned back. Knightly's eyes were hooded, his lips swollen, and his chest heaving as he tried to catch his breath. He'd never looked sexier or more like he was what he said. A god among men.

"Brigid," he said, his voice a broken whisper.

She went to step away, and he kneeled before her on the floor, his palm coming to her stomach. "I am yours."

The truth of it, the desperation in his tone and on his face, undid her. Her heart raced beneath his touch at the reminder of what had been, and the fact that she was bringing *this* god to his knees . . .

She lowered down to him, and her hands came to cradle the sides of his face. Then his lips were on hers. This kiss was gentle, searching, apologetic. Brigid opened her mouth, and his tongue brushed against hers and the kiss shifted into an urgent, pleading brush fire of want and desire. Her arms came around him, and he slid his beneath hers, and then he was lifting and carrying her to the bed. Knightly's kiss was pleading, but his hands were slow, methodical in the removal of each item of her clothing until she was ready to tackle him and shred his pants off with her teeth.

"I have waited an age for you, and I would have waited forever," he said, between kisses he peppered down her collarbone. "Don't make me rush this."

She nodded in surrender, and then she surrendered again and again.

As their bodies intertwined and she gave herself over to him once more, Brigid knew this was something she could never forget.

They slept for hours, curled together in the small alcove of the bed. Memories drifted in as Brigid slept, of their life before, what it had been and what it could be and would become.

And what it became when Knightly eventually left.

When they woke, they took their time exploring each other again.

"So, the card," Brigid said, trying not to blush as she looked down at the Lovers and thought of all the things Knightly had done to her body that morning.

"Yes?"

"I think it means we need you to be a part of our spell."

"Your plan, you mean. The one you didn't want to let me in on?"

"Yes, that one."

"I'm a part of Team Brigid now?"

"You're on probation."

He reached up, brushed his thumb against her lower lip, and leaned in for a kiss that left her thighs clenching together. "For now. I have a feeling I'll get off with good behavior."

Brigid let out a laugh and got dressed. Once they were both presentable, he followed her outside. They walked up the path through the little wood that separated the caravan from the road back to Brigid's house, and that's when they saw it.

A thick fog had rolled in across the land. As dense as campfire smoke but tinged in a purple haze.

"What is this?" Brigid asked, dread pitting in her stomach.

"The Damned," Knightly said. "The mist coming in before they do."

"That's an ocean of mist."

"And I don't think I've ever seen that many Damned." He pointed in the air, and Brigid followed his direction to where Sluaghs filled the sky, hovering over the land.

A roar sounded from behind them, then a hundred high-pitched giggles entered from every direction.

"It's coming from the direction of the caves," Knightly said. "The coven has set them loose."

"They're insane," Brigid said, as she turned and hurried back to the caravan. "We need to get to Ophelia and Finola. We've been working on a spell and with your help, maybe it will work. We can send them all back."

"What do you need?" Knightly asked, following her back inside.

Brigid looked at the freshly organized herbs in the cabinet. "That's a start."

⚷

Finola wriggled against the restraints binding her wrists, trying not to breathe too deeply in the small cabin once used for drying meat. She was accosted by a plethora of smells, ointment and smoke and herbs and a pinch of stink that reminded her of feet. Finola had forgotten the cabin, on the outskirts of town, even existed. Yet here she sat, annoyed and stuck. She was not one to side with freaky, power-hungry witches. No matter how pretty the one with the dark hair, who kept checking her out when she thought Finola wasn't looking, was. She simply did not have a desire to become a corrupt shadowy monster of herself. She'd worked too hard on the current version of Finola, and she was quite happy with who she was, thank you very much.

"I didn't realize my options were make a bargain with you or magically have my wrists bound," Finola said as she tried to work her hands free. "You couldn't even bother with vibrating handcuffs or something pink. Not only do you not have proper voice modulation, but you lack style. Tend the lough, set loose monsters, chant warnings like a drunk Gregorian choir. What kind of powerful witches are you?"

Finola could swear the dark-haired witch's lips twitched.

"You talk too much," East said. She walked over to a jar on a shelf and pulled it down. She opened it and dipped her finger in a crimson, oozing liquid before she turned to where Finola sat, bound. It seemed the coven of Knight liked dark, dank spaces, so she supposed she should have known they liked their magic equally baneful and disgusting.

Their shelves were lined with mason jars filled with various substances, including, if she was seeing things correctly (which was difficult because the room had hardly a sliver of sunlight), eyeballs, fingers and toes, hair, and teeth. It was like a biology lab gone wrong.

East walked in slow and methodical steps toward Finola. She held up the finger dripping a rust-colored substance. Finola tried to lean and jerk away, but East blew the substance into her face and suddenly she couldn't move. East dragged her fingers across Finola's lips like she was painting on a smile and smirked at her when she was done.

"Not so chatty now, are you?"

Finola tried to speak but found her mouth welded shut.

"You should have made the deal. You have power, and we could have given you more. Instead, we'll have to settle for making you bait."

Finola shook her head, trying to argue, and East only grinned. "Don't believe me?"

She lifted up Finola's bound hands and tapped each of the thumbs. A light grew in the center of her palms. "Someone scried for you and knows where you are. Should we wager which witch it will be? The lost witch, the strong witch"—her grin dropped off—"or the forsaken god?"

"They're here," the other witch said, her eyes flickering over to Finola.

"Take your post, North," East told her. "It's time to play how to catch a witch."

All sounds ceased inside the cabin as the two witches shifted back into the shadows. Finola hadn't seen the other two, South and West, and worried about where they were. Unless the other two had eaten them. Sitting in the dark cabin filled with foul-smelling and horrifying jars containing some of the more terrifying substances known to woman made her feel like a real-life Gretel, and the idea that these witches might eat their own didn't seem that impossible.

From far off the wind blew, gusting against the house like the call of an incoming storm. One long squall, then another, and then a blast that blew the front door open.

Ophelia strode in, her bag across her shoulder, her hands raised. She lowered them when she saw Finola. Fin shook her head as hard as she could. She tried to warn her to keep her hands up, to turn around and run to get Brigid or, gods help her, even Knightly.

But Finola's mouth was spelled too tightly, so she said nothing, and Ophelia crossed deeper into the cabin. "Hang on," she said, "I'm coming."

Then Ophelia stepped into the double circle drawn by East in the center of the room, and the magic inside her flipped upside down. One foot inside one circle, one foot in the other. The coven had cast a splinter spell, to separate magic from the witch. Ophelia's magic was not the type to go quietly, so it simply shifted deeper in her, and the revolt between the vibrations of the world trying to pull out what it needed, and the magic tucked deeply into her, sent her stumbling to her knees.

She clawed at her face and chest, trying to get the power out, her nails biting into the skin, blood smearing across her cheeks as she let loose a keening cry.

Finola strained in her chair, trying to break free, trying to save her sister.

East stepped out of the shadows and walked toward Finola, not bothering to spare a glance at Ophelia as she writhed on the floor, still trying to tear her own magic free.

"Now," East said, her tone as flat as ever. "Are we ready to make that deal?"

⊶0

Brigid was worried about her friends. As the skies darkened and the ground beneath them trembled, she and Knightly searched her house. Then they scoured the cliffs before they drove into town looking for Ophelia and Finola. Knightly, Brigid discovered, was a far worse driver than Ophelia, but she was so concerned for her friends she forgot on this ride to be afraid.

The Damned were everywhere. On their way outside of Brigid's property, they had to pull over several times, climb out of the car, and work together to pull the wind and rain and drive them back. One even ambled out into the road in front of their car, dancing like it was at a ceili, its legs flying and arms waving about as they drew closer to town. She had to ask Knightly not to mow it down like a befuddled sheep as he gunned the engine.

"It would just make it stronger anyway," he said, before speeding around it and into the heart of Evermore.

Brigid was relieved when they stopped seeing them right outside of the town. The perimeter was holding. Her biggest fear was they would arrive in the village to discover no one had seen Finola or Ophelia.

What they found was much, much worse.

"I think I know why we only had the one Damned trying to stall us in the middle of the road outside of town," Knightly said, as Brigid stared in shock at the sight before her.

Townspeople littered the ground, newly familiar faces lying on their backs, staring up at the sky and emitting soft, high-pitched giggles. Two of the villagers had grown spots along their face and arms. Three had grown horns and four sprouted wings. Ophelia's Thorpe was contorted into a ball, moaning as he writhed along the floor.

"They are all Damned," Brigid whispered. "Oh gods, this is how it happens?"

"Never this fast or with a group," Knightly said. "The coven is growing desperate."

"I laid my best protection charms around the lough. Set up altars and blessed the shore. It was for nothing if the coven was able to access it anyway and pull all those creatures from it."

"They didn't pull them out," Knightly said. "As I said, they set them free. When threatened, the coven attacks. The Damned we saw moved north, down from the caves."

"All of them?"

Knightly nodded.

Brigid tucked her hair behind her ears, wished for a better way to tie it back. "We have to help these people." She looked around again. "I thought for sure we'd find Ophelia and Finola here, and while I'm glad they aren't seeing this, where could they be?"

Knightly slipped an arm around her shoulder, his heat drawing her close. "It's a trap."

Brigid stumbled a step back at his words. "What?"

"It's straight out of my playbook. Finola and Ophelia aren't here because they're somehow being used by the witches."

"Which means?"

"Best guess? They're using them as bait."

"That's impossible." At his stoic face, she reached out and shoved him. "How could they be bait?"

"*I* didn't take them," he said, rubbing his chest where she'd sent him stumbling. "I know how the coven works. If they aren't here, or their usual spots, there's a strong chance they're with the witches. If they are, East and the others will be waiting for us to show, and until we do, they're in a holding pattern." He looked back to the affected villagers. "You have time to make a difference here."

Brigid took the herbs from her bag. "That they are taking a move from your playbook is disgusting, so you know." She mixed her ingredients with the water from the fountain in the center of town. "Thankfully they aren't me, and I am not afraid of them." She ground the water and herbs into the cauldron. "And I will have my friends safely returned or it will be their bones I'm grinding," she said, as she used a pestle to mix the herbs and water.

Knightly assisted her in sorting the unperfected poultices and applying them to those fighting the magic of the Damned.

"I can't believe you used the mighty cauldron to create tinctures," he said with a smile.

"It has the power to feed so that no one goes hungry, yes? Maybe it can have the power to heal so no one goes Damned."

Once they had tended to everyone, they did their best to re-salt the perimeter and headed for Knightly's car. They had done all they could for the villagers.

"Where are the witches?" she asked. "How do we reach them?"

"They have a cabin on the edge of town, but it would be better to draw them out," he said. "They'll have planned for you to come."

"Then we need to find out what they are planning without going in."

"How do you want to do that?"

"When I used the cauldron in the lough and pulled my memories, I opened myself up and they were able to meet me on the astral plane. What if I do it again, but without throwing open all the doors like an invitation. What if I knock on the right door and see if I can reach Finola and Ophelia?"

"What if you get lost in the astral plane or they show up and try and attack your physical body while your spirit is out-side it?"

"That's what you're for," she said. "You wanted to protect me? Now is your chance. You guard my body and I'll take the fight to them without their knowing."

He ran a hand through his hair, cut his eyes to hers. "If I say no, you'll do it anyway."

"Oh yes, without a doubt."

He blew out a breath. "Where do you want to conduct this fight?"

"Your lough. It's a door of its own, and if I'm lucky, it might amplify my power on the astral plane."

"And if you're unlucky?"

"I end up Damned and you send me back."

"I'm starting to hate this plan."

"Knightly," she said, "it's our best shot, and we don't have time." She thought of the timepiece in Finola's shop and shuddered. "I need you to trust me."

"I trust you, Brigid Heron. It's the rest of the world that I have my doubts about."

—0

The lough was as dark and cold as ever, the shoreline littered with a murky substance that looked like seaweed but smelled like rotting roses. She walked to the water's edge with her shoulders back and head held high. She did not want to admit the fear that was quaking under her skin, but Brigid was terrified.

Everything rested on her shoulders, and she refused to lose anyone else she loved.

She lifted the cauldron from the bag she carried, set it in the water, and filled it up. Knightly stood beside her, his eyes scanning the horizon. Brigid looked at him and tried for a smile. "Here goes."

"That's not the most encouraging toast I've ever heard."

With a smirk, she gave a bow and added, "As I will it, so mote it be," and drank the water of the lough.

She closed her eyes, and her consciousness shifted free. Brigid wasn't back in the petrified forest though, this time she was standing before her house. Whispers drifted down from on top of her porch.

She drew closer, and Ophelia materialized. Sitting on the stoop, watching a man walk away. He was tall and thin, with bronze hair and a five-o'clock shadow. Deep blue eyes and a nose that looked like it'd been broken once or twice. It only added to his looks, though. Like he was a rebellious librarian. Thorpe.

He moved in a slow, measured way, without the ailment from

the Damned that was affecting him in the center of the town only a half hour before.

The whispering grew louder, and Brigid realized it was coming from Ophelia, who was talking not *to* anyone, but to herself about herself, as though she was narrating her own story.

"When she was younger, Ophelia discovered she could breathe easier when it stormed. She wasn't sure if it was that the water washed away her worry or if the darkened skies simply offered a protective cover, but she found peace in the darkness. As the skies overhead shifted into slate gray interspersed with chalky white clouds, she took in a deep inhalation. The kind that filled down to the basin of her lungs, that refreshed her entire body. She needed the air, because panic over dying was taking root."

"Dying?" Brigid said, she walked to her. "Phee, you aren't dying. I'm here."

The light grew bright and dimmed out, and the vision shifted. They were staring at row after row of stacks in the bookstore. They followed them, turning down a corridor, and then Ophelia was opening a door and going down a narrow stairwell that led under the bookstore into a small, clean apartment.

Her narrating began again.

"Ophelia had always carried a soft spot for the space, much as she carried one for the man who owned it. There was a lot of natural wood and the scent of what she used to call 'Thorpe spice' in the air. Lemon and sandalwood. It smelled like the promise of love."

They walked through the little apartment until they found Thorpe in the second bedroom that he had converted into an office. His head in his hands and hair sticking up from where he'd tugged it too hard at its roots.

"Hey," Ophelia said, a wellspring of emotion in the word as she crouched down beside him.

He turned. His eyes were bloodshot, face pale. Blue lines snaked out from his lips, curving toward his cheeks.

"What is happening to me?" Thorpe croaked, the words barely audible.

Ophelia ran her fingers over his face, to the pulse racing in his neck. Brigid watched the fear rushing into her as she realized Thorpe was Damned.

"We have to get to Brigid," Ophelia said, and wrapped an arm around him. She tugged him forward and up the short flight of stairs to the car waiting outside. She went to start it, then slumped against the wheel, a wave of dizziness coursing through her. She looked down at her hands, and they turned into claws.

"Oh no," Ophelia said. "Ophelia was Damned too. They were all Damned."

"No," Brigid said, placing a hand on her friend's face. "You're not Damned, you're trapped in the astral plane."

Brigid ran her fingers over Ophelia's hair and face, down her sides, until she found what she was looking for. A small door, like the kind you would see in a children's doll house. It was the secret place into where Ophelia housed her magic. Her center of power. She knocked on the door, and then pressed her palm to it. Magic pure and strong, and as honest and true as Ophelia, knocked back against her hand.

"They want your power," Brigid whispered. "Of course they do. We won't let them take it from you though."

The first line in the *Book of the Goddess* was the greatest spell of all. Giving yourself to another. Brigid used her finger to draw a door in her side, much like the one Ophelia had created to hide her magic. She knocked on her side and then reached in through the door and wrapped her fingers around a pinch of her own essence. Gold flakes of freedom, a bit of the Goddess inside of Brigid. She carefully pulled it out and slipped it into Ophelia.

Ophelia's eyes turned to Brigid, the haze behind them cleared and the narrating stopped.

"Brigid?" she whispered, taking her hand. Right before the astral plane went dark, and Ophelia's grasp was ripped from her own.

EIGHTEEN

Brigid's name was called, over and over, as she stumbled in the dark, and the pure, unfiltered panic in the voice had Brigid running. She came to a halt as the sun rose over a woman sitting in a chair in the center of a body of water. Brigid drew closer and found Finola, not seated but standing on the chair, staring into the ocean.

The water, which normally ranged from murky black to navy blue, was a slightly revolting, wholly unnatural, lime green.

"It's the phosphorescence," Finola said. "The shoreline is full of rotting fish. It smells like wet gym socks and zombies."

She turned and looked over to Brigid, then pointed up to the sky. It was ash gray, the wind growing more and more vicious by the second. "Brigid," she said, "you have to hurry." Finola turned back to the water. A bubble popped beneath the surface. One, then another, then twenty, then a hundred, then a thousand. The water shifted and parted.

"Fin—"

"Run," Finola whispered, her voice urgent.

A large yellow eye rose to the surface of the sea. It blinked and looked up, down, and then directly at Finola. The eye blinked again and moved closer. Water rushed over the chair, splashing against Finola's legs.

Lightning lit the sky and the wooden planks shook beneath Brigid's feet. A deep, unrelenting growl rose from the sea, and a wave as high as three buildings followed.

Brigid didn't have time to blink. To speak. She couldn't even form a scream before the wave crashed down on Finola and the water yanked her friend off the chair and into the ocean with the creature.

Lightning lit the sky, thunder rumbled off in the distance. Brigid turned her face to it, as a tremor ran down her spine. She sat on the dock, her hands over her face. She tried to think. She opened her hands, palms up to the air. She nudged at the kernel of fear, at what it hid. The air around her thickened and sweetened. Her toes tingled. A vibration worked its way up her spine, a memory unfurling here in the astral plane.

Brigid was standing in a field, staring up at the sky. The Goddess stood, watching.

"What if I can't do this? What if I fail?"

"You can't fail if you get back up."

"What if I don't want to get back up? What if I am tired of being on my own."

"Then know I will always help you, and you are never alone."

Brigid took a deep breath, found herself dizzy and nauseated, and someone pressed her forward, her head dipping between her knees.

"You really do like to do things the hard way," the voice said. Knightly.

He'd said that to her before. Hadn't he?

She looked up at him, and Knightly's mouth relaxed, relief shifting across the sharp angles of his face. Brigid's eyes tracked his severe cheekbones, over his chin and mouth, the way his eyes warmed.

"You know, I think I changed my mind. You make a rather improper villain."

"Actually," he said and his eyes chilled. "I am an excellent one." Knightly's face twisted and reformed, his dark hair lengthening into long pale locks, his eyes widening and his lips filling out.

Brigid stumbled away from him.

"Hello, Brigid," East said, her features settling and her smile gleaming like a knife catching the light.

"Where is he?"

"You truly care?" East's lips twitched. "You made a bargain with a treacherous king. Do you really think he loves you?"

"I think I am the person who will end you if you do not return him and my friends to me now."

"Your friends are dead, Brigid Heron," East said, waving a hand and turning the water of the lough into a hard reflective surface. Ophelia lay unmoving on the floor of what appeared to be a cabin, her body trapped in two circles, her eyes unseeing and open. Across from her Finola was slumped over, tied to a chair, her lips tinged blue, her clothes and hair soaking wet. Brigid's throat closed in horror, and East reached out and tapped the surface of the water with her shoe. It cleared, and beneath it floated Knightly, his fists punching into the barricade, trying to break free. Brigid rushed forward, and East snapped her fingers and the surface cleared as the lough bubbled. Mist formed over its surface, and below it the water frothed and rose, sucking Knightly under.

"No!" Brigid called out.

The water sloshed, and then a yellow eye blinked from beneath it.

East pointed to the opposite side of the shore, where a creature somewhere between a snake and a dragon crawled from the water. Brigid swallowed hard as she kept her gaze on the sleek body of the Oilliphéist—its head that of a dragon, its body of a serpent, and its wings black as an oil slick.

This had to be a nightmare, trapped inside the astral plane. But as the gurgling of the water stopped, and the vortex suddenly began pooling water inward, she knew it was real. The whirlpool shifted into a geyser, and water rained down on her. She slipped, falling to the shore, fighting not to be dragged into the lough.

"This is *my* power, this was always meant to be how it ends," East said, her voice rising over the wind and rain. "Goodbye, Brigid Heron."

The mist closed in around East, and she was gone.

The water sloshed over the shoreline, the whirlpool expanding out, a tentacle of water rising and wrapping itself around Brigid's ankle, yanking her loose from where she grappled to climb free, and sucking her down into the water.

⊷

Brigid was underwater, being tossed up and down, over and over, like a rag doll in the wash. She couldn't make heads or tails, and she couldn't get free of the hold the freezing water had on her. She tried to look for Knightly, but the murky water was impossible to see through. Brigid was going to die in the lough, like her friends, like those who she had loved before, and she would never get to say goodbye to her daughter.

She kicked harder, flailing her arms, punching out at the water, and her lungs began to contract.

She stopped fighting to conserve energy, and let the water

pull her deeper, but as she went she began to lose consciousness, the ability to hold her breath fading.

Brigid wanted to live. She didn't *want* to give up. But she was so tired. Her chest heaved, fire rushing through it as it fought to expand and contract, and she let out a scream as the water rushed in.

Peace would come now, she thought, as she spotted a hazy golden light cutting through the water, wrapping itself around her. Maybe she would find Dove in the next life.

Brigid's eyes fluttered closed.

Darkness slipped in.

And then a vibration rippled up her spine. Light pressed against the lids of her eyes, and she flickered them open. Heat rushed through her; a choir of nineteen voices singing burst through the haze in her mind. The water parted and strong hands reached down, grasping Brigid's wrist and yanking her up.

Brigid coughed as she was laid on the grass, and rolled to her side, gasping as she drew in one painful breath after the other.

When she finally looked over her shoulder to see who had come to her rescue, there was no one there.

Instead, resting in the grass, were two halves of a coin.

Brigid picked them up and held them together. She knew this coin.

"Reknit, regrow, resow," she managed in a hoarse croak. The two halves came back together, and Brigid looked into the surface of the coin.

The last piece of a lost memory coming back together. Knightly sending the coin, showing Brigid how to save Dove, Dove being pulled into the lough, and Brigid begging the Goddess for help. The Goddess sending Brigid after her daughter, and then her words from long ago during her training.

"I will always help you, and you are never alone."

"I'm never alone," Brigid whispered, and with a shuddering breath rolled onto her knees and clamored to her feet. "Thank you, Goddess."

Across the lough, the mist continued to pour in, and Brigid saw a form unmoving at the edge of the shore. She ran stumbling to it, relief flooding her at the sight of Knightly. By the time she made it to him, he was coughing up water. She helped him sit, but he healed much faster than she, and was recovered and standing within mere moments, scanning the horizon.

"Where did that poor excuse for a witch go?" he growled, slicking his hair back and shaking the wet from himself.

"Into the mist," Brigid said, a sob rising. "But Fin and Ophelia, they're—"

"Whatever she told you was a lie, or at the very least an omission."

"It didn't look like one."

"What did you see?"

Brigid told him of Ophelia lying across the floorboards and Finola slumped in the chair, describing what she saw around them.

"They're in their cabin, I know the way," Knightly said.

"One of us will need to deal with the creatures she's pulled from the lough," Brigid said, scanning the shoreline. "An Oilliphéist is just there," Brigid said, nodding at the serpent dragon slithering along the banks. She tracked its movements, and beyond it the shadows stretching toward the shore.

More mist rolled in, spreading out from the center of the lough, and blanketing around them. The creature slithered from sight.

"I can't see the shadows," Brigid said, her eyes roaming to the edge of the perimeter. "They were moving in, and now I can't see them at all."

A soft hiss filled the air, and the rustle of grass sounded from far off, then shifted closer.

"I can stay and fight," Knightly said.

"No, you go, you'll get there quicker. If they are dead"—her voice broke, and she forced the words out—"bring them back regardless."

"They won't be, and I will not let you down," he said, before he pressed a kiss to the top of her head, pulled down the smallest sliver of sunlight, and stepped into his shadow, and then into the mist beyond.

Brigid took a step to the far side of the shore, trying to track where the Oilliphéist had gone. Ink pooled around her feet, spreading past them, and inching forward toward the fields beyond.

"Shadows slinking through the cracks in the world," she said. The Damned were breaking through. "They can't have a god, and they cannot have this world."

She reached into her pocket to see if she had anything on her she could use to cast a protection spell. She felt the flat paper of the tarot card, and then her fingers brushed against cool metal.

The coin. Knightly's mirror magic.

She pulled it out and peered into it. She saw a meadow, with grass a brilliant leafy green, and trees that reached the clouds. A stream raced by one especially fat tree trunk, and Brigid squinted at the image. She'd been there, to that river.

A foot came into view, followed by the jumping body of a girl wearing a veil of clovers attached to her floral crown.

Dove.

Brigid burst into tears at the sight of her, fear and relief warring in her body as the mist and the serpent dragon drew near.

"I'm sorry, love," she whispered, and Dove looked up.

She stared hard at Brigid, and Brigid's mouth dropped. "Can you hear me?"

Dove's face broke into a bright grin. Her mouth started moving, fast, but Brigid couldn't understand a word she said.

"I can't hear you. I have to read your lips. Slow down."

Hi. Mom.

The tears fell fast and free, as Brigid absorbed every bit of perfection from those words.

"I can't get to you. Can you come through the river?"

Dove's smile dimmed and she shook her head.

"I'll reach you, I promise. I will bring you home."

Dove shook her head.

"What do you mean no?"

She pointed to the fields beyond her. Tapped her chest.

"The fields? What about them?"

Dove took her crown of flowers she wore from her head and held it out in front of her. She gave a low curtsy and then placed it back on her head. She pointed to herself, and slowly mouthed three words.

They. Need. Me.

Brigid's breath caught. They. The Damned. The beings in the Otherworld. A kingdom needs a king, or in this case, a fairy queen.

Dove was Brigid's, yes, but she was also her father's daughter. Blood of a witch with magic of a goddess in her veins as well as that of a demigod.

"You were born to rule," Brigid whispered, understanding dawning.

Dove nodded, her eyes shining and bright.

I. Can. Protect. Them. Like. You. Protect. Me.

Brigid bit down hard on her lip to keep the sob from breaking through.

Love. You. Mom.

Brigid's smile, though watery, was fierce. "I love you too, baby girl."

She ran a finger over the mirror, tracing her daughter's perfect face. If she didn't pull her through, she would lose her when she sealed the lough. But if she didn't seal the lough, all the souls in the Otherworld would cross over. If the coven pulled them through and twisted them, they would be Damned like all the others.

Dove might become Damned.

Brigid swallowed hard. She blew a kiss to her daughter and made an impossible choice.

NINETEEN

BOOK OF THE GODDESS (P. 92):

How to Bring the Night

There are things meant to be seen and things better left hidden in the dark. To bring the night, you only have to offer a bit of your own light.

The mist was up to Brigid's shoulders when she heard the hissing from behind. She slipped the coin in her pocket and crouched down trying to see better, but it was like looking through the middle of a thick, unyielding cloud.

The wind rustled gently through her hair. The air warmed. She heard a voice calling her name. Soft, then louder, urgent.

Brigid stood up with the mist and saw Finola and Ophelia, Knightly running behind them. Hope leapt into Brigid's heart at the sight of them, and she rushed forward, falling into their arms the moment they reached one another.

"You're okay," she said, laughing and crying at the same time. Brigid felt like she might never stop crying again.

"Thanks to you," Ophelia said. "I felt you in the circle when

I was being splintered apart. It was like a piece of you shifted inside me, and I wasn't breaking anymore. I pieced myself back together and once East slipped out, I broke out of the circle, and got to Finola."

"What about the rest of the coven?"

"The dark-haired one saw me make my move, and she distracted the other two by getting them away from the cabin to check on the Damned. Said she heard them coming for the cabin."

"Really?" Brigid asked.

"I think she likes me," Finola said, shivering but managing a partial wink. "I'm rather lovable."

"You are," Brigid said, pulling her back in for another hug.

Knightly stepped up once Brigid let Finola go and slid a hand to her back. Brigid leaned into the feel of it, wishing she could tell him how she saw Dove and what she had told her, and knowing there wasn't enough time.

"East has been making her own moves for a while," Knightly said. "Now that they have broken off and she's assumed the role of leader, there will be cracks in the hierarchy."

"Thank the Goddess that."

"What are we dealing with?" Ophelia asked, surveying the mist.

"The usual," Brigid said, her gaze shifting overhead to the arriving Sluagh, "times ten."

"Are you sure now is the time to cast the circle?" Fin asked, as one splash, then another sounded from inside the lough.

"I think it's the only time," Brigid said. "I was planning to use the four tarot cards we pulled, Ophelia, but I only have the Lovers. When we checked the house for you and Finola I looked for the rest of the cards, but they weren't where you left them."

Ophelia reached into her bag and pulled the deck out. "You mean these?"

Brigid grinned and pulled the Lovers from her pocket. "To your corners, please."

"Corner?" Knightly asked.

"Oh right. A god and not a witch," Brigid said, "We'll do a triangle configuration inside a circle. That way you can stand in the center. The demigod in the midst of three powerful witches. Trust me, Knightly."

"I always have."

Ophelia was the only one with her bag. Brigid's had been lost to the shoreline, Finola hadn't had one when the witches took her, and Knightly didn't need one. Ophelia pulled her herbs and salt, and they worked fast to build the circle and then a ring inside of it. Knightly pulled the wind as they worked, trying to shield them while pushing back the Damned that closed in.

Once the circle was complete, the others moved to Brigid, waiting. Brigid handed each of them a card that symbolized their story in this time and place. The Empress, Queen of Swords, and the Queen of Wands. The Lovers.

Brigid, Ophelia, Finola, and Knightly. As soon as they entered, the mist rushed in.

It poured over them, and across the land.

The Sluaghs settled along the edge of the shore, and from the edges of the land, *far darrigs*, Pookas, Aos Sí, and banshees crept in as the Oilliphéist slithered closer.

The coven came last, the witches walking in their line, East edging just a bit out in front.

"You're too late," they said. "We have all we need."

East reached into her cloak and pulled Brigid's bag from where she had lost it going into the water. From it she pulled the cauldron.

"How did she get that?" Ophelia whispered.

"She nearly had me drowned," Brigid said, "I thought my bag was lost to the lough."

"She pulls the power of the lough," Knightly said. "She finally pulled the cauldron."

Ophelia trained her eyes on it. "We have to get that back, Brigid."

"We can't break the circle." She looked to Knightly. "Can she use it?"

"Not without paying a hefty price."

East smiled and held up a binding made from wood, one that appeared to be sewn with thread. The mist receded as she waved the stick across the air, as though she were smudging it back.

"Your circle won't hold *all* of the Damned back for long." She dipped the long spindly stick into the lough and stirred the water clockwise three times. The advancing Damned stopped midstep. They turned as one and zeroed in on Ophelia and Finola.

"Witch's wand," Ophelia whispered. "Oh gods, she has our hair, Fin."

"Change of plans," Brigid said. "You two get into the triangle. Knightly and I will take the circle and fight them off."

They switched places, a hurried flurry of movement. Knightly called the wind down and Brigid turned to a spell from the *Book of the Goddess*, twisting it to fit her need.

> *"I call the night into the Damned*
> *Unseeing and unbidden.*
> *Take from them their sight to see*
> *And keep those I protect hidden."*

The spell spread out across the Damned, their eyes going from black to opaque, their hands shifting in front of them as they careened into one another.

East nodded to the other three witches, and they fell out of formation and made their way around the lough, each moving in from a different direction. East stamped her feet into the earth three times, and the Damned stilled. She lifted the wand in her hand, gave a low whistle, and the three other witches ran for the circle.

North mouthed something to Finola, but she was too far away for her to read her lips. Knightly stepped in front of Brigid as she slid in front of Finola, and East threw the witch's wand straight for Ophelia, who caught it.

The Damned turned as one and took off running for her.

"Shit, toss it to me—" Finola cried, as Ophelia jumped out of the circle, dragging her feet across the herbs, and breaking its protection spell.

The other three witches didn't follow Ophelia, as she had anticipated, but instead dove for Finola, tackling her to the ground.

The Damned closed in on Ophelia.

"Run," Brigid yelled to Ophelia before she checked on Finola, who had thrown off the witches and was holding her own. Knightly raced to fight East and Brigid took off running to the Damned, asking a silent prayer of forgiveness for what she was about to do.

As a witch and a healer, Brigid followed a creed. It was simple, it was right. *And harm none.* The Goddess had taught her many spells, and each of these spells had a counterpart. A light to the dark, a dark to the light. Because you needed both sides to make something whole. And there was purpose and necessity to both, for there was a season for living and one for letting go.

The spell to heal began with a song.

"Rise up from your pain and dis-ease,
Your body is healed and you are now free."

Brigid needed more than the Damned's eyesight to fail them, and so she called on the counterspell.

"Lay down low beneath the ancient trees,
Your heart has grown weary and you now know peace."

She stood in the center of the creatures as they rushed to her and circled around her, and she sang. Over and over until death spread through the monsters like decay through a rotting corpse.

As she sang, she walked over them, and crossed to where the witches advanced again on Finola. She turned her song to them, and they let go of Fin, their hands covering their ears. They fell to their knees, tears falling from their eyes, their mouths falling open and eyes bulging.

"Brigid," Finola cried, shaking her arm.

Brigid sang on, the song rooting in, the sorrow and pain of a hundred years lost pouring from her.

"Brigid!" Fin slapped a hand over Brigid's mouth and leaned into her. *"Please."*

She blinked, surprised to find Finola facing her, then looked down and the horror of what she had done set in. The three witches twitched on the ground, as they slowly came to, and the Damned lay scattered across the shoreline like fish dragged in from the tide and left to rot.

"It's enough," Finola whispered, her eyes going to the witch closest to her with dark hair. "You can stop."

Brigid nodded, swallowing past the knot in her throat, her eyes seeking Ophelia. She didn't see her anywhere.

"Where is she?" Brigid asked. "Where's Ophelia?"

A scream pierced the night, and Finola and Brigid turned for the sound. Ophelia was frozen, caught along the eastern shore, arched back as though she were trying to escape an invisible force.

A heavy grunt sounded from the opposite side of the lough, and Brigid looked to see Knightly, caught in a similar pose, his face contorted.

"You think you're so clever," East said, as she stepped out into the water, the cauldron tucked under her arm. "That your little circle could hold me back or stop me. Like I couldn't predict what you would do. I've lived centuries, Brigid Heron, including the one you were gone. I understand your fatal flaw, how you must save everyone you can simply because you couldn't save your poor mother, because you were too weak and too scared. Your daughter would suffer the same fate, but because I am a benevolent god, I will take pity on her and make her mine. I will be the mother she never had."

Brigid stepped forward and East tutted at her. "Now, now. Your little god and witch are caught in a spell of my own making. A splintering. Ophelia was lucky enough to escape it before"—she shot Brigid a smile that looked like it was made to chew glass—"but this time should you come any closer, I'll bind them fully to me. Knightly will likely end up with a few missing appendages, but what is that to a god? Ophelia on the other hand, she'll be as dead as my Damned." East's eyes flashed as she surveyed the carnage. "They didn't deserve this fate." She turned to look at Ophelia. "For you to strike down what I needed."

Brigid tasted fear in the back of her throat and kept her eyes on East. "You have the lough. You have the cauldron. Why would I move a single muscle?"

East's eyes narrowed, but she continued her walk farther into the water. "Not just a muscle, if you even attempt to astral project." She made a clamping sound with her teeth. "I chop them to bits." Then she laughed, and the skin along Brigid's arms broke out in goose bumps.

Brigid's eyes drifted to Knightly's. His eyes were on East. Brigid looked at Ophelia, and her eyes were closed, her mouth contorted in agony.

Brigid held herself still and tried to think of a way out.

As she did, East moved waist deep into the water. She dipped the fingers of her left hand in, and combed them through, calling softly to the door beneath the lough. To the remaining beings waiting to be freed. To be Damned.

The water bubbled, and a tail thrashed up to the surface. Merrow crossing over, not human and not quite fish, these were creatures who were once human but traded their humanity for the ability to travel between worlds.

"The merrow have an old grudge with you, don't they, Lugh?" East called. "You left them behind with no way out, after you called them to your world. I thought they might want to settle the score."

As the tails thrashed in the lough, East sat the cauldron into the water. She leaned over it and began to chant.

"Arise ancient power
That which is older than time
Take your place this hour
I offer you my fealty
I pledge you my line."

Brigid noticed both Knightly and Ophelia had stopped fighting, their bodies limp, suspended in the air, and a cold sweat broke out across her skin.

Mist rose from the surface of the lough and formed into a ball. It rolled across the lake heading straight for where the witch waited. East let out a delighted cry and watched the mist as it settled into the cauldron. She dipped the cauldron further into the water, brought it up to her lips. She drank deep and let out a satisfied sigh.

The seconds ticked by. Long, and slow, and painful. Brigid's eyes drifted to the broken forms of Knightly and Ophelia. Finola's concern pressed against her, an invisible weight from behind.

East sat the cauldron down, and raised her arms, power shimmering from her fingertips down her torso. She spun in a circle, the water splashing out, drawing the merrow closer to her. She threw back her head and laughed, and Finola let out a cry.

Brigid spun around and saw Finola bent over the forms of the three witches who had sat slowly recovering on the ground. Their skin shifted in color, taking on a tinge of green, then blue, then red. Spots broke out across their collarbones, horns punctured the temples on their heads.

They moved with slow precision, climbing to their feet, slowly rolling up and raising their faces as they turned to East.

"We call upon the ancients, we welcome you home."

Then one by one, they dropped, and crumbled to the earth.

TWENTY

The air was perfumed with death. A chill spreading fast across the land.

Brigid stood facing East. East turned toward her coven, the sight of them registering. The glee faded from her eyes, horror twisted her mouth, and she dropped the cauldron. East pushed through the water, hurrying to the shore, and running for her sister witches. She dropped to her knees beside them, trying to send the magic of the cauldron from her fingertips into their veins.

Tiny sparks sputtered from her thumbs and blew out.

"No, no, no, *no*," she cried, laying her hands on one and then the other. She looked up at Finola. "*You* did this."

Finola stayed at she was, crouched protectively over the body of the witch at the farthest end with the dark hair, North. "No. This is *your* fault."

East turned; her eyes wild as she looked to the lough. She scrambled to her feet and clamored to the water, falling into it, and reaching for the cauldron. As her fingers closed around it, she screamed.

Her fingers blistered, the tips blackening from where they held on.

Knightly and Ophelia fell to their knees. Brigid turned to where they were collapsed, and Finola called her name.

"Brigid, help!"

Her gaze drifted to East, crumpled in the water. She turned to Ophelia and Knightly and counted to five, watching until she saw their chests expand with breath, and then she took off running for the lough.

She jumped over one merrow, and dove around another, grabbing East by her waist and heaving her to shore. She left her on her side, gasping for air, before hurrying to Finola.

"They're dying," Finola told her, her face pale, her left hand shaking as she kept her right firmly gripped around the arm of the dark-haired witch lying in front of her. "She helped me, Brigid. We can't let them die."

Brigid's gaze drifted to the Damned, their bodies empty of the souls they carried before they were lost to the bent magic of East and the witches of Knight.

She looked at the women lying on the earth beside Finola. It was easy to imagine they were Finola and Ophelia. That had her goddess not been the Goddess, one of them might have been her.

Brigid stood and walked to the shore, she waded in, waiting for the merrow to attack, but this time they swam away from her. She reached the cauldron, leaned down, and wrapped her palms around it. A vibration wrapped around the tips of her fingers and traveled up her palms into her forearms and all the way to her shoulders and the crown of her head.

She lifted the cauldron and, careful to keep the water inside, carried it to the witches and Finola.

"Help her," Finola said, her eyes swimming with tears. "Please."

Brigid tipped the water into the mouth of each witch and waited. Breath by breath, the changes that had come over them began to recede. A spot gone here, a horn retracted there, then their pigment settling back into its rightful color. Brigid stood and saw Ophelia sitting in her circle, and Knightly out of his circle striding toward East, mutiny on his face.

"Wait," she said, rushing to meet him.

He did not slow down, he met Brigid and walked beside her, vibrating with anger. Brigid reached East first, who was crawling on her side, hacking up water and clutching at her chest.

Knightly cracked his neck to one side, and Brigid looked over her shoulder at him. "Is this what you experienced?"

"This is worse. No matter how much she wants to be a god, she is not one."

Brigid nodded, and walked around to where East lay. She knelt beside her and tipped the water to her mouth. East tried to pull away, shaking her head.

"Awaken from your pain and dis-ease," Brigid said. "May the waters bless you and set you free."

East gave a final cough, and a liter of lough water poured from her mouth. When it stopped, she wheezed in a long breath and rolled onto her back, coughing one last time and sitting up. The blisters and burns retreated from her fingers and hands.

Brigid reached for Knightly, but he gave his head a quick shake. Instead, he gave a low whistle and the merrow came swimming up to the shore.

"You were wrong," he said to East, his voice low and dangerous. "I did not forsake them; I gave them what they wanted. Independence, autonomy, and a world of their own. You offered your line, you used them for your gain and tried to barter with their lives."

Then he watched as the merrow sprang into the air out of the water and dove back in, their tails flicking out and catching

East by her side, flipping her into the water. The faces of the merrow, somehow human and yet not, rose from the water and gave Knightly an unreadable look, before inclining their heads to Brigid. Then they slipped their arms around East and took her down into the water of the lough.

"What are they going to do with her?" Brigid asked.

"Whatever needs to be done. They are just but they are not cruel, the denizens of the Otherworld."

Knightly pressed a kiss to Brigid's head before he hurried to where the three witches lay recovering with Finola.

Ophelia walked to Brigid, wrapping an arm around her shoulder.

"She's gone," Ophelia said, relief in her tone, as she surveyed the lough.

"Did she hurt you?" Brigid asked.

Ophelia shook her head. "But the lough, it's still churning."

"It wasn't enough," Brigid said, her heart breaking as she watched the water froth. "The Damned are still called to come here, even without East pulling them through."

"She opened the door," Ophelia said.

Brigid looked up at her friend and gave her head a single shake. "No, she didn't. I did, or my blood and Knightly's blood—Dove's blood—did. I didn't understand at first. Now, we must close it."

Brigid pulled the mirror coin from her pocket and looked down into it. Dove stood standing before her, her hair flowing out behind her, a flash of a smile on her beautiful face. She nodded to her mother.

Brigid pressed her lips to her fingers, and her fingers to the coin. She couldn't stop the tears that came, even as she tried to swallow her pain.

She stared into the face of her daughter, telling herself to look at how well she was. Healed, smiling, understanding, whole.

The fairy queen of the Otherworld.

Brigid took a breath, and nodded to her child, to the love of her life.

When you have only one choice, there is only one choice to make.

Brigid snapped the mirror in half as the Goddess had and sliced her palm.

Before she could cross to where she'd sat the cauldron after pouring the water into East's mouth, Ophelia took half of the mirror and sliced her own palm. Knightly, seeing what they were doing, picked up the cauldron and brought it to Brigid, dropping it at her feet, kneeling before her.

He held out a palm, and she sliced his hand, too.

"We will lose her," Brigid said.

"We will keep her safe," he said. "She is ours, so she can never be truly lost."

"Does no one want my sexy type AB?" Finola asked, her voice trembling as she gave the witch whom she'd been watching over a squeeze, and stood up to cross to them. Brigid managed only a hint of a trembling smile, but she nodded to her.

Ophelia pricked Finola's thumb, and together, the four of them, the most unlikeliest of covens, gave their blood to the cauldron.

Brigid and Knightly carried it out to the lough.

"You know what this means?" Brigid asked him, tears streaming down her face, her voice a choked whisper.

"I have always known," he said, his own voice breaking. "Dove is my daughter. A queen of the gods. Some people, my love, are too bright for this world."

Knightly released his hands from the cauldron, leaving it in hers, and Brigid slowly lowered it into the water, the weight of her world in her hands.

At first nothing happened. A gentle breeze blew past, the

leaves stirred in the trees, and then . . . a flash. Brigid thought she heard the Goddess's voice, whispering in her ear.

"To pull the light from the dark is to splinter the very vibration of magic and all it affects.
To bring both back together is to heal it all."

The moon burst from behind the clouds, light spread across the land, and golden beams rained down from above. The bodies of the Damned sank into the earth, the skies opened, and a heavy rain fell, rushing from the land into the lough. The water rose, and Brigid and Knightly ran for the shoreline where they stopped and watched the pieces of the coin washing back into the lough, down into its depths. The water met their feet, and they stepped back. Again and again as the water chased them toward where Ophelia and Finola tended the witches.

They worked to help them up and carried them to the top of the nearest hill. Then they sat and watched, unspeaking, as the water spread across the land, and the lough returned to its natural state and sealed its shores.

Once the water had stilled, and the sun had set, Brigid fell to the earth, crumbling in on herself as sobs wracked her body, and she mourned, once again, the loss of her daughter.

⚷

Grief is not a simple emotion. It does not come in a wave with the tide and rush back out when the moon calls it to the sea. Grief is the worst uninvited houseguest, it is a chasing echo, a haunting ghost, and for Brigid it had finally won.

She had sealed the lough, and her daughter in it. Now Evermore and her friends would be safe, Dove would never have to worry about being pulled over by a corrupt power looking to tap into the magic of a god, and her beloved child would take her rightful place as queen over the Otherworld.

But the hard truth was that for Brigid, Dove was hers, and Brigid only wanted her where she truly belonged. Home, by her side.

Knightly sat with his arms around Brigid, holding her, his tears falling as the sun set. Eventually Ophelia and Finola joined them, laying their hands on Brigid, wanting to be there and knowing there was nothing they could do.

After a very long time, Brigid sat up, and she and her coven, and the three remaining witches formerly of the coven of Knight sat on the hill staring at the water. The world seemed fuller with the lough restored. And so much emptier without Dove.

"I need to check on Thorpe," Ophelia said. "If the Damned here are gone, does that mean the ones circling the village are too?"

Brigid and Knightly exchanged a look. Brigid took a shuddering breath. "The people there were touched. I don't know if sealing the lough hurt or helped them. I don't know what will happen to them now."

"What about *them*?" Ophelia asked, her eyes on the remaining three witches of Knight.

"We bring them," Brigid said, her eyes shifting to where Finola stood by North. "We can discuss everything else after."

When they reached the center of Evermore, they found the ground was still covered with the bodies of the villagers. Horror set in as they moved from person to person, noting they were breathing but in the middle of changing. Frozen in an in-between state.

Ophelia's gaze tracked the ground, and settled on a familiar shape, and she let out a startled cry. *"Thorpe."* She took off running, falling across him, her hands shifting to his chest, setting her hand on his heart.

"Brigid," Ophelia cried, "we have to help them."

"Is there anything the lough can do?" Finola asked, biting her lip.

"If it's sealed," North said, leaning heavily on Finola, "it doesn't have power that can reverse this."

"Your voice," Finola said, "it's not . . ." She moved her head like a robot. "Monotone unison."

"We are untethered," she said. "Our bond was broken when East tried to sacrifice us."

"What about the well?" Knightly said. "Can you try and pull from it?"

"We took the last of the water in," North said. "The well is dry."

Brigid rubbed at her arms. "We can try to use the healing spell of the Goddess. Ophelia has some of my magic in her, which is of the Goddess. If you took in the water of the well, maybe you have an essence of her too, a bit of what remained. If we work together, we might be able to revive them."

"Brigid?" Finola said, squinting toward the opposite side of the town square. "If all the townspeople are half-Damned, then who is that?"

They turned to where Finola was looking and saw a person in a cloak bent over a crumpled body.

Brigid's breath caught in her throat at the familiar sight. Knightly let out a sound that was somewhere between a laugh and curse. They exchanged a look, and Brigid smiled.

She turned back to the others. "The spell is simple. Lay your hands on each person and with true intention, invite healing into them." She gave them the words, and then turned and walked across the square to the cloaked figure.

Brigid would know that silhouette anywhere. Tall, confident, and welcoming. Brigid reached her, and the Goddess turned, tilting her chin and smiling the kind of smile you make when you've found something precious that has been lost a very long time.

"Hello, my child," the Goddess said, before throwing back her cloak, revealing her fiery crown of flowers and flaming red hair. Then she reached for Brigid and pulled her to her. The Goddess smelled of kindling from her hearth, a fresh spring, and lavender. Brigid's favorite smells all wrapped up in one being.

"You've had quite the adventure," the Goddess said, when she let her go. Then the twinkle in her eye dimmed, when Brigid nodded, unable to form the words.

"Your Dove. She has taken her place as fairy queen of the Otherworld."

"I found her to lose her again."

"You found her to help her find where she belongs."

The Goddess looked past Brigid to the witches moving through the group, laying their hands on the half-Damned, trying to send their energy into them and heal them whole. "You have found a coven of your own."

"Partly," Brigid said. "Half of them tried to kill me."

The Goddess pursed her lips. "And now they work at your side, following your lead. Not all who make poor choices are bad people. You will be a great leader, I think." She narrowed her eyes. "Lugh finally got what he wanted, I see."

"To be trapped here?"

The Goddess looked back to Brigid. "To be loved. Unwanted demigod with no people or home to call his own, overlooked by nearly everyone, including that gregarious foster father. Who gifts a piece of themselves and their magic as a way of courting? A narcissist, that's who."

"I thought you hated Knightly."

"I hated his poor choices. They brought chaos and disruptions. But I could not hate him, he was simply lost and longing." She smiled at Brigid. "Much as you were lost and longing."

"There was a moment when I was in the lough, and I thought I might die," Brigid said. "Then there was this light, and it reminded me of you and your eternal flame. I saw it, and somehow, I was pulled from the lough when I thought all hope was lost."

The Goddess brought a hand to Brigid's face and cupped her cheek. "How many times have I had to tell you, dear Brigid. You are never alone." She released her and took a step back, sweeping her cape out behind her. "Now, why don't you take me to your coven, and we can work together to repair the damning that has been done. Evermore, I believe, is much deserving of this awakening."

Ophelia and Finola did not know how to respond to meeting Brigid's Goddess. Being Finola and Ophelia, they settled for throwing their arms around her and then awkwardly apologizing when they stepped on her cloak. The Goddess threw back her head and laughed, before taking Ophelia's hand. "You have my light in you." She looked to Brigid, and Brigid nodded. "And you have the same look in your eye of being the best kind of trouble." She looked over at Finola. "As do you."

"We get it from our dear old Granny," Finola said, winking at Brigid.

The Goddess turned to the three witches who stood back, worry tugging their mouths into compressed lines. "The witches of Knight," the Goddess said. Then considering them changed her mind. "Or maybe you are witches of yourselves." She walked to them and lay a hand on their cheeks, one at a time, much as she had done to Brigid minutes before. "You were hurt and mistreated, and you did not deserve what happened to you. You hardened your hearts, but you are not lost. You can always redeem yourself." She smiled. "You also have power, and it is a bit unruly yet. I can help you train it, if you would like. I have a well that appears to know you, and it's been neglected for some time. Perhaps you would like to help me restore it?"

"We would love that," they said, speaking in unison.

Finola groaned. "And it's back."

North blushed, and South and West locked arms around each other.

"You might also decide who you'd like to be this time," she said. "If who you were no longer suits you. It's never too late to become the person you would like to be."

"Jewl," North whispered to Finola. "My name is Jewl."

"Finola," Fin said, holding out her hand, a heart-stopping grin spreading across her face.

Finally, the Goddess turned to Knightly, who sat on the fountain in the center of town a few feet away.

"Lugh," she said, raising a brow.

"Brighid," he said, matching her expression.

"I see you made a mess of things, again."

"And do you also see I've sorted it out?"

"Perhaps."

She reached into her pocket and pulled a coin from it. Knightly stood. "Where did you get that?"

"It was first bound to me when Brigid gave it to me. It might make its way back to her, but it always makes its way back to me." She flicked it in the air, and he caught it. He looked down into it, and relief spread across his face.

"Thank you," he said, his voice full of an emotion Brigid couldn't name. Awe and gratitude, but deeper.

"Use it wisely," she said.

"I will." He cleared his throat.

"Yes?"

"There's one more thing," he said. He reached inside his suit and pulled a shard of a mirror coin from where he kept them. He pricked his thumb, crossed to the Goddess, and held out his hand. She smiled, a knowing glint in her eyes, and offered her palm.

"May the lough of dreams, created by Manannán, return to the Goddess, and may she guard and keep it well."

She closed her palm and inclined her head to him.

"And may Fairy Hill be opened once more to the former king of fairy and his true love," she said. "So long as it is used not as a way to thieve the fair people of this town, but as a way to spread love."

Knightly closed his eyes and nodded. "You have my oath, and my gratitude."

"But not your fealty?"

He opened his eyes, and they drifted to where Brigid stood. "No. That belongs to her. Always."

Then the Goddess and the witches of Evermore, and the once forgotten king, healed the mostly Damned so they were whole again.

The Goddess had returned, and Evermore was on its way to being ever more prosperous and free as the curse lifted and the borders opened once more.

TWENTY-ONE

The Goddess, Brigid, and their coven worked overnight healing the people of Evermore and well into the following day. The next evening, as the sun set across the ocean, the people of Evermore rejoiced, and the witches of the island followed the Goddess to a well to learn an ancient power that would heal and save, and Brigid Heron and Luc Knightly walked up the hill down the road from her house to where a fairy ring sat.

Sorrow wrapped itself around Brigid, as she thought of all they had accomplished, and all she had lost.

"I miss her," she said, her heart in her voice.

Knightly wrapped an arm around her and inclined his head. "I know."

Brigid took a breath and looked out to where the cliffs waited. "I can't believe you returned the lough," she said, as he lay a green blanket over a flat fairy stone for her to sit on.

"It was never mine," he said. "Much as I wanted it to be, and I've learned my lesson of taking things that aren't mine."

"Why are you looking at me like that?"

"Because I want you to be mine."

"I think it's pretty clear at this point, I'm no one else's."

"I mean for always."

"Is that why you brought me to the fairy ring? I don't think it will fit on my finger."

"I brought you here because I have something better than a ring, even a magical one."

"I'm waiting."

Lugh reached into his pocket and pulled out his coin. He passed it over to Brigid, who looked down at the face of her daughter. Her heart squeezed in relief and her eyes filled with tears. "I saw the Goddess give this to you." She peered closer. "It's everything to see her face again. She looks happy, doesn't she?"

"Yes," he said, peering over her shoulder and watching their daughter lean over a river and splash water the color of sea glass onto a giggling merrow. "But it's not enough."

He crouched down in front of the ring of stones and lifted his hands, brought them together and apart, and whispered, "Show me."

The air thickened and wavered. Inside of the ring the ground shifted, the land beyond—cliffs and rolling hills—was replaced with streams and valleys, tall trees that were the size of houses and Brigid was fairly certain grew books.

"The Otherworld," she said, her eyes widening. "You can see into the Otherworld."

"Only this section," he said. "The lough opened but my way home through my door here did not. I managed to cross over for a single day, and it closed. It took a portion of my magic to manage it, and after I returned, I was able to see into the Otherworld, but only here, this view, like I'm peering through a keyhole trying to see the whole of a universe."

"Have you seen her?"

"No." He shook his head. "I looked for you and for her for a century here, but never saw either of you."

"Oh." Brigid frowned. "Then what good is this?"

Knightly grinned. "When the Goddess accepted my returning of her lough, she returned something that belonged to me."

"Which is?"

"She opened the ring, Fairy Hill, as she calls it. Not for the use of transporting mortals who seek a life of play in the Otherworld, but for me and my true love to pass back and forth for a single purpose."

"To see Dove," Brigid said, hope swelling in her chest.

"To see our daughter."

Brigid let out a wild cry of victory, relief, and joy. She reached for Knightly, fisting her hands in his shirt and yanking him to her. She kissed him fiercely, passionately, as he wrapped his arms around her, and then he tugged her into the center of the fairy ring and the world beyond.

⌐O

OPHELIA: Welcome back to *Ever More* podcast, the only podcast bringing you the best and brightest, the truest, and most magical of all podcasts.

FINOLA: That's right, Rodney, we're talking about you and your bloody podcast with those subscribers you paid for. Don't think I don't have the metrics to see what you're up to.

OPHELIA: What Fin means is congratulations, Rodney, on getting a job. We know your ma is so proud that you might be moving out of her attic one day soon.

Today we have Farmer Joanie and Father O'Malley, who are here to share their experience during the Damned Days, when the town was turned into the Island of

Monsters. We're continuing with our series of interviewing survivors who are now thrivers, and the two with us today have a particularly fascinating story.

JOANIE: Thanks for having us, and congratulations on being nominated for an Audie Award for your other podcast, *Witchy Ways*. I'm learning so much about harnessing the healing power of the earth and my inner goddess.

FINOLA: Thanks so much, what do you think about Joanie's new skills, Father O'Malley?

FATHER O'MALLEY: [awkwardly clears throat] I think advancing oneself is always a noble cause.

FINOLA: Uh-huh.

OPHELIA: Anyway, can you two tell us where you were when the Damned struck? I think you might be two of the only people who didn't get touched.

JOANIE: I was tending my sheep, when O'Malley was riding by, he'd seen the floating ghosties—

OPHELIA: The Sluaghs.

JOANIE: Ah, yes, always forget the name. And came to check on me. We hurried into my house and hid. It's not much of an exciting story, I fear.

FINOLA: It sounds like Father O'Malley had a very noble cause himself, in helping you.

JOANIE: Yes, I suppose you could say that.

FINOLA: I also noticed, when we checked on you later that day, that your shirt was on inside out. Did you two happen to wind up in a bit of stray sod at one point, as some of the others have experienced?

JOANIE: [long, *long* pause] Um, yes, you know what, we did. I forgot all about it in the celebration after you all dispatched the Damned and the Goddess returned.

O'MALLEY: Right. Yes. We're lucky we got out.

OPHELIA: Indeed. Well, we are so glad you all stopped by today, and to hear that your sheep are once more thriving now that there aren't monsters trying to eat them.

JOANIE: Oh yes, and we'll have a nice batch of dyed wool sweaters and socks for sale at our booth for the Samhain Festival. I can't tell you how exciting it is to have the town opened and people returning to visit. It's wild how they all think they've been meaning to visit for years and are finally able to come.

OPHELIA: It's a bit of magic, that.

FINOLA: When you say *we* will have a booth, Joanie, who do you mean?

O'MALLEY: Ah, I'm second in command with Joanie for the booth.

JOANIE: A portion of the proceeds go toward the church and the renovation of the abbey on the cliffs.

OPHELIA: What a wonderful cause.

FINOLA: Noble even. Maybe these shirts can be made so they can be easily worn inside out or right side in, too?

OPHELIA: Well, you've heard it here first, Evermorians, there will be beautiful new sweaters and socks for winter courtesy of our very own Joanie and Father O'Malley. Don't forget to get your tickets to Samhain Fest, which I've heard told our very own Brigid Heron will be presenting a new elixir that is guaranteed to open your third eye and help you find your passion in this world if you're feeling a little lost. That's all for now, I'm Ophelia Gallagher.

FINOLA: And I'm Finola McEntire.

OPHELIA: Remember to be kind to one another, say yes to any adventures that tempt your heart, and embrace your magic.

FINOLA: Or the fairies will get you if you don't watch out.

ACKNOWLEDGMENTS

First and foremost, I must thank my divine editor, Monique
Patterson. It is a *severe* understatement to say that working with
you is a dream come true. Thank you for your constant support
and encouragement, and for pushing me to be the best writer I
can be. I am so incredibly lucky to have you as my editor!

Huge hugs of gratitude also to my assistant editor, Mara
Delgado Sánchez, who is a constant ray of light and has never
once made me feel silly for asking any of my (often silly) ques-
tions. I am so grateful to have the best team, including Rivka
Holler, Sara LaCotti, Jessica Zimmerman, Brant Janeway, Ervin
Serrano, Gabriel Guma, John Karle and Oliver Wehner, Hannah
Jones, Jennifer Eck, Katy Robitzski, Lani Meyer, and all the
other phenomenal people at St. Martin's Press.

Thank you to Ashley Blake for always believing in me and
cheering me on. I adore you to the moon and back!

Much gratitude to my Porchies: Laura Benedict, Helen Ellis,
Patti Callahan Henry, J. T. Ellison, Ariel Lawhon, Lisa Patton,
and Anne Bogel. You are amazing and fearless writers, and I am
so lucky to call you friends.

To my Shield Wall, I could not have gotten through the past year without you. Myra McEntire, Erica Rodgers, Alisha Klapheke, Lauren Thoman, and Sarah Brown, you are truly bosom friends.

Steph Perkins, thank you for answering my endless questions, getting on the phone with me, and giving me encouragement and grace. You are a precious soul, and I am thankful for you.

V. E. Schwab, thank you for walking with me along the launch and prelaunch to *The Orphan Witch* and being such a support after it. I am grateful for your kindness, that you always answer even my oddest of questions, and for the day you gave me permission to be myself during this wild process.

Erica and Alisha, you are constant inspirations and a master class in unconditional love.

Myra, it's always *our* bullshit and I love you. So does Jason Momoa, he just doesn't know it yet.

I'm incredibly lucky to have the support and friendship of Megan Niedzwiecki, Kayleen Turner, and Nell Trotter. You are three goddesses in my life who have made it better and brighter, and you will forever be my queens of the saplings.

Thank you to Laura Benedict for being the first reader on *The Lost Witch* and pushing me and keeping me going. *You* are magic.

I owe a debt of gratitude to my dear friend Elaine Dinos. who allowed me to curl up on her porch to write the first draft of this novel.

All my love to Katy, Sara, Dallas, Juby, and Mel for constant Ya-Ya support and encouragement over the years.

Endless hugs to Lynne Street, Jenn and Chad Fitzgerald, and Ava and Harper Fitzgerald. I am so lucky to be a part of your beautiful family.

To my brother, Josh, I am beyond thankful for you. To my

nieces, Brinley and Jocilyn, you are goddesses, and you are so loved.

We lost my beloved grandmother, Frances Mack Warfield Weaver, and her sister, Bonnie "Nootie" Bishop, during the production of this novel. Two fierce and brilliant women who granted me (and most everyone they knew) fierce and unconditional love. I miss you, Granny. Every damn day.

Thank you to my daddy, Ken McNeese; my stepmother, Amelia McNeese; my stepbrother, Hayden Holliman; and my stepsister, Annbern Holliman, for believing in me and always cheering me on. Daddy, I really tried to change the byline to *Ken McNeese's Daughter*; here's to having better luck next time!

I could not do what I do without my best friend and the love of my life, Marcus Crutcher. You are and always will be my everything. I do what I do for our children, Rivers and our Doll, who are the best humans and most magical creatures to ever walk this earth.

Finally, this book is for my mother, Marilyn Jo Weaver. Beautiful, fierce, and stronger than any person I know, she has taught me more lessons than I can pen to page, including that those you love are always worth fighting for. I love you, Meme.

Thank you, dear reader, for going on this journey with Brigid. May you always be surrounded by love, and may you never be too afraid to follow your heart.

Dear Reader,

Thank you for reading *The Lost Witch*! Brigid's journey is a tale of a phenomenal woman who refuses to give up...even when she can't remember what she's fighting for. It's a celebration of magic and sisterhood, family, myth, and monsters.

This novel was inspired by the strength and compassion of Brighid the goddess and Saint Brighid. It was also born from my deep love for Ireland, and the time my husband and I spent there after suffering a miscarriage. I rediscovered hope during the month I stayed on the Emerald Isle. The awe-inspiring beauty of the country coupled with its remarkable history enchanted me. The incredible, kind, and tenacious people we met as we traveled across the Republic of Ireland shared their stories and hearts with us. Their generosity of spirit went a long way to healing me. While this novel is a fictional play on Irish mythology, it is a tribute to the legends and the joy of a rich and beautiful land.

Loss is inevitable. It is impenetrable. But so is love.

May love always soften your fall, may the road rise to reach you, and may the wind always be at your back blowing you home.

I love this story with my whole heart, dear reader, and I hope you will too.

Paige Crutcher

Paige Crutcher

 ST. MARTIN'S GRIFFIN

1. In the opening chapter of the novel, when the Goddess denies Brigid her heart's desire of having a child, Brigid makes a deal with the mysterious and devastatingly handsome demigod Knightly. She trades him information for the thing she most desires. How does her choice serve to set up the rest of the book, and would you have made the same choice?

2. Brigid makes a choice to save her daughter, Dove, and this act sets off the events that alter Brigid's timeline and curse the town of Evermore. Brigid knowingly does what she believes will save her daughter regardless of the consequences. Is there anything you wouldn't do to save those you love?

3. Brigid's loss of memory alters every choice she makes once she awakes in the cellar in 2022. She's been gone for one hundred years, with no recollection of where she went or why, or how she ended up in the present time. How might you react if you woke up a hundred years in the future with no memory of where you'd been or how you'd ended up there?

4. The village of Evermore has been under siege by mythical creatures and a coven of witches who serve Knightly. They are trying to access the ancient power of the lough so they can claim its power, the creatures, and the village. Were you surprised when it was revealed that Knightly wasn't working with the witches but against them and wanted to team up with Brigid?

5. Brigid awakens to discover two witches living in her home. It's a journey for her to learn to trust these other witches and the genuine love they have for her. What do you think was the pivotal moment for her when she chose to embrace them as a coven of her own? How do you think the story would have gone had Brigid not had Ophelia and Finola working alongside her?

ST. MARTIN'S GRIFFIN

6. Two turning points of the novel center around Brigid's daughter. The first, when she finally remembers her, and the second, when Brigid learns the very thing she is working toward, sealing the lough, means losing the one thing she wants— getting her daughter back. If you were faced with the choice Brigid was given, of saving her daughter or the town and the people in it she loved, how might your choices be similar or different to hers?

7. The relationship between Knightly and Brigid evolves as her memories return. Would you say their chemistry and romance was more of a slow burn, and if so, did you find yourself rooting for the pair to come back together? At what point did you feel this way?

8. *The Lost Witch* is told with multiple timelines and points of view. If you could reread this story from another character's point of view, which character would you choose and why?

9. Who would you say is the villain of *The Lost Witch*? Would you agree that most people live more in the gray than in the black and white, and each character has qualities that are both antagonist and protagonist in nature?

10. In the beginning of the novel, we learn Brigid Heron lived a life where she was both alone and lonely. How would you say she feels about her life at the end of the novel, and do you think learning that the Goddess and Dove were both trying to help her and Evermore in their own ways might change how she looks back on the past? Is there a time in your life where once you had perspective on an event, it reframed what you'd experienced?

ABOUT THE AUTHOR

Photo courtesy of the author

PAIGE CRUTCHER is the author of *The Orphan Witch*. She is a former journalist, and when not writing, she prefers to spend her time trekking through the forest with her children, hunting for portals to new worlds.